Sow tl

S J Richards

SOW THE WIND

For Jen (aka Aunty Spoiler as far as Matt and Abby are concerned) who has given me terrific support from the very start of my writing journey

The Luke Sackville Crime Thriller Series

Chapter 1

"Thanks," Jackie said to the barmaid as she took the tray of drinks.

She returned to the table with a tonic water for herself, a Pepsi with a straw for Oscar and halves of cider for the other two.

Andrea and Finn were deep in conversation while Oscar stared aimlessly out of the window.

Jackie took a sip of her drink and watched as the couple argued back and forth about whether the Green Party had anything worthwhile to offer.

To her mind they were stereotypical tree-huggers. Both Andrea and Finn wore bangles on their wrists and had long braided hair that fell away down their backs. Finn coupled this look with a ridiculously tiny beard that was little more than a chin patch. Both were enthusiastic and seemed to genuinely believe that their actions were changing the world for the better.

Fools.

They were playing.

She was deadly serious.

Oscar was very different and Jackie felt sorry for him.

He meant well, that much was for certain, and he was a passionate believer in the cause. Indeed it was more than a cause for him, it was his number one hobby, the focus of every minute of his waking day and in all probability his dreams too.

Oscar's problem was that he was what her dad would call a bungalow. There wasn't much upstairs, and what there was was targeted in one direction and one direction only. She was reminded of dogs that sniff out drugs at airports; very little in the way of genuine intelligence but one hell of a lot of focus.

"Gosh, I'm excited about today," he said. "What do you think, Andrea? We should generate headlines, shouldn't we?"

Jackie couldn't help smiling. If it went the way she planned there would certainly be headlines.

After all, that was what it was about. Maximising media coverage was her aim and Oscar was going to help achieve that. Before the day was over they were going to be splashed everywhere. It wouldn't just be the likes of Facebook, Instagram and X either. The broadcast media would lap it up. If they were lucky they'd be number one item on the evening news.

Andrea looked across at Oscar and nodded her head. "Yes, Oscar," she said in that patronising tone that went straight over his head but which irritated Jackie no end. "It should be noticed."

"I'm going to video it," Finn said, grinning and holding his iPhone up. "It'll be on YouTube within minutes and hopefully go viral."

"Tik Tok as well?" Oscar asked.

Finn nodded. "Yes, that too."

Oscar gave a little tremble of anticipation. "I'm looking forward to seeing his face. Do you think he'll be scared?"

"Keep your voice down, you idiot," Andrea hissed.

Oscar giggled. "Oh." He put his finger to his lips. "Silly me."

Jackie picked up her glass of tonic water and sat back as the conversation continued, in lower tones now as they started discussing the man they were targeting.

A woman sat at a table nearby waiting for her husband to bring their drinks. Much her own age, in her early forties or thereabouts, she saw her looking and smiled.

Jackie returned the woman's smile and reflected on what an odd group they must appear. She was comfortably the oldest, while Andrea and Finn were both thirty-one and

Oscar was young enough to be her son.

Although Oscar was twenty-three, his mental acuity was more in keeping with someone over a decade younger. However, this suited Jackie down to the ground. It made him easy to manipulate.

"When are we leaving?" Oscar asked, struggling to contain his excitement.

"In a minute," Jackie said.

"Are many coming?"

"I've let the media know," Finn said.

"I meant supporters. How many supporters?"

"We've put the word out," Andrea said. "We'll have to see how many are committed enough to join us."

"I want hundreds."

Andrea tutted. "That won't happen, Oscar."

"I want hundreds," he repeated somewhat petulantly.

Andrea stood up. "Come on. We'd better head off."

"I'll see you outside when I've paid for our drinks," Jackie said as Finn and Oscar stood up.

"Can I have a quick word, Oscar?" she added as he started to follow the others.

"Of course."

Jackie waited until Andrea and Finn had left the pub and then reached into her bag and retrieved the object she had bought that morning.

She smiled at Oscar and passed it to him.

"What's that?" he said.

"You need to put it on your hand."

He looked confused. "Put your right hand out," she said. When he'd done so she slid it over his fingers and was pleased to see it was a good fit.

Oscar raised his hand above the table and Jackie quickly pushed it down again. She glanced across to the next table and was relieved to see that the woman and her partner were focused on each other and hadn't seen anything.

"Take it off and put it in your pocket," she whispered.

"I don't want anyone to see it."

"Won't it cause damage?" he asked as he removed it from his fingers.

"Enough to bring us to people's attention, and that's what we want, isn't it?"

He nodded and grinned like the proverbial Cheshire cat. "Yes, definitely."

"But if anyone asks about it, say you found it. Okay? Don't say I gave it to you."

He tapped the side of his nose. "I found it by the side of the road."

"Exactly." She stood up. "Come on, let's join the others."

Chapter 2

"What the hell are they doing?" Teddy said. He turned away from the window and gestured to his wife who was sitting forward on one of the armchairs writing invitations. "Come over here and look at this."

"Can't you see I'm busy?" Maria said. "I should have done this a few days ago and they needed to go in the post today. Do you think we should ask the Waddings?"

"They've got some sort of soapbox." He paused. "Oh, fuck!"

Maria looked up at this. "What is it?"

Teddy sighed. "It's that 'Sow the Wind' mob."

"Who?"

She put the pile of invitations on the coffee table, stood up and joined him at the window.

"They're one of those weird environmental groups," he said.

"I've never heard of them."

There were only four protesters, two men and two women. One of the men, who had filthy-looking long hair and a tiny goatee, was holding up a banner with the words 'SAVE OUR CHILDREN' written on it in capital letters. Next to the words was a red circle with a stylised black coffin inside.

"That's their logo," Teddy said. "They've been handing out leaflets at the House but this is the first time they've done anything like this."

The man was accompanied by a much younger, gormless-looking man and two women. One of the women had to be his partner with her dirty dreadlocks and hippy clothes, while the other was the oldest in the group, a dumpy woman in her forties with greying hair and oversized glasses.

Teddy tutted. "What a bunch of wasters," he said. "If I see that bastard I'll tell him what I think of him."

"Who are you talking about?" Maria asked.

"Curtis Pinnington. Their brochure says he backs them and I can't say I'm surprised. I wouldn't put anything past him."

"Wasn't he elected at the same time as you?"

Teddy nodded. "Yes. He's an Independent and a complete nuisance. Arsehole too. No one likes him except his constituency." He gave a dry laugh. "And the media. He's full of soundbites and they devour them like sharks at a bloodbath."

"Why do you think they're here? Is it because of what you said about fracking?"

"Has to be. All I said was that we should be open to it if it's proven to be safe and sustainable. It seems like a balanced view to me. People like that though..." He gestured to the group at the end of their front garden. "... aren't reasonable."

They watched as the older woman stood on the soapbox and turned to address a man who had appeared at the gate.

"I recognise him," Teddy said. "He's a journalist."

As they watched a few more people arrived, one of them carrying a second hand-crafted banner above his head. He'd drawn the same image of a coffin in a red circle, this time accompanied by the words 'STOP EXPLOITING THE EARTH'.

"What are you going to do?" Maria asked.

Teddy looked at his watch. "I need to get to the House. I'll finish getting ready and head off."

"Are you going to speak to them?"

"No way. They're seeking publicity and I'm not going to indulge them."

Maria returned to the armchair as Teddy made his way

upstairs.

Once he was in their bedroom he reached for his tie and reflected on the fact that he'd been a Member of Parliament for three years and this was only the second time there had been a protest at his home.

The first had been by a woman who wanted him to back her in her pursuit of a twenty-mile-an-hour speed limit in her village. He'd gone outside, engaged her in conversation and learned that her five-year-old son had been killed by a motorist doing thirty. Teddy had promised to back her campaign and had even asked a question in the House about it.

It had done wonders for him.

Nothing had happened concerning the speed limit but that wasn't the point. He had supported her and boosted his profile. That was what mattered.

Dealing with Sow the Wind was altogether different. He didn't see how he could use them to his advantage and ignoring their presence was probably the best action. He would walk past them with his head held high and if they bombarded him with questions and demands, as was highly likely, he would be aloof, say 'no comment' and leave it at that.

Teddy tightened his tie against his collar, donned his suit jacket and headed back downstairs.

"I assume they're still here," he said when he returned to the lounge.

"Presumably," Maria said without looking up. "I decided to invite the Waddings after all."

He walked to the window. A few more had arrived but it was a fairly sorry bunch. Eleven people in all including the journalist. If they wanted to get publicity they were going to be sorely disappointed.

"Okay. I'm off," he said as he bent down to peck Maria on the cheek. "Wish me luck."

"With what?"

"Them." She was focused on her invitations and didn't reply. "I'll send you a message when I leave this evening. It could be a late sitting today."

"Okay."

He left the room, grabbed his briefcase from the hall and opened the front door.

Chapter 3

"Teddy Overton stands for everything we despise," Jackie shouted, though raising her voice was hardly necessary given the ten people in front of her were all within spitting distance.

Not that she cared. Her focus was the journalist. She needed him to have words to quote when he spread the news about what had happened.

She gesticulated behind her at the house. "Overton supports exploitation of the land. Who in their right mind wants oil exploration wells dug deep beneath our schools and hospitals?"

"We don't!" Finn exclaimed.

"He's evil," someone shouted.

"And now let me introduce Andrea Mason," Jackie said. "Andrea co-founded Sow the Wind and is one of this country's leading proponents of a clean earth policy."

Jackie stepped down and Andrea took her place on the soapbox.

"It's a proven fact that fracking causes earthquakes," Andrea began. "Our children will suffer. We will all suffer."

"It's a scandal," Finn said.

"I want a world where our energy comes from natural sources," she went on. "Where we harness the power of the sun and the wind rather than pouring money into the pockets of the men at the top of the gas and oil companies. They are corrupt, our government is corrupt and we need to put a stop to it now."

"Hear! Hear!" Jackie said and others joined in.

"There he is," Finn said.

Jackie turned to see the MP emerging from his front door.

Andrea held out her arm and pointed at him. "I see," she said with a considerable amount of sarcasm, "that the right honourable gentleman has decided to join us."

Someone laughed while Overton merely glared at her as he walked down the path towards his front gate.

"Why do you support fracking?" Andrea demanded as he drew near.

His eyes widened. "No comment," he said.

Jackie walked up to him until her face was only inches from his.

"We deserve an answer," she hissed.

"What do you have to say, Overton?" Finn called from behind her.

The MP's shoulders seemed to sag. He glared at Jackie. "Out of my way, woman."

"What do you mean 'woman'?" she said. "I'm a person and I'm one of your constituents. Don't I deserve an answer? Or are you a misogynist as well as a denier of climate change?"

"I'm not…"

He managed to stop himself from completing the sentence and tried to step around her, but she moved to one side to block him again.

He closed his eyes for a second, turned and started walking back towards his house.

Jackie followed him. "Are you going to run away indoors, Overton?" she asked. "Is that what you want to do? Are you afraid to answer our questions?"

"Coward!" Andrea called from the soapbox.

Jackie could sense he was on the edge and that one more provocation would push him over. What was more, she had done her research and knew exactly which button to push.

She lowered her voice so that only he could hear her. "Is it your wife you're running back to," she hissed, "Or is Louise Pinnington in there?"

Overton stopped walking and turned around.

"How do you know about Louise?" he hissed.

Jackie said nothing.

He stared at her for a moment before coming to a decision. "I've had enough of this nonsense," he barked. "I'm going to the House. Let me pass."

He put his hand on her shoulder to encourage her to move to one side. Jackie immediately fell backwards onto the ground as if she had been pushed.

"He hit her!" someone shouted.

Jackie was pleased to see Oscar recognise this as his cue. He ran forward at full pelt, took his right hand from his pocket and swung with all his might at Overton's jaw. The MP ducked but was unable to evade the blow and there was a sickening crack as Oscar's fist connected with his left temple.

For a second there was no reaction, then everything seemed to move in slow motion. The MP's legs gave way from the ankles up as his eyes closed. Slowly, agonisingly slowly, his body folded and he collapsed to the ground.

Oscar turned around triumphantly, anticipating smiles and cries of support, but was greeted with silence as the small crowd gazed in horror at the man now lying on his side. Blood was pouring from a gash in his head and oozing from his left ear.

Andrea jumped down and ran to Oscar. "Come with me," she said. "We need to get away." She grabbed his hand and then let go again. "What's that?" she asked as she looked down at the black metal ring encircling his knuckles.

"It's not mine," Oscar said. "I found it by the side of the road."

"Take it off and drop it," she demanded.

He did as she asked and let her lead him out of the garden where Finn joined them as they walked quickly away from the house.

A woman from the crowd ran past them to the prone

figure on the ground. "I'm a nurse," she said as she knelt next to him and lifted his head. "This looks bad," she added, almost to herself.

Jackie stepped back and watched as others in the group came forward. At their front was the journalist who was holding his phone in the air, videoing what was happening.

"I've called an ambulance," one man said.

A few seconds later Maria Overton emerged from the house.

"What's happened?" she said as she dashed forward to kneel beside the nurse. She stroked her husband's cheek. "Oh god, Teddy. Wake up!"

Jackie turned to follow the others. She needed to get away before the police arrived.

It had all gone to plan.

Oscar had done well.

Chapter 4

FOUR MONTHS LATER

Luke Sackville, previously a Detective Chief Inspector with Avon and Somerset Police and now Head of Ethics at Filchers, sat in the corner of The Good Bear Cafe with his double espresso.

He'd arrived early to prepare his thoughts. This was a big change for the team and he wanted them on board, especially Sam. As his deputy, she was the one who would have to take on the lion's share of responsibility. She was well able to, he knew that, but it meant less casework and more admin so it was a big change for her.

He looked up to see the youngest member of his team approaching.

"What's this about, guv?' Josh asked as he sat on the opposite side of the table. "I mean, a breakfast meeting, and not in the canteen. Has to be big news." He paused, looked over at the food counter and then back at Luke. "Are we having breakfast?'

Luke smiled. "This is a work meeting, Josh. Filchers is paying and you can have whatever you want."

"Wowza!" He started to stand then thought better of it. "Best to wait for the others, I guess. No rush." He paused. "Do they do a Full English?'

"Yes. It's very good."

"Gucci!"

Luke looked past Josh, whose eyes were now scanning the menu on the wall, to see Sam standing outside the cafe. She was talking to someone out of sight and from the expression on her face it appeared to be a serious conversation. After a few seconds, she turned and entered the cafe.

As she walked towards their table she shook her head, clearly annoyed with something, then put on a smile.

"Hi," she said.

"Is everything okay?" Luke asked. "You seemed to be arguing with someone."

"No. It's nothing."

"Was it about parking?" Josh asked.

"No." She hesitated. "It was Ollie. He's offered to wait outside and take me into the office when we're finished."

"That's good of him," Josh said.

Smarmy, creepy bastard, Luke thought but said, "I could have given you a lift."

"I told him that but, well…" She shrugged. "So, what's this all about?"

Luke smiled. "Not you too. You'll have to wait until the others arrive but it's nothing earth-shattering I assure you."

"They do a great Full English," Josh said.

"I've already had breakfast," Sam said.

"Me too but, you know…" He pointed to the food counter, said, "Gift horse," then indicated his mouth, grinned and added, "Mouth."

"Here are the others," Luke said as he saw Maj at the entrance holding the door open for Helen.

They were an odd duo, Maj's Somalian heritage in complete contrast to Helen's pale skin, evidence of her upbringing in the windy hills around Edinburgh.

Helen sat next to Luke while Maj sat opposite.

"Thanks for coming," Luke said once he'd placed the order for drinks and, to Josh's delight, their food. "The reason for this is that my role is changing. As you all know, I've been moonlighting as a consultant for Avon and Somerset Police. That's now moving to a formal arrangement."

"You don't mean full-time?" Maj asked.

"No. It's going to be two to three days a week."

"Are you returning to homicide, guv?" Josh asked.

"I wasn't in homicide, Josh, I was in the Major Crime Unit. And no, not directly." Luke turned to Sam. "Sam, are you okay to deputise for me when I'm not here?"

"Yes, that's fine," she said, then added hastily, "Do I have to go to Edward Filcher's meetings?"

He smiled. "Don't worry, I'll try to keep you out of them."

"Thank goodness."

"Aye," Helen said. "The less time spent with that wee twaddlepot the better."

"Actually, Helen," Luke said. "I was thinking you'd be the best person to attend his weekly meeting."

"You've got to be…" She paused as she saw the grin on her boss's face. "Ah. You're kidding."

"What do you mean by a formal arrangement?" Maj asked.

"Avon and Somerset will be buying my services through Filchers. There will be a contract for me half-time as well as day rates for the rest of you so that you can be pulled in on an ad hoc basis."

Josh sat forward in his chair. "So I might be a police officer?" he asked.

"No. You won't be a police officer but you might be a police consultant."

Josh grinned. "Wait 'til I tell Leanne."

"Helen," Luke continued, "Would you mind helping to draft the contract?"

"Not at all."

"There's one more thing I wanted to talk to you all about." He paused. "What are your views on climate change?"

Maj, Helen and Sam gave him quizzical looks while Josh merely said, "Our food's here," as a man emerged from the kitchen bearing food. "What was that, guv?" he added as two plates were put in front of Helen and Sam and the waiter returned for more.

"I was asking about weather patterns."

Josh nodded. "Gotcha." He looked across at Helen's plate. "The black pudding looks good."

"I want your views on it," Luke explained

"The black pudding?"

Luke sighed. "No, son. Changes in the weather."

"Right. I see." Josh's breakfast was placed in front of him and he cut into a sausage, impaled it on his fork, said, "It's going to rain this afternoon," and popped it in his mouth.

"You numpty!" Helen said.

"What?" Josh said through a mouthful.

"We'll talk once there's less distraction," Luke said.

*

"As you all know," Luke said, once their plates had been cleared, "Filchers has been competing for Globo Energy's outsourcing contract. It's worth £80 million over six years and I can tell you now that we've won. Over the next few months, we'll be taking on their admin and finance functions which involves over 400 staff transferring to us. It'll be public knowledge when the press release goes out later this week, but you need to keep it quiet until then."

"That's great news," Sam said, "but I'm guessing there's something else."

Luke smiled. "You're right. Filchers pitched the Ethics Team as an example of the company's innovation and Globo wants to call on our services. But before I tell you why, let me go back to my earlier question. What are your views on climate change?"

There was a brief discussion with everyone agreeing there needed to be a greater commitment, both in the UK and abroad, to reducing emissions.

"So in summary," Luke said when they'd finished, "you have concerns but none of you are members of the climate movement."

They all nodded.

"Good. Have you heard of Earth Conflict or Sow the Wind? They're climate activist groups."

"Wasn't Sow the Wind in the news a few months ago?" Sam asked.

"Aye," Helen said. "I remember that. One of their members injured an MP."

"That's right," Luke said. "Oscar Briggs, a member of Sow the Wind, hit Teddy Overton on the side of the head with a heavy-duty carabiner, the kind used in mountaineering."

Sam shivered. "I remember it now. He was hurt badly, wasn't he?"

Luke nodded. "At first they feared permanent brain damage, but now they're saying he'll make a full recovery. He stood down from parliament though."

"I'm not surprised. What happened to the man who attacked him?"

"He was found guilty of grievous bodily harm and given a community order and a rehabilitation plan. He avoided prison because of his vulnerability. He has learning disabilities."

"I haven't heard of Earth Conflict," Sam said.

"Me neither," Maj said.

"Nor me," Helen added as Josh shook his head.

"By all accounts it's less than two months old," Luke said, "but the two groups are similar. If you look at their websites you'll see that they both promote peaceful environmental protests and non-violent civil disobedience. However, members of Globo's senior executive are concerned that one or both of them may be more militant than they make out."

Josh grinned. "Are we going undercover?"

"Two of you four are, yes."

Josh's hand shot up.

"The Gents is back there," Helen said, pointing to the sign for the toilets.

"No, I…"

"I'm not looking for volunteers," Luke said. "The opposite in fact. Given we're talking about potential militancy, in other words violent action, there may be some risk involved, so please feel free to opt out if you don't want to be considered."

"Heaven forbid we should ever do anything risky," Helen said with a smile.

"You've got the option, that's all I'm saying."

"Well, I'm in," Helen said.

"Me too," Maj and Sam added.

"Definito," Josh said, his hand still in the air.

"Good, but you can put your hand down."

Josh pulled his arm down. "How are you going to decide, guv?"

"I need some more information from Globo first." Luke turned to Sam. "I hate to say this after the assurance I gave you earlier, Sam, but I need you to join me in a meeting with Edward Filcher."

Chapter 5

"It's five to," Luke said. "We'd better head upstairs."

"Mmm. I guess so," Sam said as she picked up her pad and pen.

"Don't worry, Sam. He's harmless."

He walked to the Ethics Room door and opened it for her.

"You're right," she said as she passed him and they started down the corridor. "Filcher may be pompous but at least he's not racist or misogynist. Oh, I forgot. He's both of those, isn't he?"

Luke laughed. "He's not the best specimen of humanity but he's our boss and we're stuck with him."

"I guess so."

Filcher's secretary was seated at her desk when they arrived on the Executive Floor.

"Good morning, Gloria," Luke said. "This is Sam Chambers."

"Hi, Gloria," Sam said as she leaned forward to shake her hand. "Nice to meet you."

"And you too, dear," Gloria said. "I've heard a lot about you."

"From Mr Filcher?"

Gloria laughed. "Oh no. He struggles to remember my name, and I've been working for him for over a decade, so there's little chance of him remembering yours. No, it was Ellie, the Chief Executive's PA, who told me what high regard Ambrose holds you in."

Sam was pleasantly surprised and a little shocked by this. Ambrose Filcher was the CEO and founder of Filchers and she hadn't imagined he was aware of her existence, let alone that he rated her.

Gloria's phone rang.

"Excuse me," she said as she picked it up. She listened for a few seconds then said, "I'll be right down," before ending the call and standing up. "Why don't you two go on in?" she suggested. "That was reception. The two Globo visitors have arrived. I'll go and fetch them."

Luke gave a peremptory knock on the door of his boss's office, heard a shout of "Enter", pushed the door and held it open for Sam to go in first.

Filcher was holding a photo up to the wall behind his desk. "Got you!" he mumbled as he managed to locate the hook. He let go and then held his fingers millimetres from the bottom corners of the frame in case it fell. After a few seconds, he slowly pulled his hands away and took a pace backwards.

"What do you think, Luke?" he said without turning around.

"Is it Liz Truss and you?" Luke asked.

"Liz and me," Filcher confirmed, nodding his head up and down but keeping his eyes fixed on the photo. "The ex-Prime Minister and me. Fund-raising dinner. Met her there. Formed a close bond."

"You both look a lot younger."

"It was a few years ago. 2009. Before she was PM."

"And you've been friends ever since?"

"Yes." Filcher was still facing away. "Not met her again, but yes. Close bond." He gestured along the wall to the photo of him and Boris Johnson which was of a similar vintage. "I fly high."

"You do, Mr Filcher. And often by the seat of your pants."

"Indeed." He sighed. "Ah well, enough about my successes." He turned around, spotted Sam and beamed. "Ah, Helen," he said. "Thank you for coming."

"Sam," Sam said.

"Eh?" He looked around the room. "Where?"

"My name's Sam."

"Of course. Hah! I knew that."

"Sam's going to deputise for me," Luke said.

"Eh?"

"When I'm at Avon and Somerset Police."

"Oh, yes." Filcher tapped the side of his nose. "Working for the Chief again, eh? Hush, hush."

"It's not a secret, Mr Filcher."

"It is with me. I can always be trusted." He turned and admired the photo again, lifting the left-hand corner a smidgeon to ensure it was straight. "Exactly like my old friend Liz. You can trust her with anything."

"I'd certainly trust you as much as I would her," Luke confirmed, trying to avoid Sam's eyes as he said it.

Filcher turned his attention back to Sam. "Covering for Luke, eh? A challenge for you."

Sam nodded. "Yes, but I can only do my best."

"Exactly. Even if it's not good enough. Remember, my door is always open. Especially to women."

"Especially to women?"

Filcher nodded. "I recognise it's difficult. For women I mean. Having babies. Husbands to look after." He laughed. "And work on top of all that. Pressure mounts. But you can always come to me."

"That's very good of you."

"I know."

There was a knock at the door and Gloria pushed it open. "Your visitors are here, Mr Filcher," she said and stood back as a woman and man, both in their mid-thirties, came into the room.

"Please come in," Filcher said. "Ah. You already are. Excellent. I am Edward Filcher."

The woman shook his hand first. "Liz Rathbone," she said.

"Lovely." He shook her hand and then turned and pointed to the photo of him and Liz Truss. "Not related to the other Liz, are you? Hah!"

She raised an eyebrow. "Hopefully not.'

"Mmm." He turned to the man. "And you are?"

"Daniel Craven."

He shook his hand and then turned to Luke and Sam. "This is Luke Sackville," he said, and waited for Luke to shake their hands before continuing with, "And this is, ah… Sorry, I don't know your surname, Helen."

"Sam," Sam said.

"Of course. Hah! This is Luke's deputy, Helen Sam."

"Hi, Liz," Sam said as she shook her hand. "I'm Sam Chambers." She turned to her colleague "Hi, Daniel."

"Hi, Sam," he said as they shook hands.

"Please sit wherever you like," Filcher said then watched in horror as Daniel pulled the chair out from the end nearest his desk. "Except there," he added hastily and pointed to the chairs on the far side. "They are more, ah, suitable."

Daniel shuffled over and Liz followed him around.

Luke and Sam sat opposite while Filcher took his customary seat at the head of the table.

He smiled at the two visitors.

"I was saying to, ah…" He smiled then said, "…Sam. Yes, Sam. I was saying to Sam. We look after women at Filchers. Always will. Make sure they're cared for. They need more help than men. Sad but inevitable."

"Is that so?" Liz said.

"Sadly, yes." Filcher looked at Daniel. "You too."

Daniel raised an eyebrow. "Me too?"

Filcher nodded. "Inclusion. In the numbers. Very important. Always seek to maximise it and, ah…" He wafted his hand in Daniel's general direction. "…include everyone. Regardless of their, ah…Where are you from?"

"Swindon."

"Hah! Very good. But originally?"

"I was born in Swindon."

"Ah. Your parents then…"

"I think we should start the meeting," Luke said, fearful that his boss was about to work his way through every African country. He looked across at Liz and Daniel. "Could you start by outlining Globo Energy's concerns?"

"Yes, of course," Liz said. "I'm Globo's Head of Security, and Daniel is my deputy."

"Congratulations," Filcher said.

Liz glanced briefly in his direction before continuing. "We started monitoring Sow the Wind after the incident with Teddy Overton," she said. "That in itself appears to have been a one-off, but we were concerned because one of their founders has a reputation as an anarchist."

"Do you mind if I take notes?" Sam asked.

Liz smiled. "Of course not. Her name is Andrea Mason. She founded Sow the Wind with her then-partner Finn O'Sullivan."

Sam wrote these names down.

"Then-partner?" Luke queried.

"It appears they've parted ways, and in more ways than one. O'Sullivan left Sow the Wind and started Earth Conflict roughly two months ago."

"And you're now monitoring both?"

"As much as we can, but it's difficult from the outside. Only signed-up members are allowed to their meetings for a start."

"What makes you think we can help?"

"You have your Chief Executive to thank for that."

"My uncle," Filcher said. "Ambrose Filcher is my uncle," he added as if he hadn't been clear enough.

"Is he?" Liz asked.

Filcher nodded.

"I see," she said. "It all makes sense now."

"Our surnames being the same?"

She smiled. "Not that, no. I now understand how you got to the level you have."

"Ingenuity, integrity and innovation," Filcher said. "Runs in the family. The three ins."

"I was thinking more of the three p's," Liz said.

"Three p's?"

"Partiality, patronage and partisanship."

"Hah! Very good."

"You were saying," Luke said, "that Ambrose is the reason you're here."

She nodded. "He told Brian Glover, our Chairman, that some of your team had gone undercover in the past to investigate criminal activities."

"We've worked for the Chief Constable of Wessex Police," Filcher said proudly. "She's a good friend of mine."

"Isn't Craig Reynolds the Chief Constable?" Daniel said.

Filcher's eyes widened. "Um…"

"Do you want us to go into both Sow the Wind and Earth Conflict?" Luke asked.

"If possible, yes," Liz said.

"We're going to need false identities," Sam said.

"I can help with that," Daniel said. "I have people I can call on."

"Family and friends in Nigeria?" Filcher asked.

Daniel's eyebrows furrowed. "No," he said.

"Senegal?" Filcher continued. "The Gambia?"

"I used to be in Border Force," Daniel said. "UK Border Force."

"Ah."

"Thanks for your time," Luke said quickly, fearful that his boss was going to continue putting his foot in it. "Sam and I need to talk about how to go about this and do some background research. We'll get back to you as soon as we can."

"Thanks," Liz said.

They exchanged business cards, shook hands and Gloria escorted the two visitors back to reception.

"I could have sworn the Chief Constable's name was Sara, not Craig," Filcher said after they'd left. "Still, we all make mistakes."

Some more than others, Luke thought as he and Sam said goodbye and set off back to the Ethics Room.

Chapter 6

Sam was proofreading one of her reports when Luke appeared at her desk.

"Why don't you and I grab a coffee," he said. "It'll give us the chance to talk about the Globo Energy project."

"That makes sense."

She stood up and followed him out of the Ethics Room.

She was pleased. It wasn't often they had the opportunity to talk one-on-one, and she found his views on work, and life in general, refreshing. He was a good listener too, and if she ever needed advice he was her automatic go-to.

Not that her boyfriend Ollie wasn't a decent listener, but he wasn't as empathetic. Perhaps it was because he was a professional cyclist, and lived in a completely different world from the one she and Luke inhabited. He could also be a trifle self-obsessed, something no one would ever accuse Luke of.

When they reached the canteen they bought their drinks and carried them to a corner table by the window. It was still a while until lunchtime so they had the place to themselves.

"Are you sure you're happy with deputising two or three days a week?" Luke asked once they were seated.

"Yes, it should be fine."

"Good. Remember, if you have any concerns whatsoever you only have to ask."

"Thanks, Luke. I appreciate it."

He smiled. "Don't for one second think that you're not up to it. You're an incredibly important part of the team and it wouldn't perform half as well without you."

Sam felt her cheeks go slightly pink as he said this. Words of praise from Luke meant the world.

"However…" he started to say.

Oh, Christ!

Had she done something wrong? Was the real reason for their tete-a-tete that someone had complained about her? She'd confronted that bully in the media sector the other day. Was that it? Had she been too abrupt with him?

"Are you okay, Sam?" Luke asked. He leaned forward and put his hand on her arm.

She swallowed.

She wished he wouldn't do that, she really did.

"I'm okay," she said. "You were saying?"

He pulled his hand back.

"I was saying that you deserve your promotion. However, I think it means you can't be one of the two to go undercover.

"Oh, is that all?"

"Yes. Why?"

"Nothing." She took a sip of her coffee. "I guess you're right." She saw movement over his shoulder. "Oh, someone's coming over."

Luke turned to see Cora Evans walking towards them.

"Cora," he said as she approached. "I don't think you two have met, have you? This is Sam."

"Hi," Sam said.

"Hi, Sam," Cora said. She smiled at Luke, put her hand on his shoulder and gazed into his eyes.

There was affection in that look and Sam felt like she was an unwelcome intrusion.

"Sorry to interrupt your discussion, Luke," Cora went on, still looking into his eyes and still smiling. "I wanted to check the timings for tonight."

"Shall we meet outside at seven?"

"Great." She squeezed his shoulder. "I'm looking forward to it." She let go and turned her smile on Sam. "It's good to meet you at last. He's forever talking about you. Anyway, I'll leave you to it. See you later, Luke."

"See you later."

It had been a brief encounter, but Sam could see why he had fallen for Cora. She was very attractive plus she was a Client Director which made her the same grade as Luke. It was clear he was drawn to successful women and they were well-matched.

Good for him.

Not that she and Ollie didn't go well together. They had a lot in common. Okay, he could be a tad jealous at times, and moody on occasions, but no one was perfect. They'd been together for several months now and he'd even suggested they move in together. She wasn't ready for that though, not yet anyway.

She realised Luke was talking.

"Sorry," she said. "What was that?"

"I was saying that Josh, Helen and Maj would all be up for going undercover," Luke said.

Sam laughed. "Especially Josh. He's already planning how to tell Leanne if we pick him."

"I know, and he'll be mortified if we choose the other two. Plus he did an excellent job in a similar role back in June."

"Yes, Luke, but pretending to be a teenager was hardly a challenge for him." She paused. "You're right, though. He carried it off brilliantly."

"Josh it is then. Now we have to decide between Helen and Maj."

They both took a sip of their coffees while they considered this.

"It would be Helen's first time doing this kind of work," Sam said after a few seconds.

"That's true, but I don't see that being a problem for her."

"No, and I think she'd relish it. Plus I find it easier to

picture her as an environmental campaigner."

"Good, it's decided."

Sam started to stand up but Luke held his hand up to stop her.

"Just a second, Sam," he said. "There's one other thing I need to talk to you about, and I'm afraid you're not going to like it one little bit."

Her heart sank.

Here it was. She'd been right all along and she was about to be told off, probably because she'd been forceful with that bully.

She sat back down. "Okay," she said. "Give it to me straight. What have I done?"

Luke drew his head back and furrowed his brows. "Nothing."

"Then…"

Luke laughed. "Did you think you were in trouble?"

She blushed again and was immediately annoyed with herself. Going pink in the cheeks was getting to be a habit.

"I might have done," she admitted.

"Well, rest assured you're not. No, the other thing I need to talk to you about is Glen Baxter."

She didn't like the sound of this one bit.

"Go on," she said with a slightly wary tone.

"Liz Rathbone rang me about half an hour ago. She asked if I could set up a meeting between her and our Head of Security." He chuckled. "She didn't want to mention it when we were with Filcher in case he wanted to be in on the meeting."

Sam echoed his laugh. "Out of the frying pan into the fire."

"You're right. If she thought Filcher was hard work wait until she meets Glen."

"Does she want to see him because of our undercover work?"

"No, and I think the less Glen knows about that the

better. She wants to let him know what Globo expects in terms of security when Filchers takes responsibility for their administration and finance departments."

"And?"

"And I arranged the meeting for this Friday, completely forgetting I've got to be in Portishead that day."

"Why were you going to be in the meeting?"

Luke raised one eyebrow. "We're talking Glen Baxter and a senior member of Globo Energy who happens to be female. Why do you think I was going to be there?"

"Fair enough. So you want me to chaperone?"

"Please.'

"Okay." She shook her head and then shrugged. "Still, I guess he can't be any worse than Filcher was."

"Oh yes, he can. Believe me, Sam, he's more than capable."

Chapter 7

"Have you decided, guv?" Josh asked as soon as Luke and Sam returned to the Ethics Room.

"Yes," Luke said. "Helen, Maj, could you join us please?"

The five of them sat around the table.

"Well?" Josh said. "Who's it going to be?"

Luke smiled inwardly at his eagerness, but let the edges of his mouth drop and shook his head.

"I'm sorry, Josh," he said. "Sam and I discussed who would be best and agreed that the role needed experience…"

"I've got that."

"…and maturity."

Josh's face dropped. "Oh!"

"But despite that," Luke continued, "we decided on Helen and you."

"Wowza! Me!" Josh clapped his hands together. "You won't regret it, guv."

"You don't mind do you, Maj?"

"Not at all."

"Which of us to which group?" Helen asked.

"That's a good question," Luke said. "I suggest the two of you do some desk research, discuss what you've found and come back with your recommendations."

"Coolio," Josh said.

Luke looked at his watch. "Will a couple of hours be enough?"

They both agreed that it would.

*

Helen stood at the whiteboard, drew a line down the middle and wrote 'Sow the Wind' on the left and 'Earth Conflict' on the right.

"First, we looked at Sow the Wind," she began. "As you know, it was founded by Andrea Mason who seems to have had a privileged upbringing. Her father is a merchant banker, and she was a boarder at Roedean School near Brighton, then went to Cambridge University to study Philosophy. While she was there she created The Black Cat Club."

"We found it in the Freshers' programme for 2013," Josh said. "She was described as the founding member and advertised it as being for students who…" He read from his notebook, "…*are anti-authority and believe we should move to a stateless society.*"

"Anarchists," Luke said.

"Seems like it, guv."

"We also found a newspaper article," Helen said, "about a protest outside the home of the Dean of her college. It was led by her and it was to challenge the examination rules. She seems to have dropped out towards the end of her second year."

"Perhaps she was expelled?" Sam suggested.

"It's possible."

"What about since then?" Luke asked.

"She's kept a low profile," Helen said. "Sow the Wind hasn't been very visible either. Aside from that incident where a member attacked an MP, the group has had barely any coverage. They tweet regularly, and there's a Facebook page, but they don't appear to be making much of an impact."

"Have they got a website?" Maj asked.

"Yes. It's amateurish though. It lists their principles and there's a blog, but the only article of any real interest references a letter the group sent to the Environment Minister. It was written not long before the attack on Teddy

Overton and it was from Andrea Mason, Finn O'Sullivan and Curtis Pinnington complaining about the lack of progress with renewable energy."

"It was interesting because it included their photos," Josh said. "I've printed them off." He stood up and passed them to Helen who stuck them to the whiteboard.

"Andrea and Finn look, I don't know…" Sam began.

"Dirty," Maj suggested.

She smiled and nodded. "Definitely. I can't imagine the last time they washed their hair. They look distinctly unsavoury."

"I know what you mean," Josh said. "Curtis Pinnington's a contrast, isn't he?"

Josh was right, Luke thought. Pinnington looked very much the English gentleman in an orange waistcoat over a checked shirt and red tie. He was clean-shaven and his hair was unbelievably black for a man who looked to be in his mid-fifties.

"What do we know about Pinnington?" Luke asked.

"He's the MP for South Mendip," Helen said. "He was in the Labour Party then defected to the Conservatives before they expelled him and he became an Independent. He's very outspoken and leaps from bandwagon to bandwagon."

"And party to party by the sound of it," Maj said.

Helen smiled. "Although his current focus is the environment, until a year ago it seems to have been immigration, and before that defence spending."

"That's good work," Luke said. "You said that Sow the Wind's website listed their principles. Did anything stand out?"

"Aye, one thing did," Helen said, "but it only became apparent when we saw Earth Conflict's values."

"Go on," Luke said, intrigued.

Helen took Finn O'Sullivan's photo and moved it to the right-hand side of the board. "O'Sullivan appears to have started Earth Conflict very recently. Their first blog entry was two months ago."

"That ties up with what Liz Rathbone from Globo Energy told us," Sam said.

"His is the only name on the Earth Conflict website," Helen went on, "and so far there's no logo. However, we found seven values that mirror seven of Sow the Wind's eight principles. For example, Sow the Wind's first principle is *'We wish to create a future fit for our children and our children's children'*, while one of Earth Conflict's values is, *'Our hearts and minds are intent on making the world a better place for our children and their children'*."

"Okay," Luke said, "Don't keep us in suspense."

It was Josh who answered. "Sow the Wind's eighth principle is short and to the point. All it says is, *'We oppose violence in all its forms'*."

"And there's nothing like that in Earth Conflict's values?"

Josh shook his head. "No. Completely missing."

Luke considered this for a moment. "Were there any other obvious differences between the two organisations?" he asked.

"I'd say Earth Conflict's language is more aggressive," Helen said. "What do you think, Josh?"

"I agree," Josh said. "The colours on the website are harsher too, much more in your face. Sow the Wind uses red and black but has a lot more images. Earth Conflict uses orange and loads of shouty text."

"Shouty text?" Maj said. "What's shouty text?"

"You know, lots of capital letters and exclamation marks. Very, ah…"

"Exclamationy?" Helen suggested.

Josh fired a finger gun at her. "Exactimo."

"Okay," Luke said, "So did you conclude who should join which group."

"Aye, we did that," Helen said. "We weighed up all the

evidence, ran through the pros and cons, assessed each other's strengths and weaknesses and then used a very old and well-proven system."

Josh grinned. "And I called heads correctly, so it'll be me in Earth Conflict."

Chapter 8

Josh sat in the Costa Coffee near the office waiting for Leanne to arrive after she'd finished her shift on reception.

He was excited for the evening ahead on a couple of counts.

First, he and Leanne were going round to his mum's for dinner and staying over. She was a great cook and he hadn't seen her for a couple of weeks. Okay, his little twerp of a brother was going to be there, but you had to take the rough with the smooth. Besides, he was a grown man now, living with his girlfriend in a swish apartment, well an apartment anyway. He could cope with Noah's interminable swipes and digs, of course he could.

Probably.

Second, he was going to tell Leanne and his mum about his new assignment. Golly, they were going to be impressed. The burning question was whether to tell them separately or together. Separately meant he got two doses of admiration, but together would increase the impact.

Yes, he decided, he'd wait and tell them together. He could be patient. After all, he was a responsible person, an investigative agent with years, well months, of experience at being…

He paused.

At being what exactly? What was the best way of describing himself now that he had countless, well three, assignments under his belt?

He ran through a few options.

'Undercover Agent' was the obvious one, but there was something dull about it. It lacked the resonating qualities of 'Secret Agent' or 'Undercover Operative'.

He briefly considered 'Operative Agent', but that

sounded too much like something you'd clean the toilet with.

And, if he was honest, 'Secret Agent' was a bit much. He was hardly James Bond, he was just little old Josh Ogden.

That gave him an idea.

He was going to be donning an outfit, so to speak, by pretending to be someone he wasn't. Much like a superhero.

Yes, that was it. Mild-mannered Josh Ogden becomes…

…Supermole?

…Superspook?

No. Neither of those worked.

…Superinfiltratorman?

Too many syllables.

…Superspy?

Too short.

It was important to get it right, to fully portray the job he would be doing, to…

"I said, do you want a drink?"

Josh looked up at the waitress. "Eh?"

"We're busy." She gestured to the packed tables around the cafe. "You've been here fifteen minutes without buying anything. Do you want a drink?"

"Intelligencer."

"I beg your pardon."

"I'm going to be an intelligencer."

She looked him up and down. "I very much doubt that."

"What do you think about 'counterspy'?"

She put her hands on her hips and glared at him.

"We'll have one cappuccino and one large hot chocolate with cream and marshmallows," Leanne said from behind her.

The waitress turned. "Are you with him?" she asked.

"Yes."

"Good luck with that then." She turned to give Josh

one final stare and then headed back to the counter.

Leanne bent down to kiss her boyfriend and then sat opposite. "Were you giving her a rough time?"

"I was thinking through my options."

"For what?"

Josh swallowed and his resolution to tell Leanne and his mum at the same time vanished.

"I'm going to be a Field Plant," he said.

Leanne raised one perfectly manicured eyebrow. "Like a buttercup?"

Josh laughed. "No. I'm going to be in Conflict."

"In conflict with who?"

"Lots of people. Finn for one."

"Finn?"

"Yes. I don't know the names of the others. But then, I don't know my name yet."

"You don't know your name?"

He shook his head. "Not yet."

"Your drinks are ready," the waitress called.

Leanne fetched the drinks and passed the hot chocolate over to Josh who immediately started spooning marshmallows into his mouth.

"Right," Leanne said. "Slow down and explain yourself."

Josh swallowed. "I'm going to join an environmental campaign group called Earth Conflict."

"Why? You've never expressed much interest in that kind of thing."

"It's for work." He tapped the side of his nose and lowered his voice. "I'll be undercover to find out what they're planning."

"This isn't dangerous, is it?"

Josh shook his head. "No. They may be up to, ah…" He wracked his brain for a suitable word. "…shenanigans, that's all. And it's down to me to find out what."

"Shenanigans?"

"Yes. You know, rascalry, mischief-making, that kind of thing."

"And it's safe?"

Josh shook his head again, realised that was incorrect and changed to nodding. "Definitely," he said. "Completely safe."

*

"Who wants the last roastie?" Nancy said.

"Me, Mum," Josh said. He reached forward but Noah was quicker and smiled triumphantly as he held the potato up on the end of his fork and waved it around.

"Snooze and you lose," Noah said. "However, I'll share it with you if you want," he added before licking each side of the potato and grinning.

"You're immature," Josh said.

"No, you're immature."

Josh bit his tongue. He was a man now and he wasn't going to rise to the bait.

"What were you saying about your new assignment?" Nancy asked.

"I'm going undercover in an outfit called Earth Conflict, Mum," Josh said.

"That's wonderful. Is it something to do with the Cold War?"

"No, it's about climate change and renewable energy, that kind of thing."

"Good for you. Everyone needs a hobby. Now, who wants apple crumble?"

Chapter 9

Jackie sat on the stage of the small village hall and counted the people in the audience.

There were twenty-two. It was a pretty sorry turnout but, if she was honest, better than it could have been. She looked at her watch. There were still five minutes until the start, so perhaps they'd get a few more.

A man came in just before half-past and he could have been Finn O'Sullivan's doppelganger with his ridiculous long braided hair and flower-laden jeans. The only differences were that his hair was black and, unlike Andrea's ex-partner, he had a long forked beard rather than a goatee.

Not that Finn was around any more. He'd founded his own group after he and Andrea had split. Jackie smiled to herself. Earth Conflict's profile was even lower than Sow the Wind's, and that was saying something.

The trouble was that an audience of twenty-three didn't cut the mustard. Her sponsor was fast losing patience, and she had come to depend on his regular payments. She needed to up the ante, but not make the mistake she'd made with Oscar Briggs' attack on Teddy Overton. No, this time it had to be something that thrust Sow the Wind into the headlines in a way that made their name stick.

It was six-thirty and Jackie nodded to the woman beside her and stood up.

"Thanks everyone for coming this evening," she said as she cast her eyes around the hall. "My name is Jackie Walker and I'm delighted to see so many of you tonight. Please let me introduce the founder of Sow the Wind, and one of the country's leading advocates for a green earth policy, Andrea Mason."

There was a gentle ripple of applause and Andrea stood

up as Jackie sat down.

"Thank you, Jackie," Andrea said and smiled as she looked around the audience. "Thanks for giving up your valuable time to be here. This evening I'm going to share some of the appalling actions taken by this government." She smiled. "Or should I say inactions?" There was a ripple of laughter. "We all know that the earth is facing crisis. If the energy barons continue to ravage our land and seas in the interest of profit we will all pay the cost. Only last month…"

Jackie studied the audience as Andrea shared instances, some true some fabricated, of ministers' and energy bosses' failure to live up to their pledges.

She was looking for someone to exploit, but it had to be someone who would shine a light on Sow the Wind and not on themselves. After Oscar's attack on the MP, the media had concentrated almost exclusively on his learning disabilities and his poor upbringing.

Whoever she chose had to be prepared to take extreme action for the cause, but they also had to be someone who would fade into the background once they had taken that action. The media needed to focus on why they'd done what they'd done, not on him or her as an individual. That had been her mistake with Oscar. His low IQ had been pounced on by the press as the reason for the attack, rather than, as she'd hoped, his belief in the cause.

Her eyes were drawn to the hippy type who'd arrived at the last minute. He was enjoying Andrea's stories and kept nodding and occasionally applauding.

Andrea continued speaking for about thirty minutes. When she finished there was polite applause and Jackie stood up.

"Thanks, Andrea," she said. "And now, we've got time for questions after which we encourage all of you to sign up to Sow the Wind and help save the planet."

The hippy immediately put his hand up.

"Hi," he said. "My name's Paul. That was excellent, Miss Mason."

"Andrea, please," Andrea said.

He smiled. "Andrea, you shared story after story about incompetence and money-grabbing. Isn't it time to take real action rather than shower these bastards with words?"

There was some nodding and murmurs of approval from others at this.

"Absolutely," Andrea said. "I think you've hit the nail on the head, Paul. We're planning a series of non-violent protests over the next few weeks and months which will show the profiteers that we mean business."

"Is that enough, though? Will words and placards change anything, or do we need to be more radical?"

This was music to Jackie's ears. He was her man, she was sure of it.

"We in Sow the Wind are always open to suggestions," Andrea said, "though of course we only advocate non-violent action."

"Of course," Paul said, but there was something in the way he said it that made Jackie think he'd be up for anything, violent or not.

"You should join us," Andrea said, "and share your ideas. We're excellent listeners."

"Thanks, Andrea. I think I will."

He sat down.

"Thank you, Paul," Jackie said.

A couple of hands shot up. "You," Jackie said, pointing to a woman in a flowery dress.

"Is it true," the woman began, "that Curtis Pinnington is one of your supporters, and if so is that a good thing given his somewhat chequered history?"

Andrea smiled. "Yes, he's a supporter, and I know in his younger days he might have held slightly different views from those he holds today."

"Wasn't he an advisor to Globo Energy?"

"He was, and he has admitted his mistakes, but it was what he learned in that role that led him to support Sow the Wind."

There were a couple more questions, after which Jackie drew the meeting to a close.

"Thanks again for coming," she said. "Andrea and I will be here for a few more minutes so if you want to join Sow the Wind, or have more detailed questions, we'd love to hear from you."

There was applause and Andrea and Jackie stepped down from the stage as the majority of people exited, leaving one elderly couple, a young woman who looked at most eighteen, and Paul the hippy.

The couple were the first to approach, while the young woman stood behind them, patiently waiting her turn.

"Andrea," the man began, "what do you think about the ugliness of wind farms?"

Jackie moved away from them and walked up to Paul.

"Are you going to sign up?" she asked.

"I think so," he said, "although I worry that Sow the Wind is all bark and no bite."

Jackie nodded. "I got the impression you're in favour of more radical action."

"I think it's essential. Those bastards won't take notice if all we do is bombard them with words."

"Believe me, Paul, that's music to my ears." She lowered her voice and indicated the corner of the hall near the exit. "Let's go over there where we won't be overheard."

She led him over and kept her voice low.

"We recognise the need to make an impact," she said, "but we'd be shut down in an instant if we openly advocate violence. However, those people have to realise that we're serious. After all, we're talking about the end of life on earth if they're allowed to continue as they are."

"Exactly my view," Paul said.

"That's terrific. I have some ideas I'd like to share with

you, but let's keep this between ourselves. It's best to keep Andrea out of the loop so that she can protest her innocence if necessary. When are you free?"

Chapter 10

Luke parked in Charlotte Street car park, walked down to Queen Square and then turned right onto Saw Close where he spotted Cora standing outside the theatre. She looked stunning in a white blazer over a black jumpsuit, her almost-black hair falling below her shoulders in soft waves.

Cora stood on tip-toe to kiss him then grabbed his hand. "Fancy a drink before the show?" she asked.

"Why not," he said. "The Grapes is around the corner and does a mean range of ciders.'

He led the way to the pub and ordered a white wine for Cora and a half of Midford cider for himself.

"That looks like a miniature in your massive hand," she said, once he'd taken the drinks to their table.

"I daren't have more," Luke said. "I've got to drive home after the show."

"Why not stay the night?"

He smiled. "I'd love to but my normal dogsitter, the woman who walks Wilkins during the day, is away and I have to get back to him."

Cora returned his smile and squeezed his hand. "Not to worry."

"So, what do you know about 'The Play That Goes Wrong'?'

The next fifteen minutes sped by as they discussed the play they were going to see, which didn't take long as they knew nothing about it other than it came highly recommended, and then the types of theatrical production they liked. Cora was a big fan of musicals and Luke of comedy and drama.

Conversation, as always, was easy. They avoided the trap of discussing work, although Luke had to admit that a brief discussion about the highs and lows of the day would have helped him to wind down. Jess had always been great at recognising his need to offload. It was something he knew Sam would be good at too; she was a great listener.

"We could get together on Saturday," he said as they walked up to the Theatre Royal.

"I'm busy," Cora said. "Maybe the weekend after."

"Are you doing anything exciting?"

"Nothing you'd be interested in."

They put their phones to silent.

"This is a good position," Luke said as they took their seats in the centre of row G of the Stalls.

In common with Cora and, it seemed, everyone else in the theatre, he found himself laughing out loud several times during the first half of the show.

"That was excellent," he said when the curtain came down for the interval.

"Hilarious," Cora agreed.

They stood up to go to the theatre bar where Luke had pre-ordered drinks. As they waited for people to leave their row he pulled his phone out of his pocket.

"Christ!" he exclaimed.

"What is it?"

"I've had three missed calls from Mark. Something must have happened to my mother. I'd better ring him."

He waited until they were in the corridor and then rang his brother. It was answered immediately.

"Sorry I missed your call, Mark. I'm at the theatre. What's happened?"

"It's Father."

"Father?"

"He fell off the steps in the library."

"Has he hurt himself badly?'

"It looks like it. He was unconscious when I found him and he's got a bad head wound. We're waiting for an ambulance. Hang on, I think that might be them now." The line went quiet for a few seconds then Mark came back on. "Yes, they're here. I'd better go."

"Keep me informed. I'll head down there now."

He hung up and turned to Cora.

"Sorry."

She smiled sympathetically. "Don't be silly, I got the gist. You head off and we'll speak later. It sounds like you may not be able to get home tonight. Do you want me to head for yours after the play to look after Wilkins?"

"Thanks, that would be great. There's a key under the third plant pot to the left of the front door."

He kissed her, headed for the exit and then jogged back to the BMW.

Luke was fifteen minutes into the journey to Borrowham Hall trying, and almost managing, to stick to the speed limit, when his brother rang. He clicked the button on the steering wheel to accept the call.

"Well?"

"They're worried he may have bleeding on the brain. They're about to take him to Dorset County Hospital for a CT scan."

"Okay. How does he seem?"

"Confused. The paramedics think he may have a concussion."

"Are you going with him?"

"Yes. Erica's going to stay here with Marion."

"I'll head straight for the hospital. With luck, I'll be there in an hour or so."

Chapter 11

Sam was excited that Hannah and Ollie were meeting for the first time, but also a tad nervous. It was important that her friend liked him given they had been together for over three months and were fast becoming a permanent item.

A bit too fast if she was honest.

She was still getting used to Ollie's quirks and mood swings, but it was early days and she was sure Hannah and him would get on well. After all, he was easy to talk to and had a great sense of humour.

Hannah would be on edge too, given she was bringing her new man Bertie to the restaurant. They had been going out for a few weeks longer than Sam and Ollie, and Hannah had talked about him a lot, but he'd been kept out of sight. Meeting him in person was going to be fascinating.

"What time is the table booked for?" Ollie asked.

"Nine." Sam looked at her watch. "I guess we'd better head off."

They were in The Salamander, which had become their go-to pub, and the restaurant, called 'Chez Dominique', was only a five-minute walk away.

Ollie took Sam's hand as they began walking towards Pulteney Bridge.

"I can sense you're worried," he said, "and you shouldn't be. I'm sure this Bertie guy will be great."

"I'm more concerned that you and Hannah get on."

"Of course we will. From what you've said she seems perceptive and with me what you see is what you get."

"An open book."

"Exactly." He squeezed her hand and pointed over the road. "Is that it, or are there two Chez Dominiques on Argyle Street?"

Smiling, she let him lead her across the road and they entered the restaurant. It was full but very small and had a relaxed atmosphere with plain wooden tables and chairs and modern watercolours of Paris on the walls.

Sam spotted Hannah at a table to the left and waved. Hannah looked at her, then at Ollie and smiled a smile that Sam knew only too well. It meant he'd received her approval as far as physical appearance went.

"Nice to meet you," Ollie said as he pecked her on the cheek.

"So where's the mysterious Bertie?" Sam asked.

The answer came from behind them. "Who's Bertie?" a voice said. "Hannah, have you been seeing someone behind my back?"

Sam turned to see a man who was beaming from ear to ear. "Sorry," he said, holding his hand up, "I shouldn't joke before we've even met." He laughed and held his hand out. "I'm Bertie."

"You can give her a kiss on the cheek, you know," Hannah said.

"If you're sure. I didn't want her man to think I was after her, but then who wouldn't be?" He laughed again, kissed Sam on the cheek, then held his hand out and shook Ollie's hand. "You're a lucky man, Ollie, but you needn't worry. I've only got eyes for Hannah, lovely as you are, Sam."

They took their seats, Bertie next to Hannah with Sam and Ollie opposite.

"Have either of you been here before?" Sam asked.

"I have," Bertie said, "and it was great, so fingers crossed it is again. I had the fillet steak and it was terrific. Shall we get some wine?"

They ordered a bottle of Bordeaux and the waitress gave them each a menu.

"I gather you're a fitness coach, Bertie," Ollie said, once they'd placed their food orders.

Bertie nodded. "I've been doing it for nearly five years now. I wanted to be a professional athlete but injured my knee and my career was over."

"That happened to my boss," Sam said and immediately regretted mentioning Luke. Ollie had only met him on a couple of occasions but they hadn't hit it off.

"I feel like the odd one out," Hannah said.

"Why's that?" Ollie asked.

"I'm the only one of us who didn't become, or nearly become, a professional athlete."

Bertie raised one eyebrow and looked across at Sam. "Now I'm intrigued," he said. "What was your speciality, Sam?"

"Karate," Sam said, "but turning professional was never really an option."

Bertie smiled at her. "Karate, eh? Impressive. What level did you get to?"

Conversation flowed easily and Sam found herself growing to like Bertie. He had an endearing smile, a dry and occasionally caustic sense of humour and a genuine interest in others.

"Please excuse me," Sam said when they'd finished their mains. She stood up.

"I'll join you," Hannah said.

Once they'd reached the toilets it was Hannah who spoke first.

"What do you think of Bertie?" she whispered.

"I think he's great," Sam whispered back. "What about Ollie?"

"He's certainly good-looking."

"What are you not saying?"

Hannah shook her head. "It's nothing."

"Hannah!"

"He's quiet, that's all. From everything you said, I thought he'd be the life and soul of the party."

"You're right, he has been quiet this evening. I wonder

if he's feeling unwell."

They returned to the table.

"We were talking about professional cycling," Bertie said as they took their seats. "Ollie says it's a challenge keeping himself fit during the off-season."

"It's important to have a routine," Ollie said.

"And not allow yourself to be distracted by Sam," Bertie said with a smile.

Ollie returned his smile but there was a strained look to it.

When they'd finished their desserts Bertie asked for the bill. They all paid their share and made their way outside.

"Bertie's parked in Southgate," Hannah said. "Are you walking back to yours, Sam?"

"Yes," Sam said. "I'll call you tomorrow."

Ollie grabbed her hand as they headed down Great Pulteney Street.

"Are you feeling okay?' Sam asked after they had walked a few yards.

"I'm fine," Ollie said.

"Are you sure? You were very quiet all evening."

Ollie sighed. "Well, if you must know, I didn't like the way Bertie was flirting with you throughout the meal."

"What do you mean flirting?"

"Don't say you didn't notice." Ollie laughed but it lacked humour. "It started the moment we went in when he said 'What man wouldn't want you?'."

Sam stopped walking and turned to face Ollie. "I don't recall that, and I thought Bertie was lovely. Your reaction is totally over the top."

"What about a few minutes ago? He said you'd be a distraction if you were his girlfriend. If that's not coming on to you, I don't know what is."

Sam was about to respond when her phone started ringing. She let go of Ollie's hand and pulled it from her back pocket.

"Who is it?" he asked.

She looked at the screen. "It's Luke."

"That's your wonderful boss for you, ringing late at night."

Sam ignored him and clicked to accept the call.

"Hi, Luke," she said.

"Sorry to interrupt your evening," Luke said. "I need you to cover for me tomorrow."

"What's happened?"

"My father's hurt himself and I'm at the hospital with him."

"Oh, no. What did he do?"

As she asked this Ollie started whirling his fingers around in a 'be quick' gesture. Sam turned her back on him.

"He fell and hit his head," Luke said. "They're doing a CT scan now."

"How awful. Let me know what they find and how he is, won't you?"

"I will, Sam. Sorry, but I'm supposed to be in a meeting with Filcher tomorrow. Would you mind deputising for me?"

"Of course not. What's the meeting about?"

"James McDonald set it up. The title is 'Workplace Diversity' and that's all I know, I'm afraid."

"No problem. Take care, Luke."

She hung up and turned back to see Ollie looking at her and shaking his head.

"I'm not surprised…" he started to say but she didn't give him the chance to finish.

"This is over," she said.

He sucked his jaw in. "What do you mean? What's over."

"I've had enough of your petty jealousies, Ollie. I should have done this sooner. You and I are finished."

"I'm sorry, Sam. I didn't mean to…"

"Are you listening?"

"This is ridiculous. All I said was…"

Sam was already ten yards away and didn't hear the rest of what he had to say.

She smiled as she turned onto Edward Street. Far from being upset at the end of their relationship, she felt as if a massive load had been lifted from her shoulders.

She was free and single again.

Life was great.

Chapter 12

Luke and Mark were sitting in the family room waiting for news.

"How did Father seem when they took him for his scan?" Luke asked.

"Not himself at all," Mark said. "He looked very pale and kept asking what day it was. He knew he was in a hospital, and he knew he'd banged his head, but he couldn't remember falling."

"Do you know how long he'd been unconscious before you found him?"

Mark shook his head. "No idea."

They both looked up as the door opened and a man in white scrubs entered.

"Hi, Mark," he said and then turned to Luke. "I assume you're the Duke's other son?"

"Yes. I'm Luke."

"I'm Doctor Barnabus. We've had the results back from the CT scan and I'm sorry to say that your father has a subdural haematoma as we feared. However, it's subacute which is good news."

"A bleed on the brain?" Mark asked.

Dr Barnabus nodded. "A minor bleed, fortunately. A small amount of blood has collected between his skull and the brain's surface about here." He tapped the left side of his head about three inches above the ear.

"What's the prognosis?" Luke asked.

"Your father's not a young man, but he's in good shape. That will help his recovery, but it's a question of waiting and seeing. My hope is that his confusion is a short-term phenomenon."

"Will he need an operation?"

"Possibly, but there's a good chance he'll recover without one. He's back from the scan so you can see him now."

Mark led the way back to their father's bay. Hugo was sitting up and smiled weakly when he saw them.

"I've been a ruddy fool," he said, his voice hoarse and weak.

"It's not your fault you fell over," Luke said.

"Mmm." Hugo closed his eyes for a second, and then they sprang open again. "Henry called this morning."

Luke and Mark exchanged a look. Was this part of the concussion?

"Henry?" Luke prompted.

"Mmm. Anthony's son. He said he needed to speak to you."

Something stirred in Luke's memory.

"Do you mean Henry Lavers?" he asked.

Hugo nodded.

"Who's he?" Mark asked.

"He's someone I went to school with," Luke said. "I haven't seen him since, so heaven knows why he wants to speak to me." He turned to Hugo. "Did he say what he wanted, Father?"

"No. He said he'd ring you at work."

"So you gave him the number of Filchers?"

"I didn't need to. Henry said he already had it." He closed his eyes again.

A few minutes later it was clear that their father was asleep. Luke and Mark stood up and walked to where Dr Barnabus was talking to a couple of nurses. He turned as they approached.

"He's asleep," Luke said.

Dr Barnabus smiled. "That's probably a good thing. We're going to keep him in overnight so that we can keep a close eye on him, but all being well he'll be able to go home tomorrow."

Luke followed Mark back, parked behind his brother's Maserati on the gravel at the front of Borrowham Hall, climbed out of the BMW and was immediately charged at by a screeching eight-year-old.

"Luke, it's awesome to see you," Marion said in her Californian accent as he bent down to give her a hug. She stepped back and looked earnestly up at him. "Poor Grand Pabbie. Is he okay? I was worried and I made him a card. Do you want to see it? It's awesome. I drew Borrow-ham and counted the windows to check I was right. There are fifteen and that's just the front. The sides have more and there are probably fifteen at the back too. I coloured it in. Are you going back to see him today? Can I come? I want to give him my card myself. Should we take grapes?"

Luke sighed. The girl was a motormouth, not to mention a touch precocious, but all the more charming for it.

"Marion," he said, "I think there were at least five questions in there."

"Geez. Sorry." She paused then smiled up at him. "So, what's your answer?"

Luke returned her smile. "Yes."

"Awesome." She grabbed his hand and pulled him into the entrance hall past her mother who stood just inside the front door.

"Hello, Luke," she said without looking at him.

"Hi, Erica," he said.

Erica turned her head sideways for her husband to peck her on the cheek, an affectation that made it seem like him kissing her on the lips was her ultimate nightmare. "How was he, Mark?"

"Not too bad considering," Mark said. "He'll hopefully be home tomorrow."

Erica turned to Luke. "Are you staying tonight?"

"Yes, if that's okay."

Her face said it was anything but, even though what she

said was, "That's fine." She turned and disappeared towards the kitchen, saying as she left, "I'll tell Amy to prepare your room."

"Come on, Luke," Marion said, tugging at his hand. "I want you to see Grand Pabbie's card." She led him towards the library. "I think I'll make him another one too, one that's super awesome. I'll draw him being well again and with a big smile on his face. Does that sound cool?"

Luke smiled. "I think it's an excellent idea."

Chapter 13

It was a cold, wet December morning when Sam walked into the Ethics Room but nothing could dampen her spirits, even the thought of meetings with Edward Filcher today and Glen Baxter tomorrow.

She was free of Ollie and that was what mattered. Yes, he had been good company most of the time and, yes, they had a lot in common and conversation flowed easily. However, his petty jealousies had become too much. He was forever making snide remarks, particularly about Luke, and passing them off as jokes.

She was well rid.

"Good morning, Ma'am," Josh said with a grin as she took her seat.

"Don't, Josh."

"Sorry. I couldn't resist."

"So," Helen said. "What does being our stand-in boss mean for you?"

"Nothing glamorous. A meeting with Filcher this morning and another with Glen tomorrow."

Helen pulled a face. "Oh dear. Rather you than me."

Five minutes later, Sam grabbed her notebook and headed to the Executive Floor.

She was pleased to see James McDonald, Head of Human Resources, standing by Gloria's desk when she got there. She liked him, and he had been very helpful when she'd encountered challenges after first joining the Ethics Team.

"Good morning, Sam," he said with a smile.

"Hi, James. What's this all about?"

"Diversity in the workplace. I'll explain more when we're with Filcher rather than have to say it twice."

Gloria's phone buzzed. "That's his signal," she said. "You can go in, but be aware he's in an odd mood today."

"Isn't he always?" James said.

Gloria smiled. "Yes, but he took a call earlier and, well, you'll see what I mean."

James and Sam entered Filcher's office to find him standing at the window facing away from them, his hands clasped behind his back. He was rocking his head from side to side as if in time to music only he could hear.

"Luke, James, take a seat," he said.

"I'm deputising for Luke today," Sam said.

Filcher turned around.

"Excellent," he said as he peered across at her, and to Sam's surprise he was smiling. She didn't think she'd ever seen this before.

"Have you come into some good fortune, Mr Filcher?" James said as he and Sam sat on either side of the meeting table.

Filcher tapped his nose. "No, but royalty," he said.

"Royalty?"

"More or less." His grin became even broader "Below me though."

"Below you?"

"Exactly." Filcher turned to Sam. "But above you." He tapped the side of his nose. "In line to the throne. Hah! Looked him up."

Neither James nor Sam said anything as they waited for Filcher to explain himself. However, all he said, with a wink at Sam, was "Debrett's" as he took his normal seat at the head of the table and gave a deep sigh of satisfaction.

"Now then, James," he went on. "Let's keep this brief."

"I'll do my best," James said. "Shall I outline what this meeting is about?"

"No need. Diversity. Clear as anything. And I am. We are."

"You are what?"

"Diverse. Do you need evidence?"

"Yes, but there are a range of…"

Filcher held his hand up to stop him. "No need to explain, James," he said condescendingly. "I fully understand the need to be diverse in every area of the workplace. I, for example, have a large office, while Gloria has a small desk. In between are middle-sized offices, such as yours."

"That's not…"

"Stop there, James." He put his hands together as if in prayer. "I am aware that there is also class to consider. Samantha here, for example…"

"Sam," Sam said. "I was christened Sam."

Filcher tutted. "There you are. Sam, eh? Point proven. We run the full gamut."

"Of?" James prompted.

"Of class,' Filcher replied as if it was only too obvious. "From Sam upwards to the lower middle class…" He waved his hand from side to side in front of James. "…then to me…" He pointed at himself. "…and finally to minor royalty." He lifted his hand and indicated the ceiling.

James and Sam looked where he was pointing.

"He's not there literally of course," Filcher added when he saw them look upwards. "Ah, where is he, Samantha?"

Sam thought of correcting him again but decided it was a waste of time.

"Who?" she asked.

He winked. "The Earl of Wareham of course."

"Ah, I see," James said. "You've found out."

"Indeed. Should have known sooner. Know now though. Makes all the difference."

Sam looked from James to Filcher and then back to James.

"I'm completely lost," she said.

"I'll explain later," James said. He turned back to his boss. "You've misunderstood what's meant by diversity, Mr

Filcher."

Filcher shook his head. "Not at all. I understand there is more to it." He held up the thumb of his left hand. "One, office space." His index finger joined his thumb. "Two, class." Then his middle finger. "Three, wealth." He smiled and added his ring finger but James interrupted before he could continue.

"You're talking about the wrong kind of diversity," he said.

Filcher's brows furrowed. "Eh! What?"

"This meeting is to discuss racial, ethnic and gender diversity."

"Exactly," Filcher said without missing a beat. "We are that too."

"I don't believe we're doing enough," James said.

Filcher harrumphed. "Not true." He pointed at Sam. "She is an example."

"She?" Sam said.

Filcher nodded. "Yes." He paused. "Plus that coloured man in Luke's team. Magic or Magi or something."

"Maj," Sam said.

"That's the fellow. He's ethnic. Racial too." James started to speak but Filcher was on a roll now and wasn't to be stopped. "There's another one too. Helen Hogg. Hah! She hits all three."

"All three?' James asked.

"Yes, she's a woman, and..." He paused as if what he had to say next was a major revelation. "...she's also Scottish."

*

It was another forty minutes before James managed to bring the meeting to a close.

"Do you think he understands now?" Sam asked as they

stood by Gloria's desk.

"Not a chance," James said. "It takes three or four meetings to make anything new sink in, and that's for something straightforward. Diversity is so alien to his way of thinking that he may never get to grips with it."

"Good luck."

He grinned. "Thanks. I'm going to need it."

"What was all that about the Earl of Wareham?"

"Oh, that. I guess you've never heard his formal title before."

"Formal title?"

James raised an eyebrow. "You don't know who his parents are, do you?"

"I assume his father is Ambrose's brother, but…"

James shook his head. "Not Filcher, Luke."

Sam looked at him, her face a picture of confusion. "What are you talking about?"

"Luke's parents are the Duke and Duchess of Dorset. His official title is the Earl of Wareham."

Chapter 14

"How did it go?" Helen asked when Sam returned to the Ethics Room.

'Painfully," Sam said. She paused. "Helen, do you know anything about Luke's parents?"

Helen shook her head. "Only that his poor wee mother's got dementia. Why?"

"I was wondering, that's all. Maj, Josh, has Luke ever told you what his parents do for a living?"

Maj looked up. "I think they're retired," he said.

"That's right," Josh said. "Oh, and they live in Dorset."

The others returned to their work and Sam sat down at her desk, logged into her computer and found herself staring at the screen as she mulled over what she'd just found out.

The fact that Luke was the son of a Duke didn't bother her, but why had he kept it a secret? Was he afraid she'd be like Edward Filcher and look upon him differently if she knew?

She liked to think he knew her better than that. They'd been working together for almost six months and grown close.

In a professional capacity only, of course.

They worked well together, had done from day one. There had been times when she'd thought there was more to their relationship than that, but nothing had ever come of it which was almost certainly for the best.

Besides he seemed to have fallen hook, line and sinker for Cora Evans and she was probably more his style. Cora was a strong, positive, career-focused woman who was intelligent as well as good-looking. She had it all, and they were clearly close.

Her phone rang and she looked down to see Luke's name on the screen. All thoughts of his lineage and current paramour disappeared from her mind in an instant.

There were more important things to consider.

She clicked to accept the call.

"How's your father?"

"They found a bleed on the brain."

"Oh no! Are they going to operate?"

"Probably not, and they're hopeful he'll make a full recovery."

"I hope so, Luke. How are you feeling?"

"Tired, but otherwise fine."

She wanted to ask more, to be certain he was okay. It had to be hard when both your parents were seriously ill.

"If I can help in any way," she said, "you only have to ask."

"Thanks, Sam."

Neither of them spoke for a few seconds, but the silence was comfortable, and Sam found herself wishing he was in the office rather than many miles away.

"How was the meeting on diversity?" Luke asked eventually.

"Hard work," Sam smiled. "You know what Filcher can be like."

Luke laughed. "I do indeed. And you've got Glen tomorrow so that's a double bonus."

"Ha, ha."

"I'm going to have to stay here for at least another day."

"Don't worry, Luke. I'm fine to cover and you need to be with your father."

"What's happening about Sow the Wind and Earth Conflict?"

"We're meeting shortly to agree on our approach."

"Good. Let me know how you get on."

"Take care, Luke."

Sam hung up and called over to the others. "Luke's

father is hopefully on the mend," she said. "Are you all okay to start our meeting now?"

They all moved to the table in the centre of the room and Sam could immediately see that Josh was desperate to say something.

"The wee laddie's come up with a project name," Helen said by way of explanation.

Josh nodded enthusiastically. "Greta," he said. "You know, because of…"

"Greta Thunberg," the others said in unison.

"Exactimo!"

"Project Greta it is," Sam said.

"Given Helen's going to be undercover," Maj said, "shall I take on whiteboard duties?"

"Good idea," Sam said.

Maj stood up, pulled the whiteboard over and wrote 'Project Greta' at the top, leaving the dividing line down the middle with 'Sow the Wind' and 'Andrea Mason' written on the left and 'Earth Conflict' and 'Finn O'Sullivan' on the right.

"Liz Rathbone and Daniel Craven from Globo Energy are coming in tomorrow," Sam said, "and it's Daniel who's going to help with false identities. We don't need to go overboard, but he's going to produce a false driving license for each of you, and also create some internet pages in case someone decides to google your background."

"Coolio," Josh said.

"Josh and I were discussing it," Helen said, "and it seems to us that all we need to come up with is a false name plus a background story that's easy to remember and unremarkable."

"That makes sense," Sam said.

"I'm going to be George Bailey," Josh said, adding with a grin, "…again." He paused. "I'm single and unemployed, having dropped out of university and job-hopped across a variety of unskilled jobs working behind bars, in restaurants, that kind of thing."

"I'm going to stick with Helen," Helen said, "but use my mother's maiden name which is Livingstone. I'm a widow with no children and work as a cleaner."

"That all sounds good," Sam said. "How are you going to join the groups?"

"It's easier for me," Helen said. "Sow the Wind's website lists their events and has a form to sign up and express interest. I'm going to complete that and then go to a meeting they've set up. It's in Bristol next week."

"Earth Conflict don't seem as well organised," Josh said. "I think it's because they're new. I was wondering about asking the Globo Energy guys if they had any ideas."

"Very sensible," Sam said. "Yes, let's do that."

Maj added 'Helen Livingstone - widow, cleaner' on the whiteboard beneath Sow the Wind and 'George Bailey - unemployed, unskilled job-hopper' under Earth Conflict.

"Right," Sam said. "It seems like we're as ready as we can be. I'll let Daniel know the names you're going to use and later I'll ring Luke to update him on what we've agreed."

Chapter 15

He had been a latecomer to technology, but now embraced it wholeheartedly.

Especially WhatsApp.

The ability to communicate instantly but securely was vital in pursuing his goal, and he had found WhatsApp an invaluable tool.

It afforded him vital anonymity.

His objectives were reasonable, and as far as he was concerned the ends justified the means. However, he knew that not everyone shared that view, and it was therefore essential that every exchange was kept secret.

He wasn't going to make the mistake the then Prime Minister had made during the pandemic either. He deleted conversations, or 'chats' as WhatsApp called them, as soon as their aims had been achieved. The same went for contacts.

There was no way he was keeping those details on his iPhone for anyone with half a brain to see.

In that respect he was old-fashioned. He kept contact details in his diary, coded so that no one would understand them even if they got hold of it.

Not that they would. He was very careful.

He turned his phone off and replaced the SIM card with the one he reserved for these confidential discussions. Neither the card, nor his payments for using it, could be traced back to him.

He wasn't just careful. He was smart.

Next, he pulled his diary out and entered the details of his contact into his smartphone. Their codename was Robin, a suitably androgynous name given he didn't know whether they were male or female.

He hesitated, but only for a second, then looked down at the three other names on his list. Any of them would do and he would let 'Robin' decide. Whichever was easiest would be a good start and get the ball rolling.

He mentally crossed his fingers that his contact was online, typed a simple 'Hello Robin' and hit enter.

The reply was almost instant.

'Hello, Taylor.'

He couldn't help smiling at the nickname he had come up with for himself. His father had been a tailor and thoughts of him brought back fond memories.

However, now wasn't the time to dwell on the past. There was serious work to be done.

It was time to kick things off and he set about briefing Robin.

Robin - I have three names for you.

You want them all dealt with?

No. Just one for the time being.

Then why three names?

It may be necessary to dispose of all of them over time.

I understand. Do you want me to choose?

Yes.

On what basis?

Whichever is the easiest target.

When?

As soon as possible while minimising the risk.

I understand.

Update me when you have

made progress.

> *Very well.*

Good luck.

> *Thank you.*

He typed in the three names, hesitated for a second and then hit enter.

It was unfortunate that these people had to die for the cause but none of them was a great loss in the grand scheme of things. Their sacrifice would make the world, his world, a better place.

This was a huge step forward.

Chapter 16

"I want to come to see Grand Pabbie," Marion said. She waved her handmade get-well-soon cards in the air. "I need to give him these and I want to check he's a-okay."

Luke couldn't help smiling. They'd started lunch ten minutes earlier and she hadn't stopped talking since.

"I'm not sure a hospital visit is appropriate for a girl your age," Erica said.

"I think it's a good idea," Mark said as he helped himself to another slice of ham from the centre of the table.

His wife glared at him but his eyes were fixed on his fork.

"She's giving you an evil," Marion said. "You're in trouble."

"It's probably adults only," Erica went on as she tried to catch his eye.

"No, they allow children," Mark said, now cutting his ham and still oblivious to the silent message his wife was trying to convey. "I checked yesterday."

"Awesome," Marion said. "When are we going? Is it soon? I can get dressed awful quickly. My hair needs brushing but I can do it on the way. Isn't this exciting? I've never been in a British hospital. Are they like the ones in California, Luke?"

Luke opened his mouth to reply but Marion continued without pausing for breath.

"I hope he's well," she said. "Poor Grand Pabbie. Did you say he had water on the brain?"

"He's got a bleed on the brain," Mark said.

Erica caught his eye now and her face made it clear that he would suffer worse than an acute subdural haematoma if she had her way.

"Have I said something wrong?" Mark said.

Erica closed her eyes and huffed loudly, then wiped her lips with her napkin and stood up.

"I'll speak to you later, Mark," she said.

He watched her leave the dining room.

"What did I do?"

"You're in the shit," Marion said.

"Marion! You can't say that."

"Why not? You said it yesterday."

"I didn't... well, I might have, but..."

"You also said 'bugger it' when you dropped that cup."

"Let's finish up quickly," Luke said, deciding it was time to come to his brother's rescue. "I'd like to be away by one if we can."

Thirty minutes later they set off for the Dorset County Hospital and Marion gave a running commentary for most of the journey.

"She's incorrigible," Luke whispered to Mark as they got out of the car and Marion engaged a passing nurse in conversation.

Mark smiled. "Isn't she just?"

A few minutes later they arrived at Hugo's bed to find him asleep. As they pulled chairs up a nurse arrived and shook his arm.

"Come on, Hugo," she said. "You've got visitors."

He blinked his eyes a couple of times and then opened them and spotted his sons.

"Good morning, boys."

"It's afternoon, Father," Luke said. "How are you feeling?"

"Head's ruddy sore."

"We're happy with his progress," the nurse said. "I'll ask Dr Barnabus to come over when he has a minute."

"Thanks," Luke said

"Here are your cards," Marion said, passing them over

to him.

"Thank you," Hugo said. "This is a magnificent drawing of Borrowham. Well done, Marion." He put it to one side, picked up the second card and stared at it for a few seconds before turning it the other way up.

"No, that way," Marion said turning it back again. "It's a drawing of the world and that's you at the centre of it."

"The big round thing with stalks?"

Marion nodded. "Those are your arms and legs. And those two thin things are Mark and Luke and the short one with a scowly face is Erica."

"Thank you, Marion. It's, ah… awesome."

Marion beamed. "Geez. Thanks, Grand Pabbie." She bent forward, put her arms around his neck and kissed him on the cheek.

"Did you ring Henry?" Hugo asked.

"I completely forgot," Luke said. "I'll ring him this afternoon."

"It would be good if you could. He was keen to talk to you."

Luke was baffled by this. Why would an ex-schoolmate, and one he hadn't been close to for that matter, want to talk to him after nearly a quarter of a century?

"The doctor's coming over," Mark said.

"Good afternoon," Dr Barnabus said.

Marion stood up and offered her hand. "I'm Marion."

"Hello, Marion." He shook her hand.

"I want to be a doctor when I grow up."

"Excellent."

"Or work in a morgue with dead bodies. I haven't decided."

"I see. An interesting choice."

"Which one do you think, doctor? I'm good with my hands."

"I, ah…"

"That's enough I think, Marion," Mark said. He turned

to the doctor. "When can our father come home?"

"Probably tomorrow." Dr Barnabus turned to Hugo. "You've made excellent progress, but I'd like another twenty-four hours to be certain you're stable. Are you still having problems with your speech?"

Hugo nodded. He looked at Mark and Luke. "I'm having trouble remembering the right word sometimes," he explained.

"It's common after a subdural haematoma," Dr Barnabus said, "and it's nothing to be overly concerned about. These things often self-correct, though it may take weeks or even months."

The doctor left and Marion and Hugo immediately started talking to each other, although ninety per cent of the words were coming from the eight-year-old. Luke could see his father was enjoying her being there though, and he was pleased they'd brought her.

"I'm going to step outside and make that call, Mark," he said and stood up.

Chapter 17

Luke leaned against the outside wall of A&E and decided to phone Sam first and then Henry Lavers.

"Hi, Sam," he said when she answered.

"Hi, Luke. How's he doing?"

This was one of many things he appreciated about Sam. She was deputising for him for the first time and had to be under a lot of pressure, but her first thoughts were for his father.

"He's coming on well," he said. "Fingers crossed he'll be coming home tomorrow."

"That's great news. And you? How are you bearing up?"

"I'm fine and my niece keeps us all on our toes, believe me. She's a real live wire."

"That's nice. Are you staying overnight in Dorset or commuting back and forth?"

"Overnight."

"In your parents' house?"

"Yes."

"There's plenty of room, is there?"

For a second or two Luke was bemused by this and then it dawned on him why she'd asked the question.

She knew about his parents' titles.

He hesitated before answering. The fact that his parents were a Duke and Duchess wasn't an embarrassment to him, and he hadn't intentionally kept it a secret from Sam, or indeed from any of the Ethics Team. The subject had never come up, that was all.

"I assume you know about my parents," he said.

"That they're the Duke and Duchess of Dorset. Yes."

"It's not a big deal, Sam."

"No, it's not." She paused for a second. "It doesn't

change anything but please, Luke, don't ever feel you need to keep anything like that from me. It won't change the way I…"

She hesitated.

"Won't change what?" Luke prompted.

"It won't change our relationship. You and I, we, ah… we work well together and need to be open about things like that."

"It's never come up, that's all."

"Okay."

There was another pause, and he sensed she was trying to pull herself together.

"How are things with you?" he asked.

"I've finished with Ollie."

Thank god, he thought but said, "Oh no. That's a shame. What happened?"

Her voice dropped so he could barely make out her words but he thought she said, "He wasn't like you."

"What was that?"

"He wasn't my type," she said, louder this time. He heard her take a deep breath before continuing. "Helen and Josh are making good progress preparing for their undercover stints."

"I bet Josh is excited."

"And some. He's going to be George Bailey again and Helen will be Helen Livingstone. It was her mother's maiden name."

"That's good. When are you seeing Globo?"

"Tomorrow."

"Great. And sorry, about, you know." There was silence at the other end. "Look," he went on, "I'd better get back to my father."

"Okay. Take care, Luke."

Luke took a deep breath as he ended the call.

That conversation had been hard but it also felt like he and Sam had made some sort of breakthrough in their relationship. He wasn't sure what it meant but it was for the best, he was sure it was.

He pulled the piece of paper out of his pocket with Henry Lavers' number on it and was about to call when his phone started ringing.

He smiled at the thought that Sam was calling back. There was more to be said, much more. However, when he looked down it was Cora's name on the screen.

"Hi, Cora."

"Hi, lover," she said.

She'd taken to calling him this more and more. If they ever met in the office it was 'Luke' but when they were alone it was always 'lover'. He didn't mind it, he guessed, but he was sticking with calling her Cora.

"How's Wilkins?" he asked.

"He's fine. Loving the attention I give him. He loves his treats too."

"He certainly does. Not too many though. I don't want him getting fat."

She laughed. "Don't worry, I'm managing his intake. Look, I'm sorry we can't be together this weekend, especially given what you're going through with your father."

"It's not a problem."

"As I said, I've had this arranged for ages and I can't get out of it."

"Is it an old friend of yours?'

"Kind of, yes. Do you fancy a meal out in a week from today?"

"That would be great."

"Terrific. I'll book something near me and then you can stay over."

"I look forward to it. Bye, Cora."

"Bye, lover."

He hung up and rang Henry Lavers, but it was a woman who answered.

"Henry Lavers' office," she said. "How may I help?"

"Hello," Luke said. "Is Henry there?"

"I'll see if he's available. Who may I say is calling?"

"Luke Sackville. He's been trying to get hold of me."

"Ah, yes, Mr Sackville. He said to put you straight through if you rang. Just a second."

There were a couple of clicks and then a man's voice came on the phone.

"Luke Sackville," he said. "My word, you're a hard man to track down."

"Hi, Henry. It took me by surprise when you tried to get in touch. You're not ringing about some kind of old boys' reunion are you?"

Henry laughed. "Nothing like that, no. It turns out you and I are working together."

"Working together?"

"Indirectly, yes. I'm Operations Director at Globo Energy. Liz Rathbone works for me."

"I see."

"Liz told me who she'd met and I thought it would be great to catch up and talk about old times. That's why I rang you at home. I hope you don't mind."

Luke was bemused by this. He and Henry had never been close at school. They had different sets of friends, Luke mixing with the sports enthusiasts while Henry had been more of an academic.

"It's good of you to ring, but I'm not sure there's much to be gained by getting together. It's not as if we were best buddies."

"You're right, of course you are. However, I must admit I have an ulterior motive. I know things about those environmental groups that might help you in your work for us."

"Why contact me directly and not tell Liz what you know?"

Henry hesitated. "I can't. It would be, ah, difficult.

Look, why don't we meet? I can explain everything then. It's not something I want to divulge over the phone."

"Okay, Henry."

They agreed a time and place and Luke ended the call.

Chapter 18

Sam had booked the Empire room for the meeting. She invited Liz and Daniel from Globo Energy to take a seat and made the introductions.

Josh poured the coffees.

"I hope you don't mind me joining the meeting as well," Maj said as the drinks were passed around. "I'm not taking an active role but I'll be beavering away in the background, doing any research Helen and Josh ask for."

"Of course not," Liz said as she took her drink. "We appreciate you all helping with this. As I said when we met Sam and Luke, we're concerned because of Andrea Mason and her anarchist leanings."

"What do you know about Earth Conflict?" Josh asked. "Their website is very vague, but if anything it suggests their views are more extreme than Sow the Wind."

"We noticed that, which is why we want you to look into them as well. However, it's been difficult to find out much about them. Finn O'Sullivan started the group about eight weeks ago after his relationship with Andrea broke down, and it's very much a fledgling operation with almost zero visibility."

"Relationship in what sense?" Helen asked.

"We believe they were a couple, but we're unclear on whether they fell out for personal reasons, or disagreed about the way forward for Sow the Wind."

"Any idea how many members they have?" Josh asked.

"I suspect it's still in single figures," Liz said.

"I've been wondering how to join. Helen's signed up for Sow the Wind, and she's going to a meeting next week, but there's no clue on Earth Conflict's website as to how to engage."

"I've got a suggestion," Daniel said. "Like Andrea, Finn O'Sullivan is still based in Bath. He was spotted by one of my colleagues giving forth in Southgate at the weekend." He pulled his phone out of his pocket, clicked a couple of times and passed it over to Josh.

"Ooh," Josh said as he looked at the photo on the screen. "Yukkedy-doo-da." He jabbed at the image. "Is that his real hair?"

Daniel smiled. "He's not the most savoury-looking of characters, is he?" he said.

Josh passed the phone to Helen.

"It's not only his dreadlocks," she said. "He just looks, somehow, well…"

"Like what?" Sam prompted.

"If I'm honest, like a hairy wee bawbag." She wrinkled her face as if something truly disgusting had passed her lips and passed the phone to Sam. "Rather you than me, Josh."

Sam passed it to Maj who returned it to Daniel.

Daniel swiped the screen a couple of times and returned the phone to Josh who chuckled before relaying it to Helen.

She stared horrified at the screen then looked up at Daniel. "Is this Andrea?" she asked. Daniel nodded and Helen shook her head. "She's practically his identical twin. If he removed that pathetic wee attempt at a beard I'd struggle to tell them apart."

"So are you thinking I approach him in Southgate?" Josh asked as the phone was passed around.

Daniel nodded as he took his phone back from Maj. "You're going to have to change your appearance though."

Josh jabbed his finger at Daniel's phone. "I'm not doing that," he said. "No way, Jose."

"Don't worry," Liz said. "I don't think you need to go that far, but at the moment you look very clean-cut."

Josh sat up straight. "Thank you," he said. "You mean I look like a business executive?"

"No," Liz said, "more like a kid fresh out of school at a job interview."

"We'll have to do something about your hair," Daniel said.

"What!" Josh's voice rose.

"Perhaps a number one all over," Helen suggested.

"No!" He was squealing now.

"That would work," Sam said. "You could go to that Turkish barber."

Small sounds were coming from Josh's throat.

"There's no need to go that far," Liz said, coming to his rescue "All you need to do is wash it, leave it to dry naturally and don't bother brushing or combing it."

"But how will I hold it in place?"

"No need. You certainly can't apply gel or mousse."

This was tantamount to blasphemy in Josh's eyes. "But…"

"A five o'clock shadow would help," Daniel said.

"That'll take him about a week," Helen said.

"I can see that," Liz said.

"Eh!"

"You'll have to dress differently too," Daniel said. "Less, uh…"

"Posy," Helen suggested.

Daniel nodded. "A shirt with a large pattern on it would work."

Josh looked from one to the other in horror as this exchange continued.

"Tangerine," Helen said. "Or pale pink."

"Torn jeans, heavily flared, would be a good look,' Sam offered.

The others all nodded while Josh sat back, his mouth open.

"Do you own any clothes like that?" Liz asked.

"Of course not," Josh said.

"In that case…" Helen began.

"No, no, no." He shook his head from side to side vigorously. "Not another shopping trip."

Sam looked at her watch. "Liz, it's almost time to meet our Head of Security." She stood up. "We'll leave the rest of you to continue if that's all right?"

"Possibly," Josh said. "They've already torn apart my hair and my dress sense. What else is left?"

"Sam emailed me photos for the identity documents," Daniel said, as Sam and Liz headed for the door, "and I prepared a false driving license for you, Helen, and a library card for you, Josh."

He removed the documents from his briefcase and handed them over.

"Why not a driving license for me?" Josh asked.

"It wouldn't work, given your age."

"What do you mean? I'm twenty-two."

"Seriously?"

Sam was smiling as she shut the door behind them.

Chapter 19

Sam led Liz to the Executive Floor where Glen had one of the smaller offices at the end of the corridor. There was a sign pushed into a slot on the door saying *'Head of Security'*.

She knocked and entered without waiting for a reply. The room appeared to be empty and she was about to leave when there was a loud shout of "Fuck!" from underneath the desk.

Sam and Liz bent over and saw Glen on his hands and knees. He was using his left hand to sweep what looked like small brightly coloured marbles into a paper cup.

He heard them, looked up to see who was there, banged his head on the underside of the desk, uttered another "Fuck!" and then ungracefully backed out.

"Are you okay, Glen?" Sam asked.

"Of course," he said as he climbed to his feet, tapping his buzz cut to check for blood as he did so. He spotted Liz. "Ah," he went on, with a grin so wide it made him look like a chimpanzee who had spotted a particularly delicious banana. "To whom do I give the pleasure?"

"This is Liz Rathbone from Globo Energy," Sam said.

Glen held his hand out, realised he was still holding the paper cup, put it on the desk and then shook her hand vigorously while continuing to grin inanely.

"Ingratiated to meet you," he said and then gestured to the cup. "Excuse the pinballs."

"Pinballs?" Liz asked.

Glen nodded. "Sweets. They're my piccalilli."

"I think you mean peccadillo," Sam said.

"Exactly." He kept his eyes on Liz and turned his smile up to eleven.

She extricated her hand and the two women sat down.

Glen descended into his chair then sat upright abruptly, raised both eyebrows, looked first at Sam and then at Liz, and took a slow deep breath. As he did so, his chest expanded so that his pecs were on display through his over-tight shirt which, needless to say, was short-sleeved to emphasise his biceps.

"So," he went on after a few seconds, ignoring the wide eyes of the astonished women opposite, "what brings the two of you to my humble abode?"

"Liz is Globo's Head of Security," Sam said after she'd recovered from his mini-Chippendales performance.

"Really?" Glen's eyebrows went up. "But you're a…" He waved his hand in Liz's general direction in a style reminiscent of Edward Filcher. Sam was suddenly aware of why Luke deemed it essential that Liz was chaperoned at the meeting.

"Woman?" Liz suggested.

"Yes. And a very suitable one too, might I add."

"A very suitable one?"

"Indeed. And there's nothing wrong with a woman being Head of Security."

"That's very good of you to say so."

"Thank you. Now, how can I help? Are you looking for some advice, since…"

"I'm a woman."

"No. Of course not. Well, I mean you are. Clearly, you are. You've got, ah…" He waved his hand briefly towards her breasts then withdrew it sharply and gulped. "What I meant was that you are younger than I am while I have a wealth of experience."

"I'm sure you do."

"And fifty-two staff."

"That's impressive."

He nodded, her sarcasm lost on him. "I'm happy to help. My door is always open."

"It was closed when we got here."

"Figuratively. It's always open figuratively."

"But not in practice?"

"No."

Liz took a deep breath and decided to move the conversation on. "Glen," she began. "Are you aware that Filchers is to be awarded Globo Energy's outsourcing contract?"

"No, I wasn't, but I understand now."

"You do?"

He nodded. "When you are transferred across you will of course be under me." He laughed. "I'll be on top, but together I'm sure we'll find a suitably comfortable position." He winked. "Rest assured that you won't have to walk the streets plying your wares."

Liz shook her head. "I won't be transferring across, Glen," she said. "The reason I'm here is to clarify the security measures Globo expects when Filchers takes responsibility for our administration and finance departments."

"I see."

"Because in effect you'll then be working for me." She paused to let this sink in. "However, hopefully we can keep our meetings to a minimum."

"But with regular intercourse?"

"We'll talk when we have to. Other than that I think we should keep out of each other's way."

"Absolutely. I wouldn't want to interfere with you."

She reached into her briefcase, pulled out two pieces of paper and passed one across to Glen. "This is a summary of what we expect," she said. "Perhaps you could read it through and let me know what you think."

Sam was relieved that the rest of the meeting passed relatively harmlessly, Glen seeming to find the correct words when it got into the detail.

"Thanks for your time, Glen," Liz said when they'd finished.

"Not a problem, Liz," Glen said. He held his hand out but she ignored it.

"You mentioned you use biometrics to secure your main security room," she said.

"That's right."

"I'll need a scan."

"Of course. I'd noticed, but I didn't like to say anything." He smiled. "How many months?"

Liz squeezed her eyes closed and pinched the top of her nose before replying. "What I mean," she said after a few seconds, "is that my fingerprints will need scanning so that I can get into the security room."

Glen nodded. "Right. I can organise that." He paused. "You didn't answer me. When's it due?"

Liz sighed.

"I'll escort you downstairs, Liz," Sam said. "Would you mind waiting outside for a second while I have a quick word with Glen?"

"Not at all," Liz said and she left the room.

"That went well," Glen said once the door was closed.

"You think so?"

"Yes." He beamed. "Very well.'

"She's not pregnant."

"Oh. Why is she having a scan?"

"She was talking about a fingerprint scan."

"She needs to be clearer and use the right words."

"Does she?"

"Yes. I found her difficult to finger."

It was Sam's turn to close her eyes and sigh. She turned without saying anything else and joined Liz in the corridor.

"He's harmless really," she said as they made their way back to reception.

"I guess so," Liz said and laughed. "You see all types in this job, but Glen Baxter is a one-off."

"Thank goodness."

"Amen to that."

Chapter 20

Jackie hesitated before ringing.

Should she tell her sponsor about Paul or would it be better to keep his name a secret for now? She decided to leave it to him to decide.

He answered after only two rings.

"Hello."

"Hi. It's Jackie. Jackie Walker."

"I haven't got long. I'm due in the Chamber for a vote shortly. Wait there."

She assumed he was finding somewhere he couldn't be overheard and sure enough he came back on the line after a minute or so.

"Have you made any progress? You're taking a long time and the payments will have to stop if something doesn't happen soon."

"I've found someone. I'm fairly sure he will do what's necessary."

"Fairly sure won't cut it, Jackie."

"I'm seeing him in twenty minutes. I can report back afterwards."

"As I said, I'll be in the chamber." He paused. "Give me a call in an hour."

"Before you go…"

"Yes?" He sounded impatient.

"I need to know how far he should go."

He laughed but there was no humour in it. "I don't want anything like what happened to Teddy Overton. Why you ever chose a simpleton like Oscar Briggs to do your dirty work is beyond me."

It's your dirty work, not mine, Jackie thought.

"I'm sorry about that," she said. "Oscar was a mistake

but the man I've found is bright as well as highly motivated. His name is…"

"Stop! I don't need to know his name. The more remote I can stay from this the better. That's why I'm paying you. My involvement will be after the event."

"We're both doing this for the cause though."

"Of course."

His reply was automatic but she didn't believe him for a moment. He was motivated by his political ambitions, nothing else.

"When you say what happens shouldn't be along the lines of the Teddy Overton incident, Mr Pinnington, what exactly do you mean?"

"Jackie, I leave that to your judgement. What is important is that I am given a platform to speak out. Whatever you set up with this man needs to be enough to put me in the spotlight. I will distance myself from the actual incident, but I will use it to promote the cause."

And yourself, Jackie thought. *In fact, mainly yourself.*

"Rest assured," he went on, "that I will drop you like a stone if you and this man you're so confident of don't deliver. I have other irons in the fire and you are dispensable."

"I understand. I'll ring in an hour."

She hung up, threw her coat on and walked to the bus stop.

She didn't like Curtis Pinnington, never had. He was always neatly dressed and had a grand smile but it was all a front. Underneath he was as slimy as anyone she'd ever met.

But then he was a career politician.

However, he did pay the bills, and if by helping him she was able to promote Sow the Wind, and the environmental causes she felt so passionately about, then it was worth putting up with his arrogant and patronising manner.

Their phone conversation had put her on edge though.

She was still no clearer on how far she should go. Teddy Overton had nearly died after Oscar hit him with the carabiner, and the media had focused on Oscar himself rather than Sow the Wind. Newspaper articles had talked endlessly about his learning difficulties and his difficult upbringing with not one jot of attention given to the reason for his actions.

Jackie decided it was something she should discuss with Paul. She was telling the truth when she told Pinnington he seemed bright. Between them, they ought to be able to come up with a workable plan.

Paul was already in the bus shelter when she got there, sitting on the iron bench under the glass covering. He still reminded her of Finn O'Sullivan, but on seeing him a second time she was struck more by the differences than the similarities. His hair and forked beard were matt black, whereas Finn's hair and goatee were brown, and he was a few years younger, perhaps still in his twenties.

"Hi, Paul," she said.

He stood up and she realised he was also a few inches taller than Finn and broader in the chest.

"Hi, Jackie. Where shall we talk?"

"I think here's as good a place as anywhere. If anyone comes for a bus we'll move on."

He sat back down and she sat next to him.

"We need to agree on a way to promote our cause," she said. "When we met it was clear to me that you're prepared to take strong action."

"Absolutely."

Jackie decided that she had to throw Curtis Pinnington into the mix if they were going to hit on the right solution.

"How much do you know about Sow the Wind's history, Paul?"

"I know Andrea Mason founded it, and I also know that Curtis Pinnington is a supporter."

"Ah, you know that do you?"

He nodded. "His enthusiasm for Sow the Wind seems to ebb and wane though. He's hardly been visible at all since the Teddy Overton incident."

"You *have* been doing your research."

He smiled. "I'm prepared to do whatever is necessary to promote our cause, but I needed to be certain Sow the Wind was worthy of my attention."

She laughed. "You haven't been checking up on me have you?" It was meant to be a rhetorical question.

"Naturally."

"Oh." This took her aback. "What did you find out?"

"That you're single, forty-six years old and a long-time environmental campaigner. Also, that you work in a call centre."

"Nothing damaging then."

"And that you gave Oscar Briggs his weapon."

Her brows furrowed. "What do you mean? That's nonsense. I would never have done that."

"It was a dubious Facebook post from a woman who said she was there at the time." He smiled. "It may be fake news but rest assured I won't hold it against you if it's true."

That was the second time in an hour someone had told her to 'rest assured' and, as with Curtis Pinnington, there was something arrogant and patronising about the way Paul had said it.

However, she didn't have to like Paul to work with him.

"Have you got any ideas for how we might improve Sow the Wind's visibility?" she asked.

"One or two, yes. I believe Andrea is going to be on television soon."

He had definitely been doing his research.

"That's right."

He explained his plan. It was audacious, dangerous and in some ways downright ridiculous. However, once he explained his thinking she realised that he had thought it through in some detail.

"Were you planning on being there?" he asked.

"I was, yes."

"I think it's better that you don't. The more you can distance yourself from what happens the better."

"That makes sense. What about you?"

"I'll slide away as soon as it's done, and I mean immediately afterwards. I suggest we don't meet again until a few days afterwards."

She stood up.

"Good luck with it, Paul."

"I don't need luck," he said. "I'm a professional."

She left him at the shelter and headed back to her flat.

What on earth did he mean by 'I'm a professional'? A professional rabble-rouser?

His plan had made sense in the end though. If all went well Sow the Wind would be in the headlines, Curtis Pinnington would get his fifteen minutes of fame and she'd be guaranteed her regular payments.

She shut the door behind her and saw that an hour and a quarter had passed since she'd rung her sponsor.

Again he answered almost immediately.

"Pinnington."

"It's Jackie."

"You're late. I said to ring me after an hour."

"It took a while but we have a plan."

She told him the details.

"Mmm," he said when she'd finished. "I'm not very keen on the fact that Gilbey will be there. He'll do whatever he can to exploit it to promote himself."

Pot calling the kettle black, Jackie thought.

"Is that a problem?"

"Of course, it's a problem." He sighed in irritation. "However, what's done is done. I'll deal with Gilbey."

"Very well, Mr Pinnington. I'll…"

She stopped as she realised he'd hung up.

Chapter 21

Josh was pleased he'd rebuffed the suggestion that Sam and Helen join him on a shopping expedition. He'd seen them in action before and it hadn't been an enjoyable experience.

He'd asked Leanne to join him though. She was safe, well relatively safe, and besides he'd probably end up buying the wrong clothes if left to his own devices.

He put aside his breakfast plate and picked up his coffee.

"I thought we'd start at Gaff," he said.

Leanne shook her head. "No, Joshy. Too modern."

"Yes, but that's me, isn't it?' He grinned. "Always trendy, always coolio."

"Not if you're going to fit in with a group of environmental activists it isn't. The place I'm thinking of is only a short walk from here, and I've seen something in the window I think will be ideal."

Josh wracked his brains but couldn't recall any clothes shops in Walcot that he would be interested in visiting.

"You must have seen it," Leanne went on. "It's bright yellow."

His eyes widened in horror. "No, no, no. You've got to be kidding. Not the place with the lava lamp in the window?"

"Got it in one."

"But that's… I mean it's…"

"It's retro. Vintage. Ideal for what we need."

"I don't want tangerine though. Anything but that."

Leanne smiled. "Come on, drink your coffee. They'll be open now. I'm sure they'll have something in your size in pink."

"Not pink either. Nor vivid green. I can cope with

white, or even a pale blue. Nothing too bright."

"We'll see, Joshy. We'll see."

Ten minutes later they were standing outside the brightly painted shop, the sign above saying, appropriately enough, "The Yellow Shop."

"That's cool," Josh said, pointing at an astronaut's outfit in the window.

"You're dressing to join an environmental group, Joshy. You can't turn up as Neil Armstrong."

"I know, but it's gucci. And look at that." He indicated a shirt and trousers in the other window.

Leanne shook her head. "No, definitely not. Khaki camouflage is not the look we're after."

Five minutes later they emerged empty-handed.

"I told you so," Josh said.

Leanne stood for a moment thinking and then grabbed his hand. "I know just the place. It's this way."

A minute or so later she came to a halt outside a charity shop.

Josh laughed. "What use is an old china set and a battered game of Cluedo?"

"Look," Leanne said, pointing through the window at a clothes rack in the far corner of the shop. "I bet there's something there."

They emerged ten minutes later. Leanne indicated the carrier bag Josh was holding with a nod of her head and smiled.

"I think that'll do."

"Why the sandals?" Josh protested. "It's December and it's freezing. I'll catch frostbite."

"You get frostbite, Joshy. You don't catch it."

"I will with those on."

"They'll complete the look. You have to admit the shirts are nice."

"Nice! One's a dirty brown with giant toadstools on it and the grandad shirt, well…"

"It's not a grandad shirt."

"You're right. No way would my grandad have been seen dead in that."

"It's bright. I admit that."

"Bright! People's eyes are going to explode when they see it. I thought you said we could avoid tangerine and pink."

"It's also red and green and yellow and…"

"…every other colour of the rainbow. Why, oh why, would anyone want to wear a patchwork linen shirt with sunflowers on every square?"

"Because they're at one with the world around them."

"Mmm."

*

"Don't touch it!" Leanne warned.

Josh jerked his hand away from the small black tub on the table and looked again at his reflection in the wall mirror. He'd gone for the mushroom shirt as a slightly more acceptable, if still appalling, first step into tree-huggerdom, but his hair was driving him up the wall. He'd washed it and it lay in a damp mess on his head.

He reached for the mousse again. This time Leanne slapped his hand away.

"Ow!"

"You're like Bilbo Baggins with the ring," she said with a grin. "That max-hold mousse has got possession of you."

"A little wouldn't do any harm," he squealed.

Leanne shook her head. "Nope." She put her hands on his head and ran her fingers through his hair. "You've got great hair," she said. "I've never felt the real thing before."

Josh's eyes were still on the tub. "I'll get cold turkey. I haven't gone a day without gel or mousse since I was a toddler."

"You'll cope." She looked down at his Skechers. "Where are your sandals?"

"I don't have to accept what you say, you know. I've done this kind of thing before. I'm an experienced, mature…"

He stopped mid-sentence as Leanne put her hands on her hips and glared at him.

"Okay," he said. "I'll fetch them."

The doorbell rang.

Josh's eyes widened. "Who's that?" he asked. "Don't let them in."

Leanne smiled knowingly.

"Who is it?" he demanded. "Have you invited someone around?'

"I think you look great, but I wanted a second opinion."

"Who? It's not Mum?"

Leanne shook her head.

"Please say it isn't Helen. She'll so take the mickey."

"Stop fretting, Joshy. Get your sandals on and I'll let him in."

"Him! It's not one of my mates, is it?"

"I'll be back in a second."

He took his trainers off, put on the pale brown, open-toed, ridiculously summery sandals, glanced again at the tub of mousse and managed through sheer power of will to keep his hands away.

His ears pricked up as he heard Leanne on the other side of the door.

"Stand there," she said. "Close your eyes and prepare yourself."

Josh swallowed, took one last look at himself in the mirror and then opened the bedroom door and stepped out.

When he saw who their visitor was he squeezed his eyes shut, muttered "Buggery-buggery-boo" under his breath, reopened his eyes and prepared for the worst.

"You can open them now," Leanne said.

Noah, Josh's thirteen-year-old brother, opened his eyes wide. A split-second later his mouth followed, then morphed into a broad grin as he looked Josh up and down.

"Are you going to a fancy dress as a magic mushroom?" he asked.

"Very funny, half-pint."

Noah's eyes went to Josh's sandals and then to his hair.

"You look like Edward Scissorhands," he said, "Only less cool. A lot less cool. Way less cool."

"Enough! I get the message."

Noah reached into his pocket, pulled his phone out and snapped off a photo before Josh could lean forward to stop him.

Josh shook his head. "No. You can't do that." He pointed at the phone. "Delete it."

"Shan't."

"Do it."

"No."

"Yes."

"No."

"Noah, I'm going undercover," Josh said, deciding that pleading on his little brother's better judgement might be the better course of action. "You can't share that photo with anyone. What if it went viral?"

"That would be great." Noah hesitated. "Are you pretending to be a teenager again?" He looked Josh up and down again. "Because no teenager in their right mind would dress like that."

"No, I'm going to join an environmental group."

"What do you think?" Leanne asked.

Noah stepped back and looked at his brother properly for the first time. "To be honest," he began, his voice serious now, "you would definitely fit in alongside those weirdos who glue themselves to the motorway."

Josh wasn't sure whether this was good news or not. Noah had just called him a weirdo, but then wasn't that the look he was after?

"Thanks, little bro'," he said after a few seconds.

"No problem." Noah's grin returned. "You need to tell me when your undercover work is finished though."

"Why? Are you worried I might get hurt?"

"No." Noah held his phone up. "I want to share this photo on TikTok and see how many new followers I get."

Chapter 22

Josh was surprised not to receive more odd looks as he walked into Bath city centre.

Perhaps his appearance was cool after all.

He caught sight of his reflection as he passed a shop window and immediately changed his mind. No, there was no way he looked cool.

However, it was important to put his toadstool-based attire and scruffy hairstyle out of his mind and become George Bailey. For the next few hours, and whenever he was with any of the climatey people, he was going to think and act like a different person.

George who was single and had dropped out of university.

George who had undertaken a series of unskilled jobs in pubs and restaurants.

George who lived in a squat in Walcot.

George who was concerned about climate change.

George who wanted to take action to help the Earth.

Yes, that was him. He had to channel his inner Bailey and that meant dropping some of his uniquely Josh expressions. 'Gucci' and 'Wowza' might make it harder for him to fit in. He needed alternatives.

Words with an environmental feel to them.

Anything with 'Earth' or 'Green' in would be good. 'Nature' too. 'Rainforest' might work, but it didn't flow off the tongue.

He decided not to overthink it. The words needed to flow out naturally. Once he was with others, and discussions revolved around making the world a better place, he was sure his quick brain would come up with terms that fitted seamlessly into the conversation.

Before he knew it, Josh had reached the bottom of Stall Street. He turned into Southgate and spotted Finn O'Sullivan immediately. He was standing in front of a telephone box that for some unknown reason had been painted white with black squiggles. Around Finn's neck was a placard with 'SAVE THE PLANET' written on it while standing beside him was a young woman, who looked to be in her early twenties, holding a second sign in the air. This one read 'Our Planet is in DANGER'.

Finn had a hippy-come-Rastafarian look to him with his baggy, orange-and-yellow pullover and pale brown, braided hair that stretched down to his waist. His fellow sign-holder, on the other hand, was decked out completely in black. Her black hair was in long pigtails making her look like Wednesday from the Addams Family, albeit a version of Wednesday with five rings through the left-hand side of her upper lip.

There was a grand total of two people watching as O'Sullivan spoke. One was clearly the mother of the second: a spotty-faced, and slightly dumpy, five-year-old boy sucking on a bright red lollipop and clutching her hand.

"Come on, Hunter," she said. "We need to go to M&S."

The boy took another lick of his lollipop. "Five more minutes please, Mummy," he said. "I like watching the funny man."

"You can have four more minutes."

"Three minutes?" Hunter said, trying to negotiate a deal but unaware of how to count numbers down.

"Okay," his mother said with a smile. "Three it is."

"Are you a whippy?" Hunter shouted.

"Hunter!" his mother said.

Finn ignored the question and carried on talking.

"Whippies take marriage-you-ah-na," Hunter went on, enunciating the last word very carefully. "Grandma told me."

"Sorry about that," his mother said. "Come on, Hunter.

Your three minutes are up."

Hunter allowed himself to be pulled away and Josh took his place as Finn resumed talking.

"Action is needed before it's too late," he said. "The government is doing nothing and it's about time they realised the mess the world is in."

"And how are you and your goth friend going to persuade 'em?" a middle-aged man called as he walked past.

"Through non-violent protests."

"Yeah, right."

Finn was about to respond when the man disappeared into Hotel Chocolat.

"Ignore him," the young woman said. She spoke in what sounded to Josh like a fake-cockney accent. "He's a tosser."

Josh stepped forward. "I'm interested in taking action," he said.

"You are?" Finn said. He stepped off his box and up to Josh who resisted the urge to retreat as the smell of unwashed skin hit him in both nostrils.

"I am, yes," Josh said, wrinkling his nose as he tried to breathe through his mouth. "What's the name of your organisation?"

"Earth Conflict."

"Gucc... Ah..." His mind went blank as he tried to think of a suitable word or phrase.

Finn stared at him.

"Cool," Josh said eventually. "Cool, because we conflict with the Earth, aren't we?"

"No, it's because we're in conflict with the powers-that-be about their attitude to the Earth."

"Right, yes, that makes more sense." Josh shook his head. "It's awful what they're doing."

"Or not doing."

"Exactly. That too. Action's needed before, ah, El Nino happens."

"And La Nina," the young woman said.

"Eh?" Josh said.

"Exactly, Shannon," Finn said. He smiled at Josh. "Do you fly?"

Josh's brain was spinning. He needed to think on his feet and be environmentally aware, but this question had him stumped. Only birds flew, didn't they? And bats of course. Wasn't there a flying squirrel in South America?

"Well?" Finn prompted.

"Do I fly?" He hesitated as Finn nodded, then it clicked. "You mean on airplanes?" he blurted out, then added quickly, "Of course you do."

He laughed, then realised Finn was still waiting for an answer.

"Me fly?" he said, his voice an octave higher than normal. "No. Uh-huh." He shook his head and brought his voice back down to its normal pitch. "Definitely not. All those gases they emit. Awful."

Finn nodded. "I'm pleased about that. And what's your view on toxic air."

I think you reek like no one's business was what came to mind, but Josh had read up on this and knew the right answer.

"It's getting worse all the time," he said. "We need a regenerative culture, one which is healthy but capable of adaptation as necessary."

"Good answer," Finn said and slapped Josh on the back. "What do you think, Shannon?"

"Interesting," she said and Josh could see she might be harder to win over.

"Do you want to join our group?" Finn asked.

"I might do," Josh said. "If you're serious about taking action. It's not for me if all you're going to do is preach at people and write letters to The Times."

Finn laughed. "You sound like you've got the right ideas," he said.

"What's your name?" Shannon asked.

"George," Josh said. "George Bailey."

"Like in the film?"

Josh smiled. "Yes. My parents loved 'It's a Wonderful Life'."

"Mmm. Where do you live?"

"Come on, Shannon," Finn said. "Leave him alone. This is hardly the Spanish Inquisition."

"I wanna make sure he's on the level, that's all."

"Don't be stupid. Why wouldn't he be? Listen, George. We've got a meeting next Tuesday to discuss our campaign of civil disobedience. You're welcome to come along."

Thoughts of missing Leanne's homemade cottage pie fleetingly passed through Josh's mind but he tried to ignore them.

"I'd like that," he said. "What time and where?"

"The Centurion Inn in Twerton. 8 pm."

"Cool. See you there."

"It might be Monday, Finn," Shannon said. "Don't you remember?"

"Oh yes," Finn said. "I forgot.' He turned to Josh. "Give me your number and I'll text you if it changes. Is that okay?"

"Coursio."

"Coursio?" Shannon said and frowned. "What kind of expression is that?"

"It's, ah… it's 'of course' without the 'of' and, ah… with 'ee-oh' at the end."

"Ee-oh?"

Josh grinned and fired a finger gun at her. "Exactimo."

Chapter 23

Helen had grown very fond of her son's girlfriend. They had only been together for six months, but it felt like a relationship that would endure. Becky was considerate and caring but most importantly of all, given Ronnie's history and his personal challenges, she was understanding.

They had come to Helen's for lunch and she had forgotten single cream, something Ronnie viewed as an essential accompaniment to her homemade apple crumble, so he had popped out to Tesco Express to buy some. This gave her the chance to find out how Becky was faring.

She threw the teabags away, added milk and took the two mugs into the lounge where Becky was leafing through an old photo album.

Helen handed Becky her drink. "Is it okay if I sit beside you?"

"Of course. Thanks for the tea."

Helen sat beside her on the sofa and Becky turned a few pages before pausing at a photo of an eighteen-month-old Ronnie in a high chair. What looked like Weetabix smothered his lower lip and he was beaming from ear to ear.

"He looks happy."

Helen smiled. "He was a bonny wee baby and always cheery."

"It must have been hard bringing him up on your own."

"Aye, being a single mother was a challenge to begin with, not least because I missed his father so much, but you get used to it. It helped that that wee chappy…" she tapped the photo, "…was so well-behaved. He was like that throughout school and went to University with high hopes."

Becky cradled her mug in both hands and sipped her tea. "It must have been such a shock when he dropped out," she said, almost under her breath.

Helen sighed. "It was. I didn't appreciate the stress he'd been under. He hid it from me, but as his mother I should have known."

"You can't blame yourself. He got in with the wrong crowd."

"Did he?"

"Hasn't he told you what happened?"

"No."

Becky put her mug on the coffee table, took a last look at the photo and then closed the album. "It was his friend Pinky," she began. "He wasn't on Ronnie's law course but their rooms were next to each other in the hall of residence."

Helen thought about this for a second. "Was he the one with very rich parents?"

Becky nodded. "That's the one."

"I remember Ronnie talking about a lad called Pinky when he first arrived. It stuck with me because it's such an unusual nickname, especially for a boy. Wasn't his father a politician?"

"Yes, and his mother's a barrister. By the end of the first year, Pinky had fallen out with both his parents, although they still sent him money. Ronnie told me that Pinky was wild but very funny and drew people to him like a magnet. He persuaded Ronnie to join him in a squat at the beginning of the second year."

"I thought Ronnie rented a house."

Helen heard the sound of the door being opened and turned to see Ronnie walking in.

"I got the cream," he said then saw the look on his mother's face. "What's wrong?"

"Becky's been telling me about Pinky and the squat."

"I felt she ought to know," Becky said.

Ronnie sat down on the edge of the armchair opposite his mother and girlfriend. "I haven't told you the half of it," he said with a sigh. He looked over at the window and Helen could see he was struggling.

"You don't have to say anything."

He turned and looked at her, then at Becky and then back at his mother.

"I need to, and I think I'm ready to. I've told Fay everything and it's taken a massive weight off my shoulders. Besides, you both deserve to know what happened."

Helen had a lot of time for Fay. She was Ronnie's counsellor and he'd been seeing her weekly for two months.

She waited while her son pulled himself together.

"I was weak and pathetic," Ronnie began. "Looking back, it's hard to believe I allowed myself to be sucked in by Pinky." He laughed but there was no humour in it. "He was nuts really. He had all these crazy beliefs about god and the universe and how the world was heading for disaster and that his parents were part of the problem. I remember his favourite saying was 'Every day is Earth Day'. He used to say it all the time."

Ronnie shook his head. "The thing is, he was so convincing. I started missing lectures because he was such a wonderful storyteller. He'd talk about people his mother had acted for, and how they'd been treated unfairly by the justice system. His morals were kind of weird but they were convincing too. He kept encouraging me and the others in the squat to stand up for what was right."

He paused and returned to looking at the window.

"Pinky was brainwashing me, I guess. I lost complete faith in the law and didn't see the point in finishing my degree. It wasn't long before I stopped going to lectures altogether." He swallowed. "I think that it was about that time that drugs became part of our everyday routine. It was pot at first, then he brought cocaine in. He called it nose candy and made it sound harmless." He shook his head. "I was so stupid."

"What happened to him?" Helen asked.

Ronnie shrugged. "I don't know. One day he wasn't there, but I was a full-on heroin addict by then and hardly noticed. I was spiralling downwards. If it hadn't been for Simon…"

"Simon Abrahams?" Helen prompted. Simon was an elder in the Jehovah's Witnesses and Ronnie's employer.

Ronnie nodded. "Simon knocked on the door one day, saw the state I was in and more or less manhandled me into his car. He took me to a rehab centre specialising in young people with addictions." He paused and rubbed below his right eye. "He didn't stop there though. Every week he came to our squat to take me to the centre and wouldn't take no for an answer. To be honest, without his perseverance, and his belief in me, I don't think I'd be here now."

"Have you heard from Pinky since?"

"No, thank goodness." He squeezed his eyes closed but couldn't hide the tears that were now flowing freely. "I should have come to you, Mum, and asked you to help me, but I was ashamed of what I'd become."

Helen stood up, held out her arms and smiled sympathetically. "Come here," she said.

He stood up and they embraced.

After a few seconds, there was a ping from the kitchen and Helen pulled away.

"That's the lunch," she said. "I'll serve up."

Chapter 24

"More crumble?' Helen asked.

"Not for me," Becky said.

"Go on then," Ronnie said.

Helen served him and he added a generous pouring of cream before tucking in.

"Do either of you know much about environmental issues?" she asked.

"I think Greta Thunberg's amazing," Becky said. "She's still only twenty-one and she's already accomplished so much."

"Don't forget David Attenborough," Ronnie said in between mouthfuls. "He's done as much, if not more, in his own way."

"It's not so much the people I'm interested in," Helen said. "I need an area to focus on because I'm joining a campaigning group called Sow the Wind."

Ronnie raised one eyebrow. "Why? You've never expressed especially strong views."

"It's for work."

It was Becky's turn to look bemused. "I thought you were a paralegal, Helen," she said.

Helen explained about Globo Energy commissioning Filchers to investigate Sow the Wind and Earth Conflict.

"Before you ask," she said when she'd finished, "I'm not putting myself in danger by joining. However, where I'm stuck is how to brand myself. As you said, Ronnie, I don't have particularly strong views on the environment. I'm as worried about climate change and greenhouse emissions as the next person, but I need to come across as passionate if I'm going to be convincing."

"Fossil fuels," Becky suggested. "You could present

yourself as desperately upset about the continuing use of coal and gas."

"Aye, but I'd be more likely to join an organisation like Extinction Rebellion if that was the case."

"I guess that's true."

"If the group is called Sow the Wind," Ronnie said, "they must be in favour of wind farms as a source of renewable energy. I'm sure I read somewhere that the UK is lagging behind the continent and that it's largely down to planning regulations. Why don't you look into that, Mum?"

"Mmm. That's a good idea. I'll do some research."

"Hang on," Becky said. "I'm sure I remember…" She turned to Helen. "Can you pass me the remote please, Helen?"

"Sure."

Becky clicked the TV on, navigated to a channel called AWX1 and then forwarded several days. "There," she said triumphantly and clicked on a programme scheduled for 8 in the evening. "I thought I'd seen Sow the Wind mentioned somewhere."

Helen read the description of the programme with interest.

Answer Time - 8 pm

Join Eleanor Tappett live as she and a studio audience demand answers to topical questions. This week the panel comprises John Gilbey, MP for South Hampshire, Andrea Mason, founder of Sow the Wind, and Erin Douglas from Sturridge Group.

*

Helen opened up her laptop as soon as Ronnie and Becky had left.

The first thing she did was research wind farms. It was

soon clear that offshore development was not an issue. Indeed, the opposite was true and the United Kingdom had been the world leader in offshore wind for over a decade.

Onshore was a different issue altogether, with planning applications taking on average two years to be considered by a local authority. Even then, only 40% of wind farms were approved. What was more, there was a maximum height limit of 125 metres despite modern lower-cost wind turbines on the continent being over 200 metres tall.

Yes, she decided, this was an area she could portray a passion for. It helped that planning regulations and legal contracts were similar in many ways which played into her strengths.

She spent another hour looking into the details, taking copious notes as she did so, then googled AWX1.

It was a channel devoted to documentaries and topical news, with its flagship programmes being 'In the Regions' and 'Answer Time'.

'Answer Time' featured Eleanor Tappett, previously a CNN anchor known for her forthright interviewing style. AWX1's promise was that the programme would focus on ensuring panellists answered the questions posed. Dodging and deviation would not be tolerated, and they were proud of the fact they were streaming the programme live. There would be no editing out of stuttered or weak responses.

So far this approach had reaped limited rewards, but it was a relatively new series and AWX1 claimed a growing viewer base though they didn't share numbers.

Helen clicked to find out more about the next programme. She saw that it was being filmed in a studio near Bristol and that people were invited to apply to be in the audience.

She filled out the online form, remembering to use the name Helen Livingstone, hit submit and was immediately sent a message on her phone confirming her place at the filming.

Chapter 25

His phone pinged and he looked down to see a WhatsApp message from Robin.

Good evening, Taylor.

Robin was unfailingly polite and business-like and it almost made him shiver. He shouldn't have been surprised, he supposed. After all, he or she was doing this for money. It was a financial transaction for them, no more and no less.

Whereas for him it was about securing the future for generations to come. He was selfless and a man of principle.

He typed his reply.

Good evening, Robin. Have you made progress?

It will be number one on your list.

Why did you choose him?

I am watching him now. He is alone which makes it simpler.

What do you mean by simpler?

No need for me to take anyone else out.

He hesitated before typing a reply. He wanted to ask how Robin would kill him but he was talking about a man's life being ended, a cold-blooded murder. Was it essential for him to know how he was going to be killed? Indeed, wouldn't it be better if he knew none of the details in case he let something slip?

He deleted what he'd written and typed a new message.

When will you do it?

> *Tonight.*

Is there any risk?

> *Do not worry, Taylor. I am*
> *a professional.*

Keep me updated.

> *I will.*

*

More than two hours had passed and he was pacing backwards and forwards.

Robin had assured him it would be straightforward, but what if he had been wrong about the man being alone? Or perhaps the police had driven past, spotted what was going on, intervened, captured Robin…

He stopped himself. It was nonsense thinking this way. Robin had come well recommended, albeit on the dark web, an area of the internet populated by cranks and psychopaths.

For the umpteenth time, he checked that he hadn't inadvertently put his phone on silent, then almost dropped it when it pinged. He looked away for a second and forced himself to turn back to his screen and read Robin's message.

> *Target eliminated.*

He shook his head as he read the two words.

They represented good news, of course they did, but they were so cold and unfeeling. It was the end of a man's life but to Robin he was merely a 'target', a means of acquiring money.

He, on the other hand, was doing this for the rest of humanity. He was a man of morals and eliminating people such as this man would make the world a better place.

It would be better if he knew nothing else, but on the other hand…

Did he suffer?

Not unduly.

Not unduly! What did that mean? He was about to ask a follow-up question when another message came through.

Will you now transfer the balance you owe me for completion?

Yes.

What about targets 2 and 3?

This was a good question.

What was the expression?

'In for a penny, in for a pound', that was it. Perhaps more appropriate was 'might as well be hung for a sheep as a lamb'.

More to the point, eliminating one person was not going to be enough. His death would be forgotten all too soon and it was important to create waves and pressure to take action. There needed to be real momentum so that the future was not thrown away.

Proceed with both of them.

On the same terms?

Yes, I will transfer the initiation fee today.

And you do not mind which

one is next?

No. You can choose.

Very well.

Goodbye for now, Robin.

Goodbye. Thank you for
your business.

Chapter 26

Luke was relieved that his father had been allowed to go home. Given his age and the nature of his accident he had come off surprisingly well. Yes, his words were occasionally muddled, but aside from that he seemed back to his old self.

Mark and Marion came to the door of Borrowham Hall to wave him off. He pulled the BMW away and caught sight of a sour-faced Erica in an upstairs window as he made his way towards the gates to the estate.

A few minutes into the journey he decided to ring Pete Gilmore. As well as being an ex-colleague, the Detective Inspector was also his main contact at Avon and Somerset Police. Luke had been due to be in the Portishead HQ for two days this week.

Pete answered straight away.

"Hi. Sounds like you're in the car."

"Yes. My father's out of hospital and I'm heading into Bath. I'm not sure when I'll be able to get to Portishead."

"No problem. It's more likely we'll need you in Bath though, depending on progress with the Dumpy Dumper."

"The Dumpy Dumper?"

Pete sighed. "I know! It's a crass and insensitive name, but that's what it's already become known as on social media. A body was found in a one-ton builder's bag on the edge of the Park and Ride in Odd Down."

"Any suspects?"

"No, and we haven't identified the victim yet either. We know it's a man, and he looks to be in his forties, but that's about it. Sally Croft's doing the post-mortem today. However, there are a couple of people we want to interview and it would be great if you could help. Any ideas which days you'll be available?

"Can we say Tuesday to start with and see how we go?"

"Sure. Let's do that. I'll be back in touch when I know more."

Luke ended the call and shifted his thoughts to Henry Lavers, an ex-classmate but unlike Pete not someone he would ever have described as a friend. Henry had said on the phone that he wanted to share information about Sow the Wind and Earth Conflict but wasn't willing to relay it through Liz Rathbone, even though she worked for him.

This in itself was intriguing. There had been something about Henry's tone that suggested he was hiding something sensitive. Was that because it reflected on Liz or Daniel, or was it something to do with their employer, Globo Energy?

He remembered that Henry Lavers had been very bright, top of the class in most subjects, but lacking any affinity with sports or physical activity. However, although academic he wasn't nerdy, nor was he noticeably unfit or overweight. Looking back, there hadn't been anything remarkable about Henry Lavers aside from his obvious intelligence. He hadn't been an extrovert, nor someone who kept himself to himself. He had a circle of friends, just not one that Luke mixed with.

They had been at school together for five years but only one incident stood out in Luke's mind. Henry wasn't a troublemaker in class but when they were in the Lower Sixth he had an altercation with Mr Kirby, the Geography teacher, known to the pupils as Rip.

Rip had called Henry to the front before a lesson and after a short exchange Henry had pushed him to the ground before storming out of the classroom. The teacher had then clambered to his feet and raced after him.

All Luke knew was that Henry had been taken to see the Head but he wasn't aware of any further punishment.

He parked in Charlotte Street car park and walked to the Francis Hotel. Once inside, one of the receptionists pointed him to the No. 10 Bar where he immediately spotted Henry on a padded blue chair at a table near the window. His hair had receded a few inches but he had otherwise aged well with just a touch of grey in his full brown beard.

He looked up from his book, stood up and held his hand out.

"You're even taller than I remember you," he said as they shook hands.

Luke smiled, unsure how to respond.

"Can I get you a drink?" Henry went on.

"Thanks." Luke dropped into the grey club chair opposite. "A strong black coffee please."

Henry called a waiter over and placed the order, asking for a double whisky for himself.

"Good book?" Luke asked, indicating the large tome on the coffee table between them.

Henry nodded. "As far as I'm concerned it's excellent and based totally on facts. It ought to be compulsory reading for all those environmental nutters."

"Do you mind if I take a look?"

"Of course not."

Luke picked the book up. It was attractively produced with a photo of two polar bears on the front beneath the words 'Apocalypse Never - Why Environmental Alarmism Hurts Us All'.

"I take it this is by a climate change denier," he said.

"Not at all. The author was a leading environmental journalist and it presents a balanced view on how we're being taken for a ride by politicians and bankers alike."

"Interesting." He placed the book back down.

"You ought to read it."

"Mmm. I might," Luke said, although he had no intention of doing so.

The waiter arrived with their drinks and put them on the table.

"Thanks. So, Henry," he went on after the waiter had left. "What's this information you want to share?"

"Straight to the point eh, Luke? I remember you were always very direct at school."

Luke waited.

Henry took a sip of his whisky, looked Luke in the eyes then put his glass down, clasped his hands together, held them to his chin and stared off to one side.

"Some of what I'm about to tell you is difficult for me to share," he began, his words tentative, "but it's important that you understand the full picture." He sighed. "The fact is, I've got myself into personal difficulties and that's part of the problem."

"I thought this was about the environmental groups we're looking into."

"Oh, it is, but…" He paused. "Oh, the hell with it." His next words came out in a rush, as if he was nervous that if he paused he would stop and be unable to continue. "I'm happily married with two wonderful sons and a wife who adores me, but I had a relationship with someone else, not for long, and it meant nothing to me, but she, well…" He suddenly came to a halt.

"Was it Liz Rathbone?"

Henry turned back to Luke, a look of astonishment on his face.

"Liz?" he said. "Heavens, no."

"So why is it relevant?"

"It was Andrea Mason."

"The founder of Sow the Wind?"

"The very same." Henry smiled apologetically. "I know it sounds odd."

"It certainly does." Luke tapped the book. "I can't imagine her sharing your love of reading matter like that for a start. What on earth did you have in common?"

"Nothing, but then our relationship didn't involve much talking." He grinned sheepishly. "I happened to see her in the street one day and took the opportunity to confront her about her ridiculous ideas and then…" He paused for a second as he tried to pull himself together. "She invited me back to her flat to discuss our differences and, well…" He sighed again, even more deeply this time. "I ended up spending the night."

"I see. Was that the only…'

Henry interrupted before he could finish. "We met three more times, always at her flat, and then we agreed not to see each other any more."

"Why was that?"

"She said her partner suspected something."

"Finn O'Sullivan?"

Henry nodded. "To be honest, it was a relief when we finished. As you said, we had nothing in common."

"Okay, Henry," Luke began. "I see now why you don't want Liz to know about your affair."

"I wouldn't call it an affair."

What would you call it then given you're supposedly 'happily married', was what Luke wanted to say, but instead he said, "Do I take it you learned something when you were with her that will be useful in our investigation?"

Henry nodded. "This can't come from me though, Luke. Liz and Ellen, my wife, are good friends. Please promise you'll keep my name out of it."

"I'll have to tell my team, but I assure you we'll keep it to ourselves."

"Good." He paused for a few seconds. "When we last met, she fell asleep after we, ah, you know…" He gulped. "Anyway, I took the opportunity to go through her bookshelf. There was a notebook with jottings in it, and it was clear from what had been written that violence was very much on her agenda."

"Go on."

"It was a list of targets." He gulped. "My name was there but it was crossed out."

"How do you know they were targets?"

"Targets was written at the top in capital letters and underlined."

"Okay. They were probably targets then. But couldn't they simply be targets for peaceful protests?"

"There was a separate list on the facing page headed 'Possibilities' and under that a list of about ten, ah, I guess you'd call them means of attack."

"Can you remember any of them?"

"I remember one was 'knife', another was 'car' and a third was 'push off platform'."

"Any others?"

Henry shook his head. "Sorry. I was so shocked I didn't fully take it in."

"What about the names on the list of targets?"

"Believe me, I've wracked my brain trying to recall who was listed, but all I see when I try to remember the details is 'Henry Lavers' with a line drawn through it."

"Anything else?"

"Yes. It was clear from the handwriting differences that two people had compiled the list."

"Andrea and Finn?"

"I assume so."

Chapter 27

Luke held his finger against the sensor, waited for the click and then pushed the Ethics Room door open.

He entered to find Helen bent forward in her chair. She was making snuffling noises, and for half a second he thought she was choking on something, then she looked up and he saw she was grinning and trying to hold back her laughter.

"I've never seen anything like it," she said and then spotted Luke. "Maj, quick. Go and fetch him before he changes back."

Maj had a broad smile on his face. "You're going to enjoy this, Luke," he said as he passed him and left the room.

Luke looked from Maj to Helen and then over to Sam. She was also smiling.

"Great to see you," she said. "I take it he's home?"

"Yes, he's doing well," Luke said. He nodded his head towards the door. "What's going on?"

It was Helen who answered. "We've got a wee surprise for you," she said. "You're going to love it."

"Come and sit here," Sam said, gesturing to one of the chairs.

Still bemused, he did as she asked.

She stood behind him and put her hands over his eyes. He immediately smelt her familiar perfume and realised he'd missed seeing her.

Missed seeing her!

What sort of nonsense was that? He'd only been gone for a few days, and besides she was one of his team, an employee.

Missed being at work.

That was what he meant. He hadn't missed Sam, of course he hadn't. And besides, he was in a relationship with Cora. There wasn't any question of…

Sam bent down and whispered in his ear. "You're going to love this, Luke," she said. "It's a sight for sore eyes."

You're a sight for sore eyes, he thought but said nothing.

A few seconds later he heard a click and the sound of footsteps then Sam said "3, 2, 1, blast-off" and removed her hands from his face.

What he saw blew his mind.

He stared in disbelief at the vision in front of him. The suited and immaculately coiffured Josh had been transformed into…

Into what exactly?

Helen started laughing again.

"Stop!" Josh said.

"You look like a Picasso painting gone wrong," Helen said between chortles.

"Those bright patches are cubist,' Sam said.

"There's a touch of Salvador Dali too," Maj added.

"Aye," Helen said. "It's definitely surreal."

"I think you look cool, Josh," Luke said.

Josh looked across at him. "You do, guv?"

Luke grinned. "No, but you've made my day. What does Leanne think?"

"Leanne?" Josh squeaked. "She chose this, this…" He waved his hands in front of his linen shirt. "… abomination."

"I know she did, son, but I meant the clothes.'

Helen let out a loud snort.

"Eh!" Josh said.

"But seriously, Josh," Luke said. "You look the part."

"Aye," Helen said. "The part of Joseph's amazing technicolour dreamcoat."

✳

Once Josh had reverted to normal clothes, and had been given enough time to wet, comb, style, re-comb, re-style and finally wax his hair, Luke called the team together for an update.

"First off," Luke began, "and this is in confidence, I met with Henry Lavers, Liz Rathbone's boss, earlier. We were at school together although we were never friends and haven't remained in touch. He contacted me because he has seen evidence that Andrea Mason may be prepared to use violence."

He outlined what Henry had seen and gave them the background about his affair with Andrea.

"If you want to pull out, Helen…" he said when he'd finished.

"Ach, no," she said. "The whole reason for the investigation…"

"Project Greta," Josh said.

"Sorry, Josh. The whole reason for Project Greta…" This was greeted by a beaming smile and double thumbs-up from Josh. "…is Andrea Mason's past record as an anarchist and what happened to the MP Teddy Overton. This doesn't change anything."

"It changes one thing," Josh said. He was still grinning. "It's extra information, another source. We need to update the crazy wall."

"I hate to say it," Luke said, "but you're right. Maj, do you mind?"

Maj stood up and pulled the whiteboard over.

At the bottom he had already written 'Globo Energy' with the names 'Liz Rathbone' and 'Daniel Craven'. He added 'Henry Lavers' and drew a dotted line connecting him to Andrea Mason.

Luke nodded. "That's good. Helen, have you got anything we should add to the board."

"Crazy…" Josh began.

"Stop it, Josh," Luke said

"Sorry, guv, but…"

Luke glared at Josh who stuttered to a stop.

"I'm going to a Sow the Wind meeting tomorrow," Helen said. "And then I'll be seeing Andrea Mason again on Thursday." She explained about being in the studio audience for 'Answer Time'.

"That's excellent," Luke said when she'd finished. "I suggest we all try to watch the programme if we can."

"I won't be able to," Josh said. "I met Finn O'Sullivan at the weekend…"

"In your dreamcoat?" Helen asked.

"No. I was, ah…" He hesitated. "Leanne made me buy another shirt. It's brown and covered in big mushrooms."

Helen stifled a laugh.

"Carry on," Luke said. "You said you met Finn O'Sullivan."

"Yes, guv. In Southgate. There was a girl there too, about my age, and she seems to be a member of Earth Conflict."

Maj raised his pen.

Josh looked at him.

"Well?" Maj asked.

"Oh, right, yes. Sorry. Her name's Shannon."

Maj added her name to the board beneath the entry for Earth Conflict and Finn O'Sullivan.

"She worried me," Josh went on.

"Because Leanne might be a wee bit jealous?" Helen asked.

Josh shook his head. "Not that, no. She was so black for a start."

"Josh!" Sam said.

Josh looked at Sam and then at Maj who was smiling.

"No. I didn't mean…" He looked back at Sam. "She wasn't… ah… She's white."

"But you said…"

"No, she was dressed in black. Like one of those goths,

you know, the ones in Whitby who are fans of Bram Stoker. She had rings in her lip too. Loads of them."

"So you took against her because she was in dark clothes," Helen said, "even though you'd gone shopping dressed as an edible fungus."

"I hadn't…" His voice was a squeak now. "It was Shannon's manner I didn't like. She was very pushy."

"You were saying," Luke said, seeing the need to drag the conversation back, "that you can't watch 'Answer Time' because you met Finn O'Sullivan."

Josh nodded. "He invited me to a meeting to discuss their campaign of civil disobedience." He paused. "I can't say I'm looking forward to meeting Shannon again."

"Because she's black?" Maj asked.

"She's not…" Josh saw the look on Maj's face and stopped. "Ha, ha."

"Where's the meeting?" Maj asked.

"The Centurion Inn in Twerton."

Maj added it to the board.

"Right, good work everyone," Luke said. "Let's have another Project Greta catch-up after Helen's been to 'Answer Time' and Josh has met with Earth Conflict.

Chapter 28

Helen didn't want to overthink clothes for her role as Helen Livingstone, would-be climate activist.

She flicked through her wardrobe and came across a pale orange skirt that she had completely forgotten about. It had been an impulse buy six or seven years earlier, and it had only been when she got it home that she realised it was made for someone six foot tall and very slim, not a woman of five foot five with an hourglass figure.

She had meant to take it back for a refund but never got around to it.

It was ideal.

Blouses were more of a challenge, but she remembered a red long-sleeved top that she thought might work. She tugged on the skirt and then put on the blouse, automatically tucking the latter in before pulling it from her waist and letting it hang.

She stood back from the mirror, looked at her reflection and smiled.

It was an abomination.

It was ideal.

The red and orange combo was almost frightening, while hanging the shirt outside the top of her skirt made her look as though she was trying to conceal a catheter.

The coup de gras, she decided, would be the ancient khaki fleece she used for gardening. She retrieved it from the boot room, donned her oldest pair of trainers and walked quickly to the bus stop without frightening herself by looking in the mirror again.

The bus was on time and it was just before eight when Helen reached The Curfew, a traditional pub just outside the city centre. Once inside Helen spotted a sheet on the wall saying 'Sow the Wind Meeting' with an arrow pointing towards the back of the building.

She headed down the corridor into an elegant space with high ceilings, picture windows and shelves of old books on one wall. Three rows of ten seats were laid out facing a dusky red Chesterfield. The room managed to be both formal and comfortable at the same time.

A dozen or so people were in the room, split among three groups. A woman in her mid-forties broke away and approached Helen.

"Hi," she said. "I'm Jackie. Is this your first time at a Sow the Wind forum?"

"Aye, it is," Helen said as they shook hands. "I'm Helen."

"Are you in any other groups?"

This seemed an odd first question and Helen wondered if this was because Earth Conflict had started up and was viewed as a rival organisation.

"No," she said, "but the more I read about the environmental challenges the planet's facing, the more I think I ought to do something about it."

Jackie smiled. "You've definitely come to the right place then. It'll be an informal meeting tonight so please don't be shy and feel free to air your views."

"I will. Are you expecting many more?"

"A few maybe. But to be honest, it's quality not quantity that matters. Sow the Wind welcomes people who are prepared to take action. That'll be the focus this evening, The last thing we want to be is a talking shop."

"That's good."

Jackie turned and addressed her next comment to a woman Helen immediately recognised from her photo on the whiteboard. "Andrea," she said. "Come and meet Helen."

Andrea turned away from the man she was talking to and for a split-second Helen thought it was Finn

O'Sullivan, the last person she expected to see given their acrimonious split. However, on second glance she realised that he had a differently shaped beard and a slightly cleaner look, if still very hippily-dressed.

"Hello," Andrea said, her voice flat. "Thanks for coming," she added although she sounded anything but.

"I think we should start," Jackie said, and it struck Helen that although Andrea Mason was the founder and main spokesperson for Sow the Wind it seemed to be Jackie who called the shots.

Andrea moved to the Chesterfield and sat at one end while Jackie invited people to sit on the rows of seats. Helen positioned herself at the end of the back row so that she could see everyone else. She counted twelve people in addition to herself, Andrea and Jackie.

Jackie remained standing. "Thanks for coming. Nice to see a few stalwarts and also a few who haven't been before. How many of you are signed-up members of Sow the Wind?"

Half a dozen hands went up including that of the man Helen had mistaken for Finn O'Sullivan.

"We have a few potential new recruits to our cause then," she said. "That's excellent."

She turned to Andrea. "Do you want to start us off, Andrea?"

Andrea nodded but didn't get to her feet. "Welcome everyone," she began. "I value your presence here tonight. I founded Sow the Wind as a do-it-together movement and I am merely a mouthpiece for what we hold dear and care about. It is only by working together that we can foster real change. The government pretends commitment to our cause, but they're deceitful. Let me give you a couple of examples of the lies they tell us. A few months ago…"

As she continued talking it struck Helen that although the woman lacked charisma, her words were powerful. They were delivered in a monotone but were nonetheless convincing and gave the impression of someone with deeply held beliefs.

After a few minutes, Andrea invited opinions and questions from the floor.

"Where do you draw the line when it comes to activism, Andrea?" a man in the front row asked. He was well-built with straggly brown hair and a strong chin over which sprouted wiry stubble.

"That's a very good question. However, don't forget what I said earlier. I'm a spokesperson not an autocratic leader. It's down to our members to agree how far we take things."

"Okay," the man said. He looked around at the others. "What does everyone else think? Is it enough to wave placards and write to MPs or should we be making our presence felt?"

Finn O'Sullivan's doppelganger was the first to answer. "We have to be proactive," he said. "Our actions need to be highly visible."

"Might that involve violence?"

"It might."

"What about damage to property?"

"Surely that depends," a woman in her fifties said.

Helen watched as the conversation continued, but was left with no clear view of where everyone stood. Andrea in particular was keen to avoid saying anything that might be construed as immoral or illegal.

It was clear that getting underneath the skin of Sow the Wind wasn't going to be easy.

Chapter 29

Luke met Pete in Redbridge House in Bath, where he was let in by a young uniformed constable who introduced herself as PC Warwick. She showed him to a small meeting room where he was sitting leafing through a report.

"This is Sally's post-mortem report for you to read ahead of our interviews," he said as he passed the document over. "Coffee?"

"Yes please."

Luke had read the report by the time Pete returned with their drinks.

"It makes interesting reading. I take it there was no fingerprint match?"

Pete dropped into the only other chair in the room. "Unfortunately not. Whoever our man is, he hasn't got a criminal record. We're having dental records checked so hopefully we'll identify him that way."

"What about missing persons? Have you found anyone matching his description?"

"Not yet, but I've asked the team to widen the search in case he's not a local. Of course, he might not even be British."

"Sally said he'd been dead for between six and eight hours and that he was killed by a single bullet to the centre of his forehead fired at close range. I also noted that she couldn't find any other injuries, aside from damage to the skin caused after death. It makes it sound like a gangland execution rather than a crime of passion or a shot fired in anger."

"I agree."

"And he was found naked?"

Pete nodded. "Yes. No sign of any documents near

him." He gave a dry laugh. "A lot of sand and gravel but no documents. The first person we're interviewing today is the man who found him."

"Okay. So who are we seeing?"

"First on is Malcolm Cooper. Then we're seeing a Gemma Turnbull. She called in because she thought she saw someone acting suspiciously. And lastly, we're interviewing Antonio Scarapucci. He phoned in to say he had information that might be useful."

"Are any of them suspects?"

"Not at the moment. Scarapucci has a criminal record for theft but he didn't go to jail for it. He received a community order and a fine."

At just before ten Luke and Pete made their way to the interview room where a middle-aged man in glasses sat with a glass of water. He was completely bald with two thin strips of grey hair down each side of his head.

"Good morning, Mr Cooper," Pete said. "I'm Detective Inspector Pete Gilmore and this is Luke Sackville. Thanks for coming in this morning."

"Not a problem. I'm still shaken up by it, to be honest." He shivered. "I couldn't believe it. I mean, you don't expect to find a body when all you're doing is moving ballast, do you?"

Pete sat opposite their interviewee with Luke next to him.

"Please call us Pete and Luke," Pete said. "Can we call you Malcolm?"

"I prefer Mal."

"That's fine. I'll record the interview and then we can get a statement typed up for you to sign. Is that okay?"

Mal nodded.

Pete smiled. "And because of the recording, we'll need you to say yes or no when appropriate rather than nod or shake your head."

"Of course. I mean, yes." He looked at the recording

device and raised his voice. "YES."

"It's not on yet, Mal."

"Sorry."

Pete clicked the button to start recording. "Interview with Malcolm Cooper in the Witness Interview Room in Redbridge House, Bath," he said and checked his watch. "The time is 10:07. Interview conducted by DI Gilmore and Luke Sackville."

"So, Mal," he continued, "please can you run through events last week leading up to you finding the body."

Mal nodded, then remembered the machine and said loudly, "YES, I CAN."

Pete waited.

Mal looked at Pete for a few seconds, then said. "You want me to describe what happened that morning?"

"If you wouldn't mind."

"Well, I was up early. I'm generally an early riser. Joanne says it's my age but I've always been like it. It was about five thirty I think. No, probably more like a quarter to six. I made myself a cup of…"

Pete held his hand up.

"Sorry," Mal said. "Am I being too quiet?"

"I think we can move forward a couple of hours, Mal."

Mal nodded then looked at the recording device and said, "YES."

There was another silence.

"When you're ready," Pete prompted.

"Ah, yes." Mal raised his voice again. "YES." He smiled before continuing. "I was first into work. We're building a shelter at the Park and Ride see, and we had these Dumpy Bags delivered the evening before. Trouble is, I got in that morning to find he'd put them in the wrong place, over fifty yards away, so I decided to get some of the sand and gravel nearer to make the mixing quicker once the other guys arrived."

"Sand and gravel?" Luke asked.

Mal almost nodded, then shouted "YES" before resuming. "We use the sand and gravel to make concrete. I thought I'd start with sand, but it seemed a bit odd."

"What seemed a bit odd?'

"Well, we ordered six bags of sand and six of gravel. Sure enough, there were twelve bags in two rows but it looked like they'd cocked up because seven of them were sand."

"Seven?"

Mal bent to the recording device. "YES. The six at the back and the one on the right at the front." He hesitated. "Only it wasn't"

"It wasn't full of sand?"

"NO." Mal smiled again, pleased that he was getting the hang of raising his voice at the right time. "It had a layer of sand but beneath that…" He paused for a second and took a sip of his water. "I stuck my spade in and it struck something and, well, it was him, wasn't it? I thought it was a stone so I put the spade on the ground and stuck my hands in to move the sand aside. I felt something softer than a stone and then… I saw him." He swallowed as the memory came back. "His eyes were open. I mean, they were full of sand but his eyes were wide open."

Mal opened his eyes wide to emphasise the point.

"What did you do then?"

"I screamed and jumped backwards. Nearly fell over I did. Then I called 999."

"What time did you get to the Park and Ride, Mal?" Luke asked.

"Just before eight."

"And when were the bags delivered?"

"It was about two minutes to six when the lorry arrived. I remember because we finished at six."

Chapter 30

Pete and Luke returned to the interview room after Malcolm Cooper had left.

"Given what Sally said about the time of death," Pete said, "the body must have been put in the Dumpy Bag between midnight and 8 am."

"And our killer then covered the body with sand from another bag," Luke said. "But why do that? The body was always going to be found so why cover it with sand?" He paused. "What time does the Park and Ride open, Pete?"

"Quarter past six."

"Mmm. Perhaps it was done to buy time."

The door opened and PC Warwick came in. "Miss Turnbull is here, DI Gilmore," she said.

"Thanks," Pete said.

"She's, ah…" The constable closed the door behind her and lowered her voice. "She's what you might call the worse for wear."

"In what way?"

"I haven't asked her but I suspect it was a client."

"A client?"

"I've come across Gemma a few times, sir. She's a sex worker." She paused. "She can be quite challenging to deal with."

"I see. Show her in please."

A couple of minutes later PC Warwick showed Gemma Turnbull into the room and Pete invited her to sit down opposite them.

Luke judged her to be around forty years old, but it was hard to tell given the copious amounts of red that was caked onto her cheeks and lips. She was stick-thin and wore a buttoned-up black leather tunic over a cream too-tight skirt that stopped just above the knees. The ensemble was finished off by spangled stilettos.

She also had a ring of purple-black around her right eye.

"Thanks for coming in, Miss Turnbull," Pete said. "Can I call you Gemma?"

She smiled, said, "Fuck, even smiling hurts," in a strong Bath accent then put her right hand up to tentatively tap at the skin below her black eye. "Gemma will do," she added.

"Good," Pete said. He gestured to her eye. "That looks painful."

"He's got one just as bad, the cocksucker. Wouldn't give me what was owed." She glared at Luke as if this was his fault. "I told him the fucking amount at the car window, didn't I? Girt great fat knobhead." She smiled viciously. "If I see him again I'll squeeze his balls until both eyes pop out, never mind about a fucking bruise. That'll teach the jizzpot."

"We're going to record this interview if that's okay," Pete said.

Gemma shrugged acceptance.

Pete clicked the button. "Interview with Gemma Turnbull in Redbridge House," he said. "It is now 11:36. Present are DI Pete Gilmore and Mr Luke Sackville."

"So, Gemma," he began. "Please tell us what you saw."

"It was Thursday night. No, Friday night."

Pete and Luke exchanged a look. "You seem unsure," Pete said.

"Fucking same thing either way, isn't it? I started work very late Thursday night. It was one am when I saw someone acting all suspicious like, so it was Friday by then."

"So it was gone midnight? The early hours of Friday morning."

Gemma sighed. "That was what I fucking said. It was one in the morning."

"How can you be so sure?"

"Had a client, didn't I? Pre-booked."

"What was your client's name."

"Dunno. Can't remember."

"You said you saw someone acting suspiciously," Luke said. "Was it a man?"

"Not sure. Could have been a woman, could have been fucking non-binary for all I know. Short hair though."

"I take it you didn't see their face."

"No. I'd have known the fucking gender if I had."

"What were they doing that made you suspicious?" Pete asked.

"Well, I was kinda looking over this punter's shoulder, making noises cos that's what they like, and I saw movement over by a load of builders' bags."

"What sort of movement?"

"It was difficult to tell."

"Because it was dark."

"That and the fact I was being bounced up and down on this guy's weenie." She paused and put her hand to her eye again. "At least that dick-squat paid what was owed."

"So what exactly did you see?" Pete asked, trying to get her back on topic.

"He or she was carrying something over their shoulders and they put it in one of the bags."

"What did you think it was?"

Gemma shrugged. "It looked like a roll of carpet or a folded-up duvet, I don't know. Something big but as I fucking said, it was dark. Clear now it was that body you found. All I know for certain is he or she was tall."

"How tall?"

She looked at Luke. "Stand up."

Luke stood up and she stared up at him amazed.

"Well, not that fucking tall," she said. "Fuck me, you're a big boy."

Luke sat down and Pete stood up.

"Was he or she as tall as me?' he said.

She thought about this for a few seconds. "Maybe. What height are you?"

"5 foot eleven."

"Probably your height or a bit taller."

"Tall for a woman?"

"Yeah."

"You're not giving us a lot to go on,' Pete said. "A man or woman who's five foot eleven or a bit taller doesn't narrow it down much."

"There is this," she said, then undid the top of her tunic and pulled a folded piece of paper from between her almost non-existent breasts. "After me punter had paid I went over and found this on the ground near the bags."

She passed it over and Pete unfolded it and then passed it to Luke.

"You didn't think to look in the bag to see what he or she had put in there?" Pete asked.

"As I said, I assumed it was carpet. Why would I want to look at a roll of fucking carpet?"

*

Pete gestured to the piece of paper on the table once Gemma Turnbull had left.

"What do you make of that?" he asked.

It was a printed A4 sheet. The background was bright yellow and there were no words but in the centre was a thick red 'X' positioned over an image of the earth in blue and white.

"It looks like some kind of logo," Luke said, "but it's not one I recognise."

"I'll get the team onto it," Pete said.

"Good, although it could be nothing to do with our killer or victim. Did Scene of Crime come back with anything?"

"Nothing useful, no."

"Fingers crossed we find out who the victim is soon. Then maybe that," he gestured to the A4 sheet, "might make sense."

Chapter 31

Third in was Antonio Scarapucci. He was in his mid-thirties, of medium build and average height with thick black hair.

Pete made the introductions, was told that Scarapucci preferred to be called Tony, and clicked to start recording.

"I came in voluntarily," Scarapucci began before Pete or Luke could say anything. Despite his name, there was no trace of an Italian accent.

"I was there," he went on, "and when I read about the Dumpy Dumper I thought you'd catch up with me, so I came in. Bound to be CCTV, isn't there? I mean it's everywhere."

"Thanks for coming in," Pete said.

"I'm not a suspect, am I?"

"Why would you be?"

He shrugged but Luke could tell he was on edge. "No reason."

"Why don't you tell us exactly when and where you were and what you saw?" Pete asked.

"I went out for a drive in my van and…"

"What time was this?"

"It was just after midnight."

"You went out for a drive at midnight?" Luke asked.

"Couldn't sleep, could I?"

"So you went for a drive in your van to the Park and Ride?"

Scarapucci laughed. "Sounds odd when you put it like that." He swallowed. "I, ah… yes, I was wandering around, trying to make myself tired."

"So that you could go home and finally get some shut-eye?"

"That was it. Yes."

"Okay," Pete said. "You've said you were at the Park and Ride at midnight on Friday so…"

Scarapucci interrupted. "It was probably about twelve-thirty by the time I got there. I took my time."

"I see. And when you got there, did you see the builders' bags?"

"Yeah. I parked close to them. Got out of the van and walked around the bags. CSI, or whatever they're called, might find marks from my trainers."

"You walked around the bags?"

"Yes. They were in two rows. Rows of six I think."

"Why did you walk around them, Tony?" Luke asked.

Scarapucci raised his hand to his forehead and ran it through his hair.

"I don't know," he said. "I, ah… I just did. I was killing time"

"Did you see anyone else?" Pete asked. "Or anything that struck you as unusual?"

"I didn't see anyone, no. The bags were full of gravel or sand. No tools or anything there, just the Dumpy Bags." He hesitated, then put his hand to his mouth.

"What have you remembered, Tony?" Luke asked.

"It must have been the body."

"What must?"

"One of the bags had sand in but the level was higher than the others."

"How could you tell? It was the middle of the night."

"I had the light on on my phone."

"Which bag had more in?" Pete asked.

"The one on the right at the front."

"You didn't see anything else? Nothing on the ground?"

Scarapucci shook his head. "That's everything."

"Okay, Tony," Pete said and smiled. "I think we're about done. I'll get a witness statement typed and you can come back in to sign it."

"Yes. Fine." He started to stand up. "Can I go now?"

"Can I just summarise what you've told me, Tony?" Luke asked. "So that I'm clear on what happened."

Tony sat down again.

"You had insomnia so you went for a drive," Luke began. "This was around midnight on Thursday night. You went straight to the Park and Ride in Odd Down…"

"Not directly," Scarapucci said, then added quickly. "I guess it's not relevant."

"We'll find you on CCTV," Pete reminded him.

"I, ah…"

"You what?"

"I went to that new housing estate near Sainsbury's first."

"In Odd Down?"

"Yes. Then straight to the Park and Ride."

"I see," Luke said. "And when you got there you turned the light on on your phone, walked around the Dumpy Bags, noticing that one had more sand in than the others, and then headed home. Is that correct?"

Scarapucci twisted in his seat.

"Well?' Luke prompted.

"I, ah… I might have gone to a third place before I drove home."

"And did you find any tools there?"

Scarapucci opened his mouth and then closed it again.

Luke leaned forward over the table. "It's obvious what you've been doing," he said. "Are they still in the van?"

"Are what still in the van?"

"We're not stupid, Tony."

Scarapucci folded his arms across his chest, shrugged, and seemed to come to a decision. "There weren't none," he said. "Not near Sainsbury's, not in the Park and Ride and not at the housing estate."

"In that case," Pete said, "take this as a warning. Right now, your attempts at petty pilfering aren't our concern. A man has been murdered."

"Yes, that's why I came in. To do my public duty."

"That's very noble of you," Luke said.

"Thanks. Can I go now?"

Chapter 32

Josh was chewing on a mouthful of chicken when his phone pinged. He looked down at the screen and almost spat it out.

"Buggeroh-buggeroo," he said.

"What is it?" Leanne asked.

He swallowed his mouthful. "The meeting's been changed to tonight."

"Earth Cornflakes?"

"Stop it, Leanne. You know full well it's Earth Conflict." He looked at the kitchen clock. "It's six-thirty. I need to get my skates on."

"No, you don't."

"Eh?"

"You need to get your sandals on," she said with a grin.

"But it's freezing out there."

"Ah, but you're George Bailey, ready for all conditions, going where others fear to tread, bravely…"

Josh held his hand up. "Okay, okay. I get the picture."

"After all," she went on, her grin even wider now, "as you put it yourself, you're a Field Plant."

"Ha, ha, bloody ha." He put another spoonful of casserole in his mouth.

"Don't you need to get ready?"

"It won't take me long," he said between chomps. "It's not as if this," he gestured to the top of his head, "needs much attention."

"No, you're right. All you have to do is wash off that max-hold and then fluff your hair into randomness."

Josh shook his head in disgust at the thought that his hair was going to be deprived of its gel. He then spent a few minutes polishing off the rest of his meal before disappearing to the bathroom.

Twenty minutes later he reappeared.

"Well," he said. "What do you think?"

Leanne put her hand to her mouth and started spluttering. "Oh, Joshy," she said as she tried to contain herself. "You're a picture."

"A picture out of nightmares. At least I can cover this shirt with my Burberry for the journey."

"Ah!" She held her index finger up. "That reminds me. I've bought you a little surprise. Wait here."

She stood up and went into the bedroom. Josh heard a cupboard door opening and closing and then she returned with a small tiger in her arms.

He stepped back in fright.

"What's that?" he squealed.

"It's your new coat."

"What!" He moved tentatively towards her. "It looks like the skin of an exotic animal."

"It's made of wool. I got it from The Yellow Shop."

"I'm not surprised. Look at the colour of it." He bent his head to one side and peered at the red symbols that ran down a white column between two strips of yellow. "Are those Egyptian hieroglyphs?"

Leanne lifted the coat to inspect it more closely. "Yes, I think you may be right."

He shook his head several times. "No way, Jose. I'm not wearing that."

"Nonsense. It'll keep you warm, plus it'll cover your bright shirt. It's got a hood too."

"Wowza! A hood. Aren't I a lucky boy?"

Leanne smiled. "Yes you are, Joshy. Now put it on."

Grudgingly, he put the coat on.

She leaned towards him and kissed him on the lips. "Now get out there and show them that George Bailey is a true environmentalist."

"I'll do my best," he said as he headed out of the

apartment for the bus stop.

*

It was just after eight when Josh arrived at the Centurion Inn in Twerton. It wasn't a pub he'd visited before, and as he looked at the outside he could understand why.

His preference was for lively city centre bars, where young professional types hung out after work and at weekends. The Centurion was more of a locals' pub and looked to date from the 1960s. It was pleasant enough, but why Earth Conflict had chosen it he couldn't imagine. He'd have thought they'd go for the kind of place where festival-goers hung out, somewhere like the Bell in Walcot.

He was greeted by a smiling barmaid when he approached the bar. She was in her mid-forties, a well-endowed woman in a low-cut blouse.

"Can I get you something?" she asked, her accent suggesting she had been brought up nearer Royal Berkshire than Twerton. She looked his coat up and down and grinned. "Did you miss the bus to Glastonbury?"

He smiled back. "I'm looking for Finn O'Sullivan."

"He's over in the corner with my daughter and a couple of others," she said.

Josh turned around to see four people deep in conversation around a low table. Finn and Shannon sat to the left with two men opposite who he hadn't seen before.

So Shannon, the mouthy girl with the mockney accent, was this woman's daughter. That was interesting.

"What do you think?" the barmaid prompted in an attempt to get his order.

He turned back, smiled and said, "Not genuine."

She looked down at her cleavage and then back up at him, one eyebrow raised.

"No," he spluttered, trying to keep his eyes directed

towards her face and away from her more-than-substantial bosom. "Not… I mean… I was, ah…" He decided his only way out was to be honest. "I was talking about your daughter's accent."

She laughed. "Oh, you mean her East End twang. It's Shannon's recovery mechanism."

"Recovery?"

"She's had a troubled past."

"Right. I see."

"Can I get you a drink?"

"A pint of Somerset red please."

He took his drink over to the table where Finn was the first to spot him.

"Hello, George. I'm glad you could come."

"Hi, Finn," Josh said. "Where's the meeting going to be?"

"Here." He indicated the table they were sitting around.

"Oh. I thought…"

"You thought there'd be more of us?" Shannon asked. "Sorry if we're a disappointment, *George*." She emphasised his name in a way he found disconcerting.

"Far from it. It's good to be one of the first."

"Good man," Finn said. "Grab a pew. This is Nick…" He gestured to the man nearest him. "And this is Brett. Nick, Brett, meet George. We got talking in Southgate at the weekend."

They nodded hello and resumed the conversation they'd been having when Josh arrived.

It was Nick who spoke first. "I agree with Shannon," he said in a deep voice without any trace of an accent. "Grabbing attention is key."

He was a large man, not overweight, but broad and with a full chest. He had bristles on his chin that went a few days beyond five o'clock shadow, and this was coupled with unkempt brown hair which fell to his shoulders and was in dire need of combing.

Josh felt the urge to smooth his own hair down but managed to resist.

"Take our time, I say," Brett said with a West Country lilt. Josh thought he was much the same age as Nick, in his late thirties or thereabouts, but he was more clean-cut and the only one of the five not wearing clothes more suited to a Music Festival. He wore a burgundy jumper and jeans.

Nick, on the other hand, sported a green, blue and red pullover that was almost as bright as Josh's sunflower-bedecked patchwork shirt.

He glanced across at Finn who had on a pale grey cheesecloth shirt that looked as dirty as his braids.

Shannon had, again, come as one of Dracula's assistants only he was sure she had more rings in her bottom lip than she had at the weekend.

The conversation went backwards and forwards for a few minutes before Finn looked over at Josh. "You've been quiet, George. What's your view?"

"I'm with Nick," Josh said. "If Earth Conflict's going to achieve anything we need to be proactive so that we can grab people's attention."

"We don't want to get ourselves arrested," Brett said.

"Why not?" Shannon demanded. "Are you frightened of prison?"

"It's not that. I think we need to take it steady, that's all. After all, we aim to achieve our goals by non-violent means, don't we?"

"If we can," Finn said.

"What do you mean?"

Finn smiled. "None of us want to resort to violence, of course we don't. However, the capitalists who run our energy companies have to recognise that dragging our planet back from the precipice will be impossible if they continue on their current path."

"What are you saying?"

"What Finn's saying," Shannon said, "is that the ends

sometimes justify the means."

"Hear, hear," Nick said.

"We have to be open to new ideas," Finn said. "We're a team after all. Talking of which, we need a plan to boost our numbers."

After much discussion, it was agreed that they would hold an open meeting within the next week or two. Shannon said she would find a venue while the four men offered to hand out leaflets.

"I can get them printed," Nick said. "Are we still going with the Earth Conflict logo we discussed last time?"

"Yes, I think it works," Finn said.

"What is the logo?" Josh asked.

"Sorry, I forgot this is your first time. I printed off a few copies last week but I've lost mine. Have any of you got a copy?"

"I've got one," Shannon said. She produced a folded piece of paper, laid it on the table and pressed it flat.

"What do you think, George?" Finn asked.

Josh looked down at the sheet of paper. Set against a bright yellow background was a thick red 'X' over an image of the earth.

"I like it," he said. "It makes sense." He pointed at the image of the globe. "The Earth's here," he said, "and this…" He pointed at the red 'X'. "…represents the cornflakes."

He looked at the others who were all looking confused.

"What's the matter? Did I…" he began and then realised what he'd said.

"Sorry," he went on. "Conflict, that was what I meant." He raised his voice. "Conflict." He tapped the image again. "This is the earth and 'X' marks the conflict." He beamed. "Excellento!"

Chapter 33

Although Helen was only in the audience for the filming of 'Answer Time', she needed to look the part in case she ran into Andrea Mason, or indeed any of Sow the Wind's members, before or after filming.

Rather than waste time she decided to wear the same outfit she'd worn for the organisation's meeting, so on went the orange skirt and red blouse. The colours almost brought tears to her eyes but what the hell? She donned the khaki gardening fleece and headed for her car.

It took forty minutes to drive to the studio, which was on a business park on the Bath side of Bristol.

Once inside she joined a short queue and the man in front of her immediately turned around and introduced himself. He was about her own age, perhaps nudging sixty, and had bright blue eyes beneath a full head of salt-and-pepper hair.

"Hi," he said. "I'm Bob."

"Hi, Bob. I'm Helen."

They shook hands and he smiled. It struck her as a very genuine smile and she suddenly wished she hadn't dressed so dowdily.

What was more, she was going to have to lie to him.

"Are you an 'Answer Time' fan?" he asked.

She returned his smile and found herself desperately wanting to tuck her blouse in. Hell, she wanted to change it. The skirt too.

"Not really. The panellists drew me in, plus I'd like to see Eleanor Tappett in action."

"She's formidable, isn't she?"

They had reached the front of the queue where a young woman greeted them.

"Hi," she said. She looked at Bob first. "Can I have your name, please?"

"Bob," he said. "Bob Matthews."

"Thank you." She looked down her list, found his name, crossed it through and then looked at Helen.

"And what's your first name, Mrs Matthews?"

"We're not together," Helen said.

"Oh, sorry. I assumed…"

"No problem. My name's Helen Livingstone."

"Thanks." She crossed her name through. "Please go on in and Jeffrey will show you to your seats."

"That was embarrassing," Bob said as they made their way inside.

"These things happen."

A middle-aged man was standing at the centre of the low stage, clipboard in hand. Behind him were two tables, the one on the right for one person while the one on the left was for three. These fronted a large screen with the words 'Answer Time' emblazoned across an image of the Houses of Parliament.

He was filling rows from the front and gestured to them to walk along the fourth in a bank of eight.

"Please don't leave any gaps. We've got a full house tonight."

Helen judged there were about twenty in each row, so that made for an audience of around a hundred and sixty if he was right and it filled up. Hardly a big audience but enough to look good on camera.

"Did you submit a question?" Bob asked once they were seated.

"No. You?"

He nodded and his smile returned. Helen noticed a dimple appear in the centre of his chin as the corners of his mouth turned up.

"I was a bit naughty. I thought I might as well be controversial, but I doubt my question will be picked."

Ten minutes later, the banked rows of seats were full and there was a pleasant buzz in the studio. Helen looked around and spotted the large, almost handsome man who had been at Sow the Wind's meeting. He was on the front row and talking earnestly to the Finn O'Sullivan doppelganger who had also been at the event.

A middle-aged man came to the front with a microphone and called them to attention.

"Good evening everyone. I'm Jeffrey, the Floor Manager for today's filming. As you all know, the programme is going out live so please don't heckle or interrupt when our panellists are answering. And don't forget to turn your phones off or to silent."

There was a small hubbub as people reached for their mobiles.

"Thanks for coming," Jeffrey continued. "Thanks also to those of you who submitted questions. Unfortunately, we won't be able to get to all of you." He looked down at his clipboard and then back up again. "Is Margaret Webb here?"

A woman in the second row put her hand up. "That's me," she said.

"Great. We'll take your question first." He went to the next name and then looked up again. "Bob Matthews?"

"I'm here," Bob called.

"Terrific."

He proceeded through another dozen names before saying, "Please feel free to applaud at any time. Audience noise always helps." He smiled. "If it's the right sort of noise of course." There was a smattering of laughter. "So, thanks again for coming. We'll be underway in about twenty minutes."

"What's your question?" Helen asked once Jeffrey had finished.

"Don't you want it to be a surprise?"

"I'd like to be prepared."

Bob tapped her arm with his hand, and she felt a frisson of electricity as he did so.

Electricity!

What was that about?

"I think I'll keep it a secret," he said and laughed. "Your honest reaction might be exactly what they're looking for when their camera is focused on us."

They continued talking and Helen found they had a lot of interests in common, although she deliberately avoided saying much about herself. She told him she was Helen Livingstone, a widowed fifty-seven-year-old who worked as a cleaner. Nothing interesting in that and the less she had to lie the better.

She kept the discussion to what they liked to read and watch on TV or at the Theatre.

After a few minutes, Bob looked at his watch. "It's ten to and the filming's going to last an hour. You'll have to excuse me while I pop to the toilet."

He stood up, saying "Excuse me," and "Sorry," as people stood up to let him pass.

Helen watched him go and felt pleased that she'd found someone to talk to. She couldn't take it further of course but still, it was good to have company.

She shook her head and smiled wryly.

What was she thinking?

She'd known Bob for twenty minutes and was now musing on 'taking things further'.

He was nice though, that was the thing. Bob was her sort of man. He was warm, personable, attractive and easy to talk to.

What was there not to like?

Chapter 34

Erin Douglas had toyed with joining Reform. Many of the party's policies reflected her views, but there were too many extremist hangers-on for her liking, the kind of people who were openly racist and much too keen to share their views with anyone who would listen.

It gave the party a bad image and those inconsiderate, loud-mouthed few were in danger of doing to Reform what Jeremy Corbyn had done to the Labour Party.

No, until Reform got their act together and kept the bad eggs away, she would steer clear of them. Besides, she wasn't deeply political. She had her views on immigration, of course she did. And what was happening in the English Channel was particularly horrifying. Something needed to be done but that was well outside her remit.

Erin was single-mindedly focused on energy.

As Public Relations Manager for the Sturridge Group, the almost invisible name behind three of the UK's leading energy providers, Erin's main role was to bang the drum for the industry. She was responsible for highlighting the benefits of the country's mainland and offshore gas and oil resources.

It was an issue she felt passionate about. People needed to realise that they and their families depended on fossil fuels and would for decades to come. She understood the fascination with wind farms and solar panels, but to think they would meet the needs of the population anytime soon was to be living in la la land.

This evening's was an important event. To be invited onto a live version of Question Time, albeit one organised by a relatively minor commercial channel rather than by the BBC, was a coup both for her and for her employer.

It also made her nervous. She'd never done anything like this before and, although live viewing figures were unlikely to go much past five figures, she had positioned her team to make the most of things on social media. YouTube would see highlights within minutes of the end of filming.

With careful editing of course to ensure that she and the Sturridge Group's companies came over in the best possible light.

It was going to be tricky though, given what she knew about the other two panellists.

Erin wasn't too worried about Andrea Mason who was a known anarchist and the name behind Sow the Wind. She was a relative nothing, and although she spoke well she had never proven herself adept at answering questions.

The Liberal Democrat MP, John Gilbey, was going to be more of a challenge. He was a career politician for a start, which made him a past master at evading tricky questions and using statistics to prove everything. What also bothered Erin was how little she knew about his views on the environment. She was unclear, for example, on whether he thought we should make the most of existing resources or plough money into researching sustainable and renewable energy.

She'd have to play it by ear.

"You can go to the Green Room now," the makeup lady said.

"Thanks."

"About fifteen minutes until we're on," a man with a clipboard added.

Erin swallowed. She hadn't thought she would be so on edge but this was her first time on television and her stomach was in knots. Be yourself, she kept telling herself. You know your stuff. Remain on your guard and you'll be fine.

She walked into the Green Room and recognised

Andrea Mason immediately. Her unkempt look was almost a fashion statement, and she had an air of superiority.

"Hello," she said, offering her hand. "I'm Erin."

"Yes, I know," Andrea said.

Erin withdrew her hand when it became clear that Andrea wasn't going to shake it and took a seat against the opposite wall.

A few minutes later the MP came in, a bustling red-faced man with a broad smile across his face. He approached Erin first. "Hi," he said. "I'm John. I'm guessing you're Erin?"

"That's right," she said as she shook his hand.

He walked over to Andrea. "And you must be Andrea."

"Yes."

Again she ignored his offered hand and he turned, shrugged at Erin and took a seat next to her.

"Hopefully, we'll have a good debate," he said. "A decent bit of to and fro never harmed anyone."

"What's your position on all this?" Erin asked.

"Ah," he said, smiling and tapping the side of his nose. "I think I'll leave that as my little surprise."

The door opened.

"Ten minutes," clipboard man called.

"Excuse me," Erin said. "I need to pop to the loo."

"Nervous?"

"A touch. It's my first time doing this type of thing."

"Don't worry about it. You'll be fine."

She smiled and left the room to find the man with the clipboard standing outside as if on guard to stop any of them from escaping.

"Have I got time to pop to the toilet?"

He looked pointedly at his watch. "If you're quick. We're on in eight." He gestured down the corridor. "It's the first door on the left around the corner."

She walked quickly to the toilet, locked herself in a cubicle, did a wee and tried to keep her mind from spinning as she thought through possible questions and how she should answer them.

This was stupid. She needed to get her act together.

She flushed the toilet, opened the cubicle door while she was still fastening her skirt and was thrown back as she felt a blow to her stomach.

"Hey!" she said as she bent forward instinctively. "That hurt."

Her immediate thought was that it had to be Andrea Mason, though why she would punch her before, rather than after, the debate was beyond her.

She remained bent forward and realised that her top was starting to feel wet. Looking down, she lifted her blouse to reveal a thin line of blood to the right of her tummy button. It was seeping out and starting to drip down onto the top of her skirt.

"What the…" she started to say, but stopped as she felt her head start to spin. She closed her eyes, stumbled back against the toilet and would have fallen had she not put her hand on the side panel. Her body felt suddenly weak and she drew her breath in to stop herself from fainting.

With one last desperate effort, Erin forced her eyes open and stepped forward out of the cubicle. Her vision was fogged but she could see that the bathroom was empty, her attacker gone. She lurched to the sink, grabbed it with her right hand and then staggered away towards the door.

She had to find someone to help her, but she was conscious that her energy was waning. She tried to call out, but the words caught in her throat.

Erin's legs gave way and she collapsed to the ground.

Chapter 35

Helen was worried about Bob. He'd been gone for ten minutes and it was almost eight o'clock.

Jeffrey appeared, minus clipboard this time, grabbed the microphone and walked to the centre of the stage.

This is it, she thought. Bob's late and they're not going to let him back in once they've started filming. Had he had an accident? Or had she done something to annoy him so he'd decided to cut his losses and head home?

They'd seemed to get on well, but given her appearance had he…

"I'm sorry," Jeffrey began, and Helen realised the man looked more tense than he had before. He wiped his brow with his hand before continuing. "The programme won't be going ahead tonight."

Helen put her hand to her mouth as several people started shouting questions and voicing disapproval.

Something must have happened.

Had Bob had a heart attack?

"There's been an incident backstage," Jeffrey said. "A very serious incident."

People shouted out more questions.

"I can't tell you any more at present," he went on. "Please stay in your seats for the time being."

One man immediately stood up. "If there's no show I'm going home. I…"

"No, sir," Jeffrey said, raising his voice. "Please sit down. We've called emergency services and we can't afford to block their entrance with cars trying to leave."

"An ambulance?" someone asked.

Jeffrey nodded. "Yes. The police are on their way as well."

He walked away and the hubbub returned, even louder than before.

A few minutes later, Helen saw Bob appear at the front of the stage. He signalled for her to come down to him.

"Excuse me," she said as she stood up.

"He said we can't leave," the woman next to her said.

"I'm not leaving. I'm going to see my, ah… my friend."

She headed down to the front where Bob grabbed her hand and pulled her around so that his back was to the audience

He kept hold of her hand as he looked down into her eyes.

"Someone's been stabbed, Helen," he said in a whisper.

"What! Who?"

"Erin Douglas. The woman from Sturridge who was due to be on the panel."

"How awful. Is she badly hurt?"

He hesitated. "She's dead."

"Oh no! Was it you who found her?"

He shook his head. "No. I was washing my hands in the Gents when I heard a scream. I went outside and a woman was standing in the corridor gesturing to the door by her side, her eyes wide and staring. As I approached her, another woman went into the Ladies and I followed and…"

Tears came into his eyes.

Helen put her free hand to his cheek. "What did you see, Bob?"

He gave a deep sigh. "A woman I've never seen before. She was lying on the ground with two women bent over her. There was a lot of blood and it was clear she was dead." He wiped under his eyes with his free hand. "Sorry I'm like this. I've never seen a dead person before."

"Don't apologise, Bob. It's understandable."

"One of the women said it was Erin Douglas. A few seconds later two men came in and ushered me out." He looked around. "I wish we could leave."

As he said this Jeffrey walked over. "Please can you return to your seats?"

Helen heard sirens outside. It sounded like more than one vehicle.

"Come on," Bob said. "We'd better do as he asks."

They returned to their seats where Bob bent forward with his head in his hands.

"Bob?" Helen said.

He lifted his head and looked at her, dampness still evident below his eyes.

"Yes."

She indicated the people around them. "We can't talk about it now," she said, "but when they let us leave do you want to go for a drink somewhere?" She lowered her voice. "It'll give you the chance to talk about what you saw."

"I'd like that," he said. "Although I'm expected back by ten."

Helen hesitated. "Of course," she said.

He saw the look on her face and half-smiled. "By my dogsitter," he explained. "Tilly was spayed a couple of days ago and I didn't want to leave her alone for a whole evening."

"Ach, right. I see. So you're not…"

His smile grew and the dimple returned. "I'm not married and I'm not in a relationship either."

"Good."

"Good?"

"Oops." Helen felt a blush come to her cheeks. "I didnae mean to say that out loud."

"You?"

"Me what?" She paused. "Oh, I see. Yes, I'm single as well."

"Once a Livingstone, always a Livingstone, eh?"

Helen had almost forgotten she'd been lying to him.

She'd lied to him, then asked him out for a drink. What sort of woman did that make her?

A lying hussy, that's what.

She decided she'd have to swear Bob into her confidence and tell him the truth.

It was the best bet, and it was clear that he was someone she could trust.

Chapter 36

Thirty minutes passed before Jeffrey returned.

"I'm sorry about the delay."

Several people called down to him at once.

"What's happened?" one man asked.

"How much longer?" said another.

"Is someone dead?" a woman at the front asked in a particularly strident voice. She stood up as she said it and everyone turned to look at her.

Jeffrey held his hand up. "The police will be along to talk to you in a minute. I'm sure they'll answer all your questions."

"The police are here," the woman at the front shouted. "I'm right, aren't I? Someone's died." She was still standing and delighted to be the focus of everyone's attention. It was as if a person's recent demise was the best news she'd heard all day.

"I've been told that a Detective Inspector Crabtree has arrived to lead the investigation," Jeffrey said.

"Aha!" the woman exclaimed. "There's an investigation. That means murder. Someone's been murdered." She turned to the woman on her left. "I told you that was the case, Florence. Didn't I say someone's been murdered?"

"Please sit down, madam."

She nodded her head up and down a few times, enjoying her fifteen seconds of fame. "I was right. There's been a murder."

Jeffrey gave her a ferocious look "Madam," he said. "Please!"

She grunted, mumbled "Murder" one final time and then grudgingly sat down.

Jeffrey sighed. "Thank you. As I was saying, DI

Crabtree will be along as soon as…"

He stopped mid-sentence when he heard a loud, attention-breaking cough behind him, followed by a stage-whispered, "Bramley."

He turned to face a man of fifty or so who gave every appearance of being a retired boxer. His nose had been broken at some point, and his cheeks were evidence of acne-filled teenage years.

"Sorry?" Jeffrey said.

"My name's Bramley. Not Crabtree. It's Bramley."

"Ah, right." Jeffrey turned back to the audience. "This is DI Bramley."

The stage whisper returned. "DCI Bramley."

"What?"

"I'm not a DI, I'm a DCI. DCI Bramley. Detective Chief Inspector Bramley." Bramley shook his head in irritation. "Give me the mic. I'll take it from here."

He took the microphone and clicked a button on its side. "I have been assigned the role of…" he began.

"We can't hear you," someone at the back shouted.

"What?"

"You've turned it off," Jeffrey said. He walked over and clicked the button.

DCI Bramley sneered, shushed him away and then dropped his hands to his side.

"As I was saying…" he began.

"Up!" Jeffrey shouted. "You need to hold the mic up to your mouth."

DCI Bramley gave Jeffrey a look that would have frozen hot coals, but lifted the microphone to his mouth.

He looked along the front row, then moved his eyes up and along the back row before taking in those seated in the middle. He nodded as if this had confirmed what he'd already known.

"You're all suspects."

The audience went berserk, and there were a few

expletives as they vented their anger.

Bramley held his hand up but there was no holding them back. The woman at the front was on her feet again, pointing at him and shouting "Murder and he thinks I did it!" at the top of her voice.

"Be quiet, all of you," Bramley said, but this only provoked them further.

He tried again, much louder this time.

"BE QUIET!"

Still nothing.

A few seconds later, and as suddenly as the cacophony had begun, the audience went silent.

DCI Bramley nodded to himself, pleased that his words had finally had the desired effect, then noticed an elegantly dressed blonde woman walking towards him from the side of the stage.

He turned towards her. "I'm sorry, madam," he said. "This is a police matter."

She ignored him and turned to the audience.

"Please can I ask you all to give DCI Bramley your full attention?" she said, her voice carrying to the back despite not having a microphone.

"He told us we're guilty, Eleanor," one man shouted.

Eleanor Tappett smiled and shook her head. "No, he didn't," she said. "He said you were all suspects which is a very different thing."

People immediately started talking again but stopped as soon as she held her hand up.

"Thank you," she said. Her face turned grave. "A woman has been murdered tonight. There were security guards on the front and rear exits which means…" she paused to ensure the message hit home. "It means that all of us are suspects. The police will want to interview everyone before we are allowed to leave."

She turned to DCI Bramley.

"Please continue, Inspector."

Bramley grunted and turned back to the audience.

"My team will call you in one by one."

"I've got a babysitter," one person shouted. "I have to be back by ten."

"I need the loo," someone else called to titters of amusement.

"Mmm," Bramley said. "We'll do this in priority order. "All of those who need to leave as soon as possible put their hands up."

Everyone put their hand up.

Bramley sighed, grunted and hissed "Useless bunch of idiots" to himself, forgetting that the microphone was pressed tightly to his lips.

Chapter 37

It was another hour before Helen and Bob were allowed to leave.

"Is that drink still on offer?' he asked as they started towards their cars.

"Definitely. I don't know the area though. Are you from around here?"

"No."

"I live on Entry Hill in Bath. Do you know it?"

"I think so, yes."

"What about you? Do you live in Bristol?"

He ignored her question.

"What about the Old Lock and Weir?" he asked. "It's on the River Avon and not far off your route home."

"Sounds good. I don't know it so I'll follow you."

Ten minutes later Helen parked next to Bob's VW Golf and they walked into the inn, a quaint riverside pub that was surprisingly busy given it was midweek.

Bob got the drinks in and Helen managed to secure a table.

"Thanks," she said as he passed over her tonic water. "That was one hell of an evening."

"It certainly was. I'll never forget seeing that poor woman's face."

They both took a sip of their drinks and Helen decided now was as good a time as any to tell Bob the truth.

"I lied to you."

He looked at her for a second and put his glass down on the table. His face became deadly serious.

"I lied too," he said.

Helen's phone rang.

"Excuse me." She picked up her phone and looked at

the screen. "It's Luke, my boss. I need to take it." She stood up and grabbed her fleece from the back of the chair. "I won't be able to hear him here so I'll talk to him outside. I shouldn't be long."

She stepped outside the pub and was immediately hit by a blast of cold December air. She tugged her fleece tight and accepted the call.

"Hi, Luke."

"I wanted to check you're okay. I saw what happened on the news."

"Ach, I'm fine. We were kept back to be interviewed but the police allowed everyone to leave a few minutes ago."

"I see. Are you on your way home then?"

"No." She hesitated and then decided there was no reason not to tell Luke the truth. "I was sitting next to a man who was in the Gents when Erin Douglas was found. I suggested a drink because he was pretty shaken up by the sight of her body."

"They're saying the circumstances are suspicious."

"Bob said there was a lot of blood. What's more, the police told the audience that we're all suspects which suggests she was killed."

"Is Bob the man who was sitting next to you?"

"Yes."

"Is he with you now?"

"No, I stepped outside the pub when you called. Why?"

"Be careful what you say, Helen."

She half-laughed. "You don't think Bob could be the murderer do you?"

Luke didn't say anything.

"You're right," she said after a few seconds, sighing inwardly at the thought of having to maintain the lie. "There's no reason to tell him anything about myself. I'll continue being Helen Livingstone, a widowed cleaner."

"It makes sense."

"Do you think Sow the Wind might have had

something to do with it, Luke? After all, Andrea Mason was there, and the woman killed worked for an energy company."

"It's possible, but it takes activism to a whole new level if that was the case."

"I guess so. I'll see you in the morning."

"Bye, Helen."

Helen returned to Bob and put her coat back around the chair.

"It's an odd time for your boss to ring," Bob said when she'd sat down.

"He saw what had happened on the news and knew I was at the filming so rang to check I was okay."

"That's very considerate of him." He caught eye contact. "There can't be many cleaners whose boss would be so thoughtful."

Helen looked away as he said this, ashamed at having told him a lie.

Had Bob seen through her story?

"Tell me the truth," he said.

Helen swallowed and turned back to face him. "What do you mean?"

"Just before you took the call you said you'd lied to me."

"Oh, that." She tried to laugh but it sounded weak even to herself. "I lied about my age. I'm fifty-eight not fifty-seven."

"Oh, is that all?" He laughed. "You're still a spring chicken by my standards. I'm nearly sixty."

"You also said that you'd lied."

"Yes, although my lie was more of a concealment than a falsehood."

"I'm intrigued."

"I tell you what, Helen," he said. He smiled again but this time the dimple failed to make an appearance. "Why don't we drink up and I can show you what I was lying about? So much better than just telling you, don't you think?'

"Oh, I don't know."

Bob stood up and held his hand out.

He was still smiling but she could tell he was on edge.

He stretched his hand towards her.

"Come on, Helen," he went on. "It'll be painless, I assure you."

She stood up, put her fleece on and stepped around the table.

"Excellent," he said.

He took Helen's hand and led her out of the pub.

Chapter 38

Luke and Pete arrived at the Good Bear Cafe at the same time, ordered coffee and breakfast and went to their usual table.

"I take it you read about Erin Douglas's murder?" Pete asked once they'd sat down.

"Yes. Nasty business."

"Want to make a guess as to who the Senior Investigating Officer is?"

Luke sighed. "You're not going to tell me it's Applejack, are you?"

"I'm afraid so," Pete said, trying to conceal his smile.

"Unbelievable!"

Luke shook his head.

He'd encountered DCI Jack Bramley several times before leaving the force, and had worked with him on one investigation since joining Filchers. It had never been a pleasant experience. The man was lazy and a downright liability. He was also cocky and arrogant, despite being about as much use on an investigation as a one-legged man in an arse-kicking contest.

"If he's SIO on that at least it'll keep him away from the Dumpy Dumper case," Luke said as the owner appeared with a plate in each hand. "Thanks, Mauro," he added as his Full English Breakfast was placed on the table.

"Thanks, Mauro," Pete echoed. He removed the top of his bacon sandwich and added a healthy squirt of HP sauce.

There was silence while they ate.

"Helen Hogg was at the filming last night," Luke said when he'd finished. He wiped his lips with a napkin and positioned his knife and fork on the now-empty plate.

"When I get into the office I'll ask her if she met Applejack."

"I'm pretty sure he'll have made his presence felt. How come Helen was there?"

"A project we're working on."

"Oh, yes? Any reason to think that your project and Erin Douglas's murder are connected?"

I sincerely hope not, Luke thought. *Not if it means I have to work with Applejack.*

"Helen was there to see one of the other panellists in action. There could be a connection but I think it's unlikely."

Pete took a glug of his coffee. "I'm hoping today is the day we find out who the man in the Dumpy Bag is. Without knowing that, the investigation's going nowhere." He paused. "Have you had any further thoughts on those three interviews? At the moment they're all we've got to go on."

Luke scratched his chin. "Mmm. I'm sure there was something crucial in there somewhere but I'm not sure what. Can you email me the statements once they've been transcribed from the recordings?"

"Will do."

*

It was nine-thirty by the time Luke got into the office.

Sam was the only one there and tapping away on her computer.

"Morning, Sam," he said.

She looked up and smiled. "Hi, Luke. Good day yesterday?"

"It was okay. Three interviews, so nothing very exciting. Do you know where everyone is? I'd like to have a team catch-up on Project Greta."

"Maj and Josh were here early for an 8:30 meeting and I

got in just before 9 so I haven't seen them."

"What about Helen?"

"Her coat's not here so I assume she's not in yet."

"That's unlike her. I'll give her a call."

Luke stepped away and called Helen's mobile. It went straight to voicemail.

He returned to Sam.

"I've left a message," he said. "She may have come down with something, or more likely she's shattered after being held back at the studio last night."

"What happened?" Sam asked. "All I know is that they cancelled the programme due to technical difficulties."

"There was a stabbing. A female panellist by the name of Erin Douglas."

Sam put her hand to her mouth. "Oh no. Was she hurt badly?"

"She was found in the Ladies and pronounced dead at the scene."

"How awful."

The door opened and Luke turned as Maj and Josh walked in.

"Josh and I have a meeting with Liz Rathbone from Globo at 10:30," Sam said. "Do you think we could have that get-together now? It's unlikely Helen's going to have anything to add given 'Answer Time' was cancelled."

"Good idea." He called over to the others. "Maj, Josh, can you spare time for a team meeting?"

"No probs, guv," Josh said.

"No Helen?" Maj asked.

"Not in yet." He explained what had happened at the studio. "I suspect Helen got to bed very late so she'll be having a lie-in," he concluded.

"Are you doing the crazy wall, Maj?" Josh asked.

"Why don't you do it?"

"Wowza!"

Josh pulled the whiteboard over, picked up a black

marker pen, looked at the other three for a second and then picked up a red marker pen in his other hand. "That's better," he said, holding both pens up. "I'm ready."

"Okay," Luke said. "Sam, you said you're meeting Liz later. Does that mean there have been developments?"

"I'm not sure. She said she wanted to see Josh and me but without Helen there. All I know is that it's to do with her boss. She said that she'd explain when we meet."

"That's intriguing given what Henry Lavers told me about his affair with Andrea Mason."

"I wonder if she knows about it and wants to tell us."

"Possibly, but if that was the case why exclude Helen since she's the one joining Sow the Wind?"

Luke turned to Josh.

"How did your meeting with Earth Conflict go, Josh?"

"There were five of us," Josh began. "Finn, Shannon and me plus Nick and Brett, who I hadn't met before."

"Please can you add them to the board". He waited while Josh wrote their names below Finn and Shannon. "What were your impressions of them all?"

Josh thought about this for a second. "Funnily enough, Finn wasn't the person who came across as the most likely to endorse violence. Shannon and Nick were much more vocal on that front. Brett kept harping on about the need for peaceful protest."

"What was Finn's position?"

"I'd say his views were more in line with Shannon and Nick but he didn't say much. He seemed content to listen most of the time."

"Any other observations?"

"Brett was dressed like a normal guy gone out to the pub with his mates, whereas Nick was wearing stereotypical treehugger clothes."

"Like you," Maj suggested.

Josh smiled. "Very much so. Even brighter clothes, although that's hard to believe." He paused. "There was one other thing. They seem to have come up with a logo and showed me a printout of it. It was something like this."

He put the black marker down, pulled out a blue one and drew a circle on the whiteboard.

"It was pale blue rather than dark blue," he said, "but this will have to do."

Josh swapped the blue marker for the red marker and added an 'X' over the top.

"That was it," he said. "Plus there was an outline of North and South America in darker blue within the circle making it clear it was meant to be the Earth."

"Was it on a bright yellow background?" Luke asked.

Josh looked at him, bemused. "How did you know that, guv?"

Luke sighed and shook his head.

"Things have just got more complicated, son. One hell of a lot more complicated."

He clicked on his phone a couple of times and then passed it to Josh.

Josh looked down at the photo. "That's it, guv." He passed the phone back. "Where did you see it?"

"It was on a piece of paper found next to a body."

"Whose body?" Sam asked.

Luke shrugged. "I wish I knew. I'm helping Avon and Somerset on what the media have called the 'Dumpy Dumper' case. You must have read about it."

They all confirmed that they had.

"So you don't know the victim's name yet, Luke?" Maj asked.

Luke shook his head. "Not yet." He pointed at the logo Josh had drawn on the whiteboard. "There are no obvious suspects so far, but finding Earth Conflict's logo at the crime scene certainly puts a few people in the frame."

"Could Erin Douglas's murder be connected?" Josh asked.

"It's possible. All I know about her is that she worked

for an energy provider. Maj, could you do some digging please?"

"Will do."

Luke turned back to Josh. "Any idea how widespread this logo is?"

"Not really, guv. The people at the pub had all seen it before, but I got the impression that Finn O'Sullivan hasn't made a final decision on whether to use it on all their materials."

"Do you know how many other members there are?"

Josh shook his head. "Not many more than those four I suspect, but I guess I'll find out tonight."

"Tonight?"

"They're holding an open meeting. I've been helping to stick flyers up."

"Presumably without a logo."

"That's right. The flyer doesn't even mention Earth Conflict. I'll show you."

He went back to his desk and returned with an A4 laminated sheet of paper and laid it on the table.

Concerned about Climate Change?

Frustrated by the UK Government?

Worried about the Environment?

**JOIN US TO DISCUSS HOW TO DRIVE
REAL CHANGE**

8PM - THURSDAY 10TH DECEMBER

BATHWICK COMMUNITY CENTRE

Sam read it, then turned to Luke.

"Is it safe for Josh to go?" she asked.

"I don't think there's any danger," Luke said. "It's in a very public place. Besides, if anyone in Earth Conflict was responsible for Erin Douglas's murder, it's people on the other side of the environmental debate they're targeting, not greenies like George Bailey here."

Chapter 39

Sam's phone rang. It was Reception.

"Hi, Sam," Leanne said. "Your visitor's here."

"Thanks," Sam said. "We'll be right down."

She told Josh and they went downstairs to find Liz Rathbone deep in conversation with Leanne. There was an eruption of laughter as they drew near.

Josh looked from one to the other and raised one eyebrow. "Are you talking about me?" he asked.

"Not everything centres on you, Joshy," Leanne said.

"That's a relief."

"But as it happens…"

"I was hearing all about your tangerine dream outfit," Liz said. She turned back to Leanne. "Did you take any photos?"

"No, but his brother did. Hang on a moment…"

"No, no, no," Josh squeaked as Leanne reached for her phone. "Definito notto! Liz is a client and those photos are private."

"But isn't the outfit part of the work you're doing for Globo?" Liz asked.

"Well, ah…"

Liz took out a business card and passed it to Leanne. "Email them to me when you get the chance," she said and winked.

"I'll do that."

"We've booked the Orange Grove room, Liz," Sam said. "It's on the first floor."

She led the way to one of Filchers' medium-sized meeting rooms. Bland as the rest, the only decorative feature to break up the magnolia walls was a framed photo of Bath's Orange Grove with the Abbey in the background.

"Thanks for seeing me," Liz said once they were seated.

"We were intrigued," Sam said, "by your request to see Josh and me but not Helen."

"I thought you might be. You'll understand when I tell you." She hesitated. "This is difficult as I feel that I'm going behind Henry's back."

"Henry?" Josh asked, avoiding Sam's eyes as he said it. They both knew full well who she was referring to.

"Henry Lavers," Liz said. "He's my boss and he's also the son of Globo's founder and a major stakeholder in the company."

"What has he done?" Sam asked.

"I, ah…" She glanced at Josh and then back at Sam. "This is more difficult than I thought it was going to be."

"I can see that," Sam said. "Do you want a glass of water?"

"That would be great."

Sam turned to Josh. "Would you mind?"

He raised an eyebrow. "Eh?"

Sam glared at him. "Would you mind fetching Liz a glass of water please?" She said it very deliberately. "And I'd like a cappuccino while you're at it."

"But… Oh, I see." The penny dropped and he gave her a double thumbs-up. "Gotcha. Ah… it's a bit of a walk to the canteen so I might be a few minutes."

"Take your time."

He grinned sheepishly and left the room.

"Thanks for that," Liz said. She took a deep breath before continuing. "Henry's married, that's the thing. He and Ellen have been together for fifteen years, they've got two sons, outward appearances suggest they're very close and in love, but…" She came to a halt. "I feel so guilty. I've been keeping this from her and she and I are supposed to be good friends."

"It'll probably be easier if you just come out and tell me," Sam said.

"You're right," Liz sighed. "The fact is there was a relationship, a sexual relationship. It was short-lived but it's left everything in a mess. Since it finished Henry's been more intense about everything. It was him that initiated this investigation and I wonder if it's because he's seeking revenge, if it's his way of getting his own back."

"By ensuring Andrea Mason is revealed to be planning violence?" Sam asked.

Liz looked over, confusion etched across her face, and shook her head. "Not at all. Things he's said make me think he wants the investigation to fail."

"But why, given he kicked it off in the first place?"

"He wants it to reflect badly on me. He resents me for what I did."

"I don't understand. What did you do?"

"It was me that ended it."

"You intervened?"

"I wouldn't call it intervening. I'd had enough of the lies and deception. As I said, Ellen is supposed to be a good friend of mine. So I told him it had to end."

It suddenly dawned on Sam that this was nothing to do with Andrea Mason.

"How long were the two of you in a relationship?"

"A couple of months. I finished with him in July and I thought he'd got over the disappointment, but now…"

There was a creak and Sam turned to see Josh in the doorway with a glass of water and a mug.

"Here they are," he said as he put them on the table.

"You didn't bring sweeteners," Sam said as he pulled a chair out and readied himself to sit down.

"But you don't…" He stopped as he saw the look on her face. "Oh, right. Of course. Two sweeteners coming up." He smiled and turned back to the door.

"No rush."

"Right."

He left and the door closed behind him.

"You were saying," Sam prompted.

"Henry's been talking to other senior managers about the way I'm running things. He's told them that I'm racist."

"Racist! That's nonsense."

"Stratford Edmunds, our Personnel Director, advised me to be careful in how I deal with Daniel. He said if my behaviour continued the company would have to take formal action."

"Are you sure it was Henry who told him? Could it have been someone else? Or even Daniel? He's your deputy so if you were ousted…"

"I can't believe that of Daniel. We get on really well. No, it has to be Henry."

"What I don't understand is why you didn't want Helen in today's meeting."

"There's something else." Liz took a sip of her water. "Daniel and I had a meeting with Henry yesterday and he told us to ensure the investigation focused primarily on Andrea Mason, that she was the one with an anarchist background and violent tendencies." She gave a dry laugh. "Anyone would think he had a vendetta against her as well as against me."

Sam hadn't met Henry Lavers but she'd already developed a distinct dislike for the man. Supposedly happily married but with at least two affairs behind him, the man sounded like a sexual predator.

"I didn't want Helen to hear that," Liz went on, "in case it made her less objective in her dealings with Sow the Wind."

"I see."

"Look, I know this is hard, but do you think you could keep my affair with Henry from Helen and Josh?"

"It's difficult, Liz. We work very closely together."

"Please, Sam. I beg you. I'm sure they can be trusted but the more people who know, the more chance there is of it getting back to Ellen."

"Okay, Liz. I promise I won't tell them."

"Thanks."

"How do you want us to play our investigations going forward."

"Exactly as you would have done if I hadn't told you all this. Stay objective and find out what you can. I'm going to be professional about this even if Henry isn't."

Chapter 40

Sam had promised not to tell Helen or Josh but Luke was a different matter altogether.

Once she'd escorted Liz to Reception she returned to the meeting room and rang him.

"Hi. Do you think we could have a word?"

"Sure," he said. "I'm in the Ethics room."

"Would you mind coming here? I'm in the Orange Grove room and I don't want the others to hear what I have to say."

"Of course. I'll be right down."

She was sitting back in her chair and staring out of the window when Luke walked in.

"You look concerned," he said.

She turned to face him. "I am. I've just heard something which has thrown everything in the air."

He sat down opposite her. "Is it Ollie?"

She furrowed her brows. "Ollie? Why would you say that?"

"Sorry, Sam. When you said you wanted to talk about something personal I assumed…"

"I didn't say it was personal. I said it was something I didn't want the others to hear." She paused. "Anyway, Ollie and I are history."

She was sure she saw a glimmer of a smile on Luke's face but it was gone as soon as it appeared.

Was he pleased that she and Ollie had split up? And if so, why? He was in a serious relationship with Cora so it wasn't as if anything could happen between them.

Between them!

Where was her brain?

Stop it, Sam.

"I'm sorry to hear that," he said.

She realised he'd said something.

"Sorry. What did you say?"

"I said I'm sorry to hear you and Ollie have finished."

"You are?"

He grinned. "To be honest, no. He and I didn't exactly hit it off and…'

He ground to a halt.

"And what?"

He looked into her eyes. "I think you deserve better, Sam." He paused. "Was the split mutual?"

"No. I ended it. He was controlling in a passive-aggressive way. Jealous too."

"Jealous of what?"

Mainly of you, she thought. *He thinks there's something between us, but that's never going to happen.*

"Any man I spoke to," she said. "Hannah's boyfriend, for example."

"You're well rid."

"I think you're right."

She paused.

Should she ask?

She wanted to but didn't want to hear his answer.

Ah well, there was nothing to lose.

She tried to keep her tone light, as if she was asking out of pure politeness.

"How are you and Cora getting along?"

"Okay." He hesitated, seemed about to say something else then sat back in his chair. "So," he went on, his voice suddenly a shade deeper. "What is it you wanted to talk to me about?"

She explained about Liz Rathbone admitting to having had an affair with Henry Lavers.

"And she didn't know he'd had a relationship with Andrea Mason?" he asked when she'd finished.

Sam shook her head. "Definitely not. I mentioned her

name and the way Liz reacted made it clear he's kept it from her."

"I don't like the idea of not telling Josh or Helen."

"Me neither. Liz made me promise, that's the trouble."

"Okay. Let's think this through logically. You learned three things from your meeting." He held his right index finger up. "One: Liz had an affair with Henry Lavers." Up went the middle finger. "Two: he's trying to exact revenge on Liz by accusing her of being racist." Luke's ring finger joined the other two. "And three: he's asked her to focus the investigation on Andrea Mason, and we believe he's done that because he also had a relationship with her."

"Mmm. Thinking about it that way, I guess there's no benefit to be gained by Helen or Josh knowing."

"I agree. What he's done, and what he's doing now, has an impact on Liz but needn't change the way we go about the investigation."

"Luke, is it okay with you if I keep in regular contact with Liz? I'll need to keep her up to date with progress, but more than that she was very open and I'd like to give her moral support."

"That's a good idea." He looked at his watch and stood up. "I've got to have a quick word with Filcher. I'll catch up with you later."

He left and Sam was about to stand up to return to the Ethics room when her phone pinged. She looked down to see a message from Ollie.

We need to talk.

She hesitated then typed her reply and hit send.

Why? We agreed not to contact each other.

Sean's in trouble again.

Sean was Ollie's friend. She had helped him and his partner out of a fix a couple of months earlier. What had he done now?

.

Why can't he contact me
himself?

> *He's embarrassed to admit*
> *what he's done.*

What's happened?

> *I can't tell you this way. It's*
> *complicated. Can we meet?*

That's not a good idea.

> *I won't hassle you, I promise.*
> *Can we meet for coffee after*
> *work today?*

Sam sighed. She didn't want to see Ollie but she liked Sean and if he needed her help…

Okay. Costa Coffee near
Filchers at 4 pm?

> *Great. Look forward to*
> *seeing you xx*

She was momentarily horrified by the two x's at the end of his last message but decided it meant nothing. It might even have been an accident that he was already regretting, a hangover from when they had been close.

However, she certainly wasn't going to reply with anything that could remotely be considered to be affectionate.

She typed something, decided it was a bit harsh, deleted it, started again, deleted that, then typed three words and hit send before she could overthink it.

See you later.

Chapter 41

"Can't I smooth it down a tiny bit?" Josh asked.

He had emerged from the shower with a towel around his middle and was now standing in front of the bedroom mirror, his hand poised above his head.

"No," Leanne said emphatically. "It needs to look unruly. However, you'll be pleased to know that you don't need to wear the magic mushrooms or tangerine dream this evening."

"That's a relief."

"I bought you a jumper." She held it up so that he could see it in the mirror. It was plain black.

"Hey, that's okay. Thanks, Leanne."

"It's not completely plain."

She turned it around to reveal four ten-inch green, yellow and red thunderbolts on the front.

"What are those?" Josh squealed. "They're like something out of an Avengers movie."

"It'll keep you warm."

"It certainly won't keep me cool."

"You're cool in my eyes, Joshy."

He grunted and she returned to the lounge while he finished getting ready.

"Well?" he said when he appeared a few minutes later.

She tried not to laugh as she looked him up and down. "I'm pleased to see you remembered the sandals," she said, "and those flared denims suit you."

"No, they don't."

She nodded. "You're right. Still, you're dressed for the part and that's the main thing. Where's the meeting?"

"Bathwick Community Centre. It's a twenty-minute walk."

"Be careful."

"Why?"

"If the police see you they might arrest you. I'm sure that jumper constitutes a breach of the peace."

"Ha, bloody ha. Wish me luck."

She walked over, kissed him on the lips then put her hand up and ran her fingers through his hair.

"Good luck," she said. "And remember it's Earth Conflict, not Earth Cornflakes."

He left their apartment and set off. After a couple of minutes, he passed an elderly man who nodded, said "Hello", spotted the jumper and increased his pace.

It started raining heavily and he was relieved when he reached the community centre, a detached Edwardian house rather than the purpose-built modern building he had expected. As he approached the door Shannon emerged.

"Evening, *George,*" she said, continuing to emphasise his name in a way he found unsettling.

"Hi, Shannon. Aren't you staying?"

"Course I am. I've popped out for a fag."

"Ah, right. Are there many here?"

"See for yourself."

"I will. How…"

Josh stopped speaking as she very deliberately turned away, walked a few steps away to a covered area and lit a cigarette.

He shrugged and walked through the open front door and into the corridor beyond. She had taken against him for some reason, but what did it matter? He wasn't here to make friends, he was here to be an operative, an undercover spy. He had a mission and it was his duty to explore every…

"Hi, George."

"What? Oh, ah… Hi, Brett."

"You looked a million miles away." He spotted Josh's

jumper. "What have you come as this evening?"

"Eh?" He looked down at the lightning bolts. "This is how I like to dress. My hair too."

"What about your hair?"

"I like it this way. Natural. Wild." He paused. "Natural."

"You already said 'natural'."

"Coolio." Josh swallowed. "Many here?"

"A dozen or so, although it may have been the free biscuits that attracted some of them."

"Chocolate digestives?"

"I'm not sure."

"I'll check."

Josh let Brett pass and entered the main room which was just big enough for a rectangular table at the front and five rows of six seats. The white walls were bare aside from a cork noticeboard covered in business cards and pamphlets.

Finn was sitting at one end of the table looking through some notes while four teenage boys were helping themselves liberally to the biscuits beside him.

It didn't take long for Josh to count the attendees. An elderly couple sat at the front in the middle, a mother and her young son were at the far end of the third row, an older man, perhaps sixty, sat alone on the fourth row and two middle-aged women were at the back.

That made eleven.

He approached the table in time to see the last custard cream being snaffled by one of the boys who turned, grinned victoriously at Josh, and then followed his friends out of the room.

That brought the number of attendees down to seven.

And the number of biscuits to zero.

"Hi, Finn," Josh said.

Finn looked up. "Hi, George. Thanks for coming."

Josh took a seat on the second row and realised he recognised the young woman at the end.

"Hi, I'm George," he said. "Didn't I see you in Southgate?" She and her son looked over and he smiled at the little boy. "Hunter, isn't it?"

"Yes," Hunter said, his mouth opening to reveal a mouthful of chocolate. "My name is Hunter Aaron Davison and my mummy's single."

"Hunter!" she exclaimed but she was smiling as she said it. "You'll have to excuse him. I'm Leanne."

"Leanne! But…"

Josh stopped.

He'd almost forgotten that he didn't have a girlfriend.

He was George Bailey.

Single, badly dressed and suffering from a hair malfunction George Bailey.

She raised one eyebrow. "But what?"

"But…" He swallowed. "Ah… I was thinking what a nice name Leanne is."

"Thanks." She turned the smile up a notch. "Hunter was telling the truth by the way. I *am* single."

"Ah… Right."

"And you are?"

"Single. Definito!"

"No." Her smile was at its maximum now. "I meant, what's your name?"

"Oh, right. Of course… George. It's George."

"Do you think my mummy's pretty?" Hunter said.

Josh closed both eyes for a fraction of a second. What should he say? He could hardly say she wasn't, but if he said she was, would she get the wrong idea?

Leanne laughed. "You don't have to answer that."

"Phew. That's a relief."

Her smile vanished.

"No!" he went on. "I didn't mean… You're very, ah…"

Pissedy-piss-piss.

He sighed.

"You're very attractive. I didn't… I mean…" He

gulped. "Are you interested in the environment?"

"Am I putting you on edge, George?" she asked, the smile back.

"No. I… But if you're here…" He gestured vaguely around the room. "Then you must want to discuss greenhouse emissions and climate change."

She shook her head and lowered her voice to a whisper. "To be honest we came in to escape the rain."

"I see."

She looked him in the eyes. "I'm glad we did though."

"Right. Good. Excellento!"

Nick and Shannon came into the room and sat at the table next to Finn.

He pointed at them. "Those two are in his cornflakes. They must be about to start."

"In his cornflakes?"

He nodded absent-mindedly, wishing they would begin the meeting so that he could escape this conversation.

Leanne tapped the seat next to her own. "It seems silly you being over there."

"Yes. Ah…"

He heard a noise and turned to see Brett standing beside him. "Shove along, George."

"Right." He moved next to Leanne. "Leanne, this is Brett."

"Hi," Brett said.

She nodded hello.

"Are you single, Brett?" Hunter asked.

"No. I'm not."

"George is single."

"Is he?"

"Yes. He said Mummy's a tractor."

"Attractive," Josh said. "I said she's attractive."

"Look, Mummy." Hunter pointed to the front. "It's the funny man we saw when we went shopping."

"You're a smooth operator," Brett whispered in Josh's

ear as Finn got to his feet.

Chapter 42

"Thanks everyone for coming," Finn began. "My name is Finn O'Sullivan. I hope you didn't come in merely to escape the weather."

"We did!" Hunter shouted, earning a hissed "Shhh!" from his mother.

Finn laughed. "And who can blame you? There's more rain than ever these days and it's all down to climate change. The authorities couldn't care less about reducing greenhouse gas emissions. All they're concerned with is lining their pockets. Our organisation, Earth Conflict, seeks to raise awareness of what they're doing to our planet. We must..." He paused. "Do you have a question?"

Josh turned to see the older man behind him standing up with his hand in the air.

"I have a question," he said. "Are you anti-establishment, Mr O'Sullivan?"

"I don't see why that's relevant."

"Were you previously a member of Sow the Wind, an organisation founded by Andrea Mason?"

"Yes, I was."

"And is it true that you left Sow the Wind because you were disappointed that Mason, despite being a self-proclaimed anarchist, wasn't prepared to use violence?"

"Not at all, Mr..."

"Matthews. Bob Matthews."

"What's your point, Bob?"

"I'm simply trying to find out where you and your organisation stand on the use of threats and violence."

"You're fucking stirring it, that's what you're doing," Shannon said angrily.

"Leave this to me," Finn said.

"She said the fucky word," Hunter stage-whispered, earning himself another loud "Shhh!" from his mother.

"So you would never threaten anyone?" Bob persisted.

"Of course not," Finn said.

"Erin Douglas spoke out against wind farms and nuclear energy. Didn't you once say that her children would suffer if she had her way?"

"I wasn't threatening her personally. I was pointing out that her views were capitalist and outdated."

"Did she deserve what happened to her?"

"Definitely not."

"May I say something?" Nick said.

Finn nodded and Nick stood up. "Bob," he said. "Do you believe in fate? That even the most tragic event can be for the better good?"

"What do you mean?"

"If the assassination attempt on Hitler in the Second World War had been successful, would that have been a good thing?"

Brett stood up before Bob could answer.

"Nick, you're talking shit," he shouted. "You can't compare Adolf Hitler with Erin Douglas. Are you advocating murder?"

"Guys, guys," Finn said as Leanne placed her hand over Hunter's mouth before he could voice his thoughts on the word 'shit'.

Shannon stood up. "You're pathetic, Brett," she said. "You've no idea what we're up against."

The elderly couple sidled along their row as quietly as they could and slid out of the room. Josh heard a noise behind him and turned to see the two middle-aged women following their lead.

"I was wrong to think Earth Conflict was a worthy organisation," Brett said, his cheeks now red. "You're evil, pure evil."

Bob turned to Brett and whispered, "Can we talk

outside?"

Before Brett could answer, Nick spoke. "I think we need to have this out, Brett," he said.

He headed for the corridor. Brett grunted and followed with Bob hot on his tail.

Shannon turned to Finn. "I'm going to see what they're up to," she said as she too exited the room.

"That was fun," Hunter said. "Can I have more chocolate?"

Finn was staring at the exit, confused and shocked by what had happened.

"Is the meeting over?" Josh asked.

"Uh… Yes, I guess so." Finn said.

He followed the others out.

Josh, Leanne and Hunter were now the only people in the room.

"Is the show over, Mummy?" Hunter said.

"Yes, darling, the show's over." She turned to Josh. "It was lovely meeting you, George. Do you have your phone?"

"Yes."

She smiled. "Add a new contact."

"Why?"

"For my phone number, silly. It would be lovely to see you again, perhaps somewhere quieter and without…" She nodded her head towards her son.

"Eh?"

"Your phone?"

"Right." He opened his contacts.

"Leanne Davison, 07503 891555."

He added her details.

She clicked on her own phone.

"What are you doing?" he asked, trying to keep the rising panic from his voice.

"Adding you of course."

She typed in 'George Bailey' and looked across at him. "What's your number?"

"Oh, yes, ah…"

He knew he couldn't give her his number so he gave her the first set of digits that came into his head.

"Thanks," she said. "It's been lovely to meet you."

She put her hand on his leg and he almost jerked it away in fright.

"I'll, ah… I'll be in touch," he squealed.

"I look forward to it." She turned to her son. "Come on, Hunter. Time to go."

"Okay, Mummy."

She smiled at Josh as she stood up. "Are you leaving now, George? We could walk together to…"

"No!" He tried to laugh but it came out as a mousey-squeak. "I need to stay. Ah… to see Finn. When he returns. In a minute. Have to stay. Talk to him."

She laughed. "Okay. See you soon."

He watched them leave, heaved a sigh of relief and called up his contacts to delete her entry.

No way was he risking Leanne, the real Leanne, seeing it.

No, no, no.

He'd learned his lesson the hard way and he wasn't going there again.

Chapter 43

The tailor's son had met Erin Douglas twice.

She had been forthright in her views on both occasions, arguing that oil and gas were the future. According to her, the planet's natural resources should be exploited not wasted, and 'new-fangled ways of generating energy' - those were the very words she had used - were a short-term, expensive fad.

She had paid the ultimate price for having such strong opinions and her death was unfortunate.

But essential.

Robin had messaged him within thirty minutes and he had been happy to pay the balance of what was owed. It was money well spent.

However, although her murder had generated headlines, the police were woefully slow at putting two and two together. Could they not see the link between what had happened to her and the death of Scott Finlay?

Their tardiness made another killing essential. With three corpses, the link between the murders would be blindingly obvious.

He had some regrets about this third target. She was less of an advocate than the first two. However, she rounded off the trio nicely and he was sure that the police, stupid as they might be, would at last join the dots.

His phone pinged and he saw it was a message from Robin.

Good afternoon, Taylor.

He was pleased. There was no time to waste and he decided to get straight to the point.

How quickly can you deal with number 3?

> *There is a problem.*

His heart stopped a beat. This was a word he didn't want to hear. Robin had come highly recommended and he was paying to bring solutions, not problems.

You guaranteed this would be smooth.

> *Someone was asking too many questions.*

Is there a chance you will be unmasked?

> *No.*

Can you be sure?

> *I have made the problem disappear.*

How?

> *By now you should know the answer to that question.*

He knew the answer, of course he did, but he was shocked by how cold and uncaring his hired assassin was. It wasn't as if Robin was working for a noble cause. The killings were purely for money and if someone got in the way they were dispatched with no more thought than swatting a fly.

He was sure that Robin couldn't possibly be a woman. Surely only a man could be so ruthless.

Some people were inherently evil.

Unlike himself. He was a man of principles.

He was about to type a reply when another message from Robin appeared.

> *There will be a cost for*

dealing with the problem.

How much?

The same as for each of the others.

Okay.

Thank you.

Are you in a position to proceed with number three?

Yes.

Please transfer the funds for dealing with the problem plus the initiation fee for the third target.

Consider it done.

I look forward to receiving the funds.

Goodbye, Robin.

Goodbye, Taylor. It is a pleasure doing business with you.

Chapter 44

Luke turned off the alarm, threw on his walking-the-dog clothes, and made his way downstairs where Wilkins was squealing and running backwards and forwards in his crate, excited at the prospect of the morning walk.

"I won't be a second, boy. I'll need something warm this morning."

Luke donned his heavy-duty coat and green wellies then released the cocker from his steel cage, attached his lead, and went out through the kitchen door.

He was immediately hit by a blast of cold air and turned the collars of his coat up. It was a typical December morning, a couple of degrees above freezing but feeling colder due to a light drizzle that was trying its hardest to be sleet.

Once they passed through the gate at the end of the back garden, he released the spaniel and watched as he disappeared into the darkness, eagerly seeking new smells or, better still, rabbits to chase. Wilkins had never successfully caught one but it didn't stop him trying.

Luke welcomed this opportunity to think things through ahead of the day. He was being pulled in conflicting directions, having agreed to see Pete at Avon and Somerset HQ while also needing to make progress on several projects at Filchers.

Project Greta was his biggest concern. He trusted his team, and Sam was proving herself to be a very competent deputy, but he would like to have spent more time with Josh and Helen. Both had challenging assignments as they tried to uncover the motives and intentions of Earth Conflict and Sow the Wind.

He wondered what had happened to Helen. It wasn't

like her to be absent from the office without letting him know. He hoped Ronnie hadn't got himself into a mess. Her son was a fragile person at the best of times.

However, she would doubtless turn up bright and cheery this morning, full of stories about the abandoned filming of 'Answer Time'.

As for Josh, the lad was coming on well. He might not always appear to be on the ball, but he was very good at adapting to situations and using his initiative.

Most of the time.

Some of the time.

Well, occasionally.

He smiled. Was it time to send Josh on another course? He'd loved learning about detecting, even if it had filled him with a new set of jargon which he had proceeded to fling here, there and everywhere. Perhaps a course on ethics or criminology would help to round off his education.

His phone started ringing but as he pulled it from his pocket Wilkins appeared from the gloom, sat back on his haunches, looked up at his master and dropped a dead squirrel on the ground.

Luke accepted the call, grunted in disapproval and tapped the corpse with the toe-end of his boot to turn it over.

"It's a sodden teatowel," he said as he realised it wasn't a rotting body after all.

"I beg your pardon."

"Sorry, Pete." He watched as Wilkins disappeared back into the blackness. "I'm walking the dog and he's dropped a damp cloth at my feet. What's up?"

"We've got a name for the body in the Dumpy Bag."

"And?"

"You're not going to like this, Luke." He paused. "His name was Scott Finlay and he was a very vocal denier of global warming."

"Meaning there's a link between his murder and Erin

Douglas's?"

"It's got to be a possibility."

"Does Applejack know?"

"Not yet. I'd like you in the meeting when I tell him. I'm worried that he'll try to edge you out, and we'll need you all the more if we're hunting a multiple murderer."

"I'll be there as soon as I can."

Luke ended the call.

"Wilkins!"

The cocker ran up and he gave him a biscuit before putting him on the lead.

"Sorry, boy. Short one today."

He set off back to the house at a brisk walk.

Fifteen minutes later, showered, suited and booted, he climbed into the Beemer and headed for Portishead.

It was an hour's drive which afforded him more thinking time.

He went through what he knew about Erin Douglas. She had worked in public relations for Sturridge and had been scheduled to speak alongside Andrea Mason. Douglas was in the panel precisely because she and Mason were at different ends of the environmental debate.

The more he thought about it the more he thought it likely that her murder and the murder of Scott Finlay were linked.

If that was the case was the killer an environmental activist? And if so, could he or she be a member of either of the groups his team was investigating?

Could it be Andrea Mason herself? She'd been at the studio when Erin Douglas was stabbed.

More to the point, had he put Helen in danger by asking her to join Sow the Wind?

Worse, had something happened to her after the filming? Was that why she hadn't turned up for work the previous day?

He tried her number but as before it went straight to

voicemail.

He rang Sam.

"Hi, Luke," she said. "I'm just walking into the office. Are you on your way to Portishead?"

"Sam, can you keep trying Helen? I'm worried about her."

He explained that the body found in the Dumpy Bag had been identified as Scott Finlay, an anti-environmentalist.

"Should I ring around the hospitals, Luke?"

"Good idea. Can you ring Ronnie too please, and ask if he's seen his mum?"

"I will. I'll do it without worrying him though."

"Thanks, Sam. If I can I'll come to the office later."

He hung up and rang Josh.

The phone rang…

…and rang.

Not Josh as well!

He was about to leave a message when an out-of-breath voice answered.

"Guv, hi."

"Are you okay, Josh?"

"Sorry. I've been running." He was still panting. "To the shop. Ran out of sausages."

"That must have been awful."

"You're telling me. Got them now though." Another deep breath. "Why are you ringing?"

"I'm on my way to Portishead and I wanted to check how it went last night."

"It was very interesting. I met Leanne, which was surreal."

"Leanne?"

"Yes. She was there with her son."

"Did you say her son?"

"Uh-huh. His name's Hunter. He's five."

"You seem very relaxed about it."

"It's not a problem. I won't be seeing her again. I deleted her contact details from my phone so there's no danger of her getting in touch."

"Right. And you're happy with that are you?"

"Definito."

Luke's eyebrow went up. He had thought Josh and his girlfriend were close. For it to end so abruptly was a real shock.

"Isn't it going to make things difficult for you at work?"

"Why would it?"

"Have you forgotten that Leanne works on reception?"

"That's not a problem either, guv. She doesn't know and I'm not going to tell her."

"She doesn't know?"

"Why would she? I'm not going to tell her. You won't tell her will you, guv?"

"I…"

Luke stopped as he replayed Josh's words and it dawned on him that this was another case of the youngest member of his team tying himself in word knots.

"Are you saying there are two Leannes in your life, Josh?"

"Only one now, guv."

"I thought as much. You had me confused for a moment."

"Eh?"

"So what about the meeting itself? You said it was interesting."

"It all kicked off, guv. A guy stood up in the audience and asked a question. Nick and Shannon came back at him and then Brett came to the guy's support and it escalated from there. Within a couple of minutes they were shouting at each other and then they all headed outside. Finn too."

"Was there a fight?"

"I don't know to be honest. I was stuck with Leanne."

"The Leanne with a five-year-old son?"

"Yes."

"I'm hoping to get into the office this afternoon. When I do we'll get the team together and update the whiteboard. You haven't heard from Helen, have you?"

"Afraid not, guv."

Chapter 45

Pete was alone in the room assigned to the Dumpy Dumper case when Luke arrived at HQ.

"Any sign of Applejack?" Luke asked as he took a seat at one of the desks.

Pete turned his chair around. "Not yet. His DI told me he gets in around 9:30. She said she'd get him to call me when he appears."

"How much have you found out about our victim?"

"Scott Finlay was forty-five and a lecturer at Bristol University in the History Faculty. I spoke to a colleague of his this morning and she told me that he'd been in trouble a few times because of his outspoken views and was suspended on full pay by the Dean two weeks ago."

"Why was that?"

"He made a YouTube video in which he'd said that environmental activists deserved to have their throats cut. Ironic really, given what happened to him."

"Was he single?"

"Yes. Lived alone in a flat in Kingswood."

"Mmm. I guess being single and suspended from work explains why no one reported him missing."

Pete smiled grimly. "The way his colleague reacted to news of his death made me think he probably didn't have many friends. She was shocked but not upset."

"I wonder if Finlay and Erin Douglas knew each other."

"Why are you two talking about my case?"

Luke turned to see the puggish face of Detective Chief Inspector Jack Bramley. He was standing at the open door with both hands on his hips.

"Is that your impression of a teapot, Jack?" Luke asked.

Applejack jerked his arms down so that they were flat to his sides.

Luke grinned. "You're not going to give us a rendition of Riverdance are you?"

"You shouldn't be here, *Mister* Sackville." Applejack took care to emphasise the word 'Mister'. "Do I have to remind you that you're a fucking civilian?"

There was a loud and deliberate cough behind him.

"What now?" he demanded, turning around and almost leaping into the air as he realised who it was.

"Oh, ah..." He bowed his head slightly as he saw who it was. "Sorry, Ma'am. I was, ah..."

"I know what you were doing, DCI Bramley," Chief Constable Sara Gough said. She was a few inches shorter than her subordinate but seemed somehow to tower above him. "Luke is here specifically at my request. He will be helping you now that we've got a double murderer on our hands."

"It's not a double murder."

"Silly me. I'm sorry, DCI Bramley." She looked very deliberately at her watch. "It's only nine-twenty-five so I dare say you're still catching up with the morning's events."

Applejack looked at her and then turned to Pete who was fighting to keep himself from smiling.

"I was about to bring the DCI up to date," Pete said.

"Good." She turned back to Applejack. "I am making you the Senior Investigating Officer for what is now a very high-profile case, DCI Bramley. We must do everything in our power to bring to justice whoever killed these innocent people."

"Of course, Ma'am."

"I want daily updates and I want them in person."

"Naturally. I'll ensure we do everything possible to catch the man who killed these two women."

"Two women?"

"Sorry. Slip of the tongue, Ma'am. These two men." He

hesitated as he saw Pete shaking his head. "I mean, one man and one woman."

"Mmm. And I'm sure you don't need reminding that we mustn't make assumptions. The murderer may be a woman."

Applejack shook his head. "That's not likely, Ma'am," he said, his voice somewhat patronising. "The first body was found in a skip."

"A Dumpy Bag," Pete corrected. "He was found in a Dumpy Bag."

"It's much the same thing." He tapped the side of his pitted and bulbous nose. "My nose tells me it had to have been a man who lifted him in."

"Because women are weak?" the Chief suggested.

"Exactly." He nodded his agreement and then saw the expression on his superior's face. "Not mentally. I didn't mean women are mentally weak."

"That's a relief."

"But, ah…"

She held her hand up. "That's enough. Please come to my office between six and six-thirty today to give me my first update."

"Between six and six-thirty?"

"I know you'll be busy, but I'd appreciate it if you could spare me a few minutes."

"Of course, Ma'am."

She turned and walked away.

"Late for you, six-thirty," Luke said with a grin once she'd gone.

Applejack grunted.

"Shall I bring you up to date, sir?" Pete asked.

"Yes. I am the SIO and I need to know everything ahead of anyone else."

"Even if the Chief comes to see me before you're in?"

"Mmm."

"I'll leave you to it, Pete," Luke said. "I could do with

catching up on progress with the hunt for Erin Douglas's killer." He turned to Applejack. "Who's your DI, Jack?"

"Benson."

"That's good news. I've worked with Laura before. She's excellent which is vital for anyone working alongside you."

Applejack raised one eyebrow as Luke left, uncertain if he should be annoyed by this comment or not.

"What did he mean by that, DI Gilmore?" he asked.

Pete chose to ignore the question and opened his notepad. "I'll run you through events on the night of Scott Finlay's murder, sir."

Chapter 46

Luke was pleased to get away from Portishead after a very frustrating morning.

And it was all down to DCI Bramley.

It was hard to fathom how the man could be SIO of a murder enquiry and yet so off the pace. And now it was clear that he was struggling to absorb information from Pete on Scott Finlay's murder.

Fortunately, Laura Benson had a good grasp of everything in the Erin Douglas case. She was relatively young, in her early thirties, and newly promoted to Detective Inspector. However, she had worked with Applejack in the past and had the measure of him.

Laura and Pete had arranged to meet after lunch and he knew that the two of them would effectively be in control of the case. Meanwhile, Applejack would flounder around on the edge trying to catch any reflected glory while tefloning away any problems.

As soon as he'd left the car park Luke rang Sam.

"Still nothing from Helen," she said. "No record of a Helen Hogg being admitted to any hospitals in Somerset and her son hasn't spoken to her since the day of the filming. This isn't like her, Luke."

"I know." He paused. "What name was she using for her Sow the Wind work?"

"Livingstone." She hesitated and he knew she was on the same wavelength as him. "I'll ring round again."

"Thanks, Sam."

He ended the call and reflected on how pleased he was to have Sam as his deputy. More than that, he was pleased to be working with her full stop.

His phone rang.

"Hello, lover."

It was nice to hear from Cora but this 'lover' business was starting to get on his nerves. It was almost as if she was trying too hard.

"Hi, Cora."

"I'm sorry but I'm going to have to pull out of our dinner this Saturday." She laughed but he thought he detected a note of embarrassment. "My friend's invited me to go to Capri for the weekend. It's all expenses paid and too good an opportunity to miss. I hope you don't mind."

Luke's immediate thought was that, no, he didn't mind much at all. Chloe and Ben were coming down at the weekend and he hadn't seen either of them in several weeks.

"Of course, I don't mind. The twins are home from Uni and it'll be good to spend time with them. Capri's supposed to be beautiful so you should have a great time. Is it the same friend you saw last weekend?"

She laughed again and there was a definite tinge of something to it. Not quite embarrassment. Perhaps nerves? But why should she be nervous? They'd been going out for a few months and were comfortable with each other so why would she think he would mind?

"Is everything okay, Cora?"

There was hesitation at the other end.

"I think so, but…" She paused for a few seconds.

Luke laughed. "Come on, out with it."

"It'd be good to talk through a few things."

"Sure. Fire away."

"Are you in the office today?"

"I'm on the way now."

"Perhaps we could meet for a coffee. I need to explain something."

"Canteen?"

"I'd prefer a cafe. What about the Costa Coffee near Filchers? Four this afternoon works for me."

"Look forward to it. I'll see you later."

He was intrigued but not unduly worried. It didn't sound like Cora wanted to finish with him, but then again if she did would it be such a bad thing? It wasn't as if their relationship went very deep. They enjoyed each other's company but it was always as if she was holding back slightly.

She wasn't as open with her feelings as Sam, that was the problem. Yes, Cora was attractive and, yes, she was fun to be with, but something was missing. For all their intimacy he didn't feel able to be totally honest with her, whereas with Sam…

Hang on a minute. Why was he thinking about Sam? He was going out with Cora. Besides, Sam had never shown any interest in him beyond what was needed for them to work effectively together.

She was out of his league too.

Way out of his league.

His phone rang again and he saw it was her. He pressed the button to accept the call and realised his cheeks were flushed.

What the heck was that about?

"Hi, Sam."

"I've located Helen."

He breathed a sigh of relief. "Thank goodness. Is she okay?"

"She's going to be fine."

"Well done tracking her down."

"I didn't. A nurse at the Royal United has just rung me."

"What happened?"

"Helen fell into the Kennet and Avon canal early yesterday morning. She banged her head and had to have stitches but other than that, and a partially shaved head, it seems she got off lightly."

"Why didn't she get in touch sooner?"

"Concussion. She slept most of yesterday but was apparently very confused when she was awake. The nurse was surprised when I told her Helen's surname was Hogg because she'd been admitted as Helen Livingstone."

"Are you going in to see her?"

"Yes. I've got a meeting at four and I'll head up after that."

"I'll give you a lift if you like." He hesitated. He was also busy at four but was seeing Cora and for some reason he didn't understand he held back from revealing this to Sam. "I've got a meeting at four as well so we can set off to the RUH when we're both finished."

"Okay. Let's meet in reception. I don't think my meeting will take long."

"Mine should be quick too. See you later."

"Take care, Luke."

He clicked to end the call and found himself smiling. Sam nearly always ended their phone calls by entreating him to take care. It was a throwaway line, he knew that, but he liked to think it indicated they were close.

Close in working terms that was.

Nothing else.

Chapter 47

Ham Woods was only half a mile from Jake's house but it was always quiet, and especially so in the middle of Winter. He'd headed straight there after he'd left work to try and clear his head.

It was a cold, drizzly afternoon. The sun had vanished, and the sky was gradually turning from grey to black, but he was too self-absorbed to give a damn.

He shook his head and kicked away a mound of leaves as he trudged slowly up the incline towards the top of the hill. Who did Amanda think she was, giving him a dressing-down in front of the others?

Okay, he'd turned up late for work for the second day running. But that was no reason for his supervisor to embarrass him like that.

Frank had revelled in it, of course. The little bastard had given him a look as if to say, 'Not the blue-eyed boy now, are you, Smarty-pants?'

Jake slowed his pace and tried to calm himself.

It was nonsense to take a simple reprimand so badly. He was nineteen, three months into his printing apprenticeship, and this was the first time he'd put a foot wrong. Heck, he worked twice as fast as most of the others and his work was high quality too.

It wasn't his fault he'd got in late either. It wasn't easy for his mum with her leg in a cast and he'd had to help her get ready.

He realised that he ought to have apologised to Amanda instead of acting all high and mighty. She was only doing her job and she would have understood if he'd explained his reason for being late. Perhaps when he went in tomorrow he ought to say sorry. He'd make sure to be on time too.

Jake stopped walking when he heard a loud crack some twenty or thirty yards into the trees to his right. Probably a muntjac deer, he thought. He'd seen them in the Woods before.

He stopped walking and crouched down, not wanting to scare it.

It was unfathomably dark in among the densely packed trees, but he thought he detected a slight movement, something darting from behind a pine tree to the ground. It could have been a deer's head but it had moved quickly with almost a stabbing movement.

He stepped off the path and took two slow paces onto the ground cover of moss and dead leaves, then rested his hand against the first of the trees and squinted to try to see the deer's outline. It was no more than ten or fifteen yards from him now and he could hear it breathing but still couldn't see it.

Dare he go closer?

Why not?

What was there to lose?

He took his hand off the trunk, took a step and immediately regretted it as another loud crack sounded. He looked down to see a broken branch beneath his trainer.

It was on him before he could look up again, barrelling into his chest with a force that told him it wasn't a muntjac. Jake stumbled backwards and onto his back. *'Fuck,'* he thought. *'It's a wild boar. I'm going to be gored to death.'*

"Get off me," he screamed but it was already gone.

He sat up, heaving a sigh of relief at having escaped, and turned his head to see not a giant pig racing down the path but a hooded figure.

It was moving fast and, after a few yards, turned a corner and vanished from view. It was difficult to tell in the twilight, but Jake thought he or she was tall. There had also been something long in the figure's right hand.

He clambered to his feet and turned back towards the trees. What had been going on in there? Why was the figure holding a stick?

He swallowed.

Could it have been a spade?

But, if it was a spade…

No, surely not. That was the stuff of nightmares.

He glanced back to where he'd first heard the noise. It was even darker in there now.

He was tempted to leave, to head back home, but what if…

No, he had to see what was in there and find out what the hooded figure had been up to. It was probably nothing, just a person who enjoyed a late afternoon walk and who had been spooked when someone else had turned up.

Who was he trying to kid?

He pulled out his phone, turned on its torch and took a tentative step towards the trees. Shining the light created shadows that made him look from left to right as movement appeared to be everywhere.

'Stop it, Jake," he said, deliberately speaking out loud to try and shake the fear away. He gulped and moved tentatively towards the first tree, stepped past it and shone the torch in a 360-degree circle around, first at body height and then at ground level.

Nothing.

He moved slowly to the second tree, did the same again.

Still nothing.

Jake took another step forward and felt something soft beneath his right foot. He raised his trainer quickly and shone the light down to reveal a small, pale grey something. Possibly a toadstool, he thought, though it had felt harder than he would have expected.

He dropped to his knees, brushed away the leaves, and screamed.

Chapter 48

Luke was about to set off to meet Cora when Pete rang.

"What's up, Pete?"

"Another body's been found. A man."

"Where?"

"In woods near Shepton Mallet. It was called in a few minutes ago."

"Murdered?"

Pete gave a dry laugh. "He was about to be buried in a shallow grave so, yes, I'd say that was a fair bet."

"Did you say 'about to be buried'?"

"A walker, Jake Whitehead, disturbed someone in the act of burying the body. Whoever it was shoved him onto the ground and fled the scene." Pete hesitated. "Unfortunately, it happened so quickly that he's not even sure whether it was a man or a woman. All he could say was that he wore a hoodie and was tall."

"Any reason to link this murder to the other two?"

"Not as yet."

"Thanks for the early notice. Keep me up to date."

"Will do."

Luke ended the call and swore under his breath.

His instinct told him that this was the same person who was responsible for the deaths of Scott Finlay and Erin Douglas. If that was the case they had a serial killer on their hands.

Key to establishing a link was finding out who the dead man was. If he was another anti-environmentalist then as far as Luke was concerned it was case-proven. The big question then was who the next target would be.

"I'm off now," he called to Maj and Josh as he left the Ethics Room.

"Give Helen my best," Maj called.

"Ditteroni," Josh added.

Luke headed downstairs, nodded to Leanne on reception as he passed her, and walked the hundred yards or so from Filchers to Costa Coffee. As soon as he entered he spotted Cora at a table towards the side of the cafe. She smiled up at him as he approached.

"Would you mind getting me a latte, lover?"

"Of course not."

"This is table nine."

He went to order their drinks and was surprised to see Sam at the back of the queue. He tapped her on the shoulder and she turned and almost did a double-take when she saw him.

"Oh," she said. "I thought you had a meeting."

"It's with Cora. She said she wanted a word outside the office. What about you? Was your meeting cancelled?"

She suddenly looked a little edgy, almost embarrassed. "No. I, ah…"

"What is it, Sam?"

She smiled sheepishly. "The truth is I didn't want to tell you who I was seeing. It's Ollie. I know you don't like him."

Several notches above don't like, was what Luke wanted to say but instead, keeping his voice as light as he could, he said, "Oh, right. Are you two back together then?"

She was about to answer when the young lad at the counter spoke. "What can I get you?" he demanded, his words delivered in a petulant tone as if she'd been keeping him waiting rather than her being the one in a queue.

"Excuse me, Luke." Sam turned to face the server. "A hot chocolate and a skinny latte, please. To drink in."

She turned back to Luke. "I'm seeing him because…"

"Size?"

She turned back. "Medium, please."

She returned her attention to Luke. "Ollie rang me and…"

"Name?"

Sam turned back for the third time. "What? Why do you need my name"

"For the side of the styrofoam cups. To show they're yours." He said this as if she was an idiot.

"We're drinking in."

He sighed in exasperation. "You should have said."

"I did."

"Mmm. Where are you sitting?"

"I haven't got a table yet."

This response clearly wasn't good enough and his sigh was even more exaggerated this time. He waved his hand towards the serving area. "Wait at the end of the counter."

She was about to respond to Luke when the server added, "Nine pounds forty."

She held her phone to the reader until it pinged, smiled at the waiter, the response being a weary shake of the head, then turned back to Luke.

"Ollie asked…"

"What will you have?" the server asked. He was now looking at Luke, the same petulant tone back in his voice.

Luke couldn't help smiling. "You don't have to explain, Sam. Go and wait for your drinks."

She headed to the end of the counter and he ordered and paid for his and Cora's coffees, telling the server they were at table nine.

He returned to the table, bent to kiss Cora on the cheek and then dropped into the chair opposite.

"So what is it you want to talk about?" he asked.

She smiled across at him but it was a touch more tentative than usual.

"I like you, Luke," she began. "I like you a lot."

"Are you about to dump me?"

"Oh no." She laughed and reached across the table for his hand. "Far from it."

My god, she's not going to propose, is she? was the thought that flew into Luke's mind. He didn't want that, not one bit.

"No," she went on. "I feel that I've been neglecting you and now I'm spending all of this weekend in Italy which means another Saturday and Sunday when we won't see each other."

Luke was listening intently but found himself half-distracted when he saw Ollie enter the cafe and walk over to Sam, now seated at the other side of the cafe.

"It's fine with me, Cora. You know it is."

"That's very good of you, Luke." She squeezed his hand.

As she did so the waiter arrived, the same man who had served them. He placed the latte in front of Luke.

"Mine's the espresso."

The server sighed in exasperation, moved the latte to Cora and placed the smaller mug in front of Luke. "Is that good enough for you, sir?"

Luke chose to ignore the sarcasm. "That's great, thanks."

"I was wondering," Cora continued once the waiter had left, "if a rota might be the best way forward."

"A rota?"

She nodded. "Yes. I'm seeing Rory for two weekends on the trot which doesn't seem fair. I wondered about alternating."

Luke raised an eyebrow. "Rory?"

"Yes, Rory." She smiled apologetically. "Of course. I haven't mentioned his name before, have I? He's the old friend I talked to you about."

"What do you mean by alternating?"

"Every other weekend. It will make everything much easier. I suggest we keep weekdays flexible though."

"Cora, are you in a sexual relationship with Rory?"

She laughed. "Yes. I thought that was obvious."

"But I thought you and I…"

"You didn't think we were exclusive did you, Luke?"

"Yes, I did."

"I'm sorry. I didn't mean to lead you on. But it needn't change anything between us."

He pulled his hand away from hers. "Oh yes it does, Cora. I'm not…" He paused. "Sharing you, or anyone for that matter, isn't something I'm prepared to do."

He stopped talking as he realised that he could hear Sam. Her voice was raised and she sounded angry. A second or two later he saw Ollie storm out of the cafe and turned to see Sam bent over the table looking upset.

"I'm sure we can make this work," Cora said. "As I said, I like you a lot."

"I believe you, but a shared relationship just isn't for me. No hard feelings, Cora, but I think it would be best if we stop seeing each other."

She smiled across at him. "No worries, Luke. I understand, but if you change your mind…"

He stood up. "I won't. Please excuse me, Cora. I need to check on Sam."

Chapter 49

"Sam, is everything okay?"

She looked up at him, her eyes rimmed with red.

"Not really."

He sat on the opposite side of her table and passed her a tissue.

"What did he do or say this time?"

She half-laughed as she wiped beneath her eyes. "It seems like you know him better than I do."

Yes, I do, Luke thought. *He's a bastard and he's not good enough for you.*

It was true and she needed to realise it. But saying it like that might offend her even though they had a close relationship, albeit one that was work-based.

However, they had often opened up to each other and he needed to be honest with her about his feelings.

His feelings about her boyfriend that was, not his feelings about her.

He couldn't do that. It wouldn't be fair. She was on the rebound and besides he didn't think he could handle the inevitable rejection. She clearly didn't feel the same about him as he felt about her.

His heart missed a beat as it dawned on him that he wanted much more than a working relationship. He wanted to reach out and hold her hand but with more sincerity than when Cora had reached out for his.

He wanted to ask her out, just the two of them, alone.

On a date.

But no, the timing was all wrong. The meeting with Ollie had to have been arranged because she was hoping for a reconciliation. It hadn't worked and that made her vulnerable. Now was not the time to take advantage.

However, it was only fair to be honest and tell her what he thought about Ollie.

"Ollie's a bastard and he's not good enough for you," he said.

She laughed properly now, and smiled across at him. "Why don't you tell me how you feel, Luke? Don't hold back."

He returned her laugh. "Go on then. Tell me what happened. Unless you don't want to of course. I understand if…"

"Don't be silly, Luke. I'm happy to tell you." She sighed. "Ollie told me that Sean Abbott had got himself into trouble again, but that he could only explain if we met face-to-face."

"So this wasn't about you and Ollie getting back together?"

"Not as far as I was concerned."

"I take it Sean isn't in trouble?"

She shook her head. "As soon as he sat down Ollie started protesting his love for me. He said he was sorry for being jealous and he'd never act that way again."

"Oh yes. He was jealous of Hannah's boyfriend, wasn't he?"

The corners of her mouth turned up and he was struck, as he so often was, by how attractive she looked when she smiled. Hell, she was a beautiful woman whatever she did, but her smile was…

He realised she had said something.

"Sorry," he said. "What did you say?"

"It was mainly you he was jealous of."

"Me! That's ridiculous."

"Is it?"

"Of course it is. We work together. That's all and that's all it's ever been."

"And ever will be, I guess," she almost whispered as she looked down at her drink and stirred the spoon around and around.

Luke was unsure what to say next. She was still upset but putting a brave face on it. Ollie must have said something that offended her.

"Why did he storm off?"

She looked up at him and laughed again. "The fact I told him to fuck off and never come near me again might have had something to do with it." She paused and her smile vanished as she recalled their conversation. "He won't let go, Luke. I tried reasoning with him, told him to get over himself, but he kept going on and on about how good we are together. My 'fuck off' was the only way to get rid of him."

"Hopefully, he's got the message. And if he hasn't he'll have 6ft 6 of ex-rugby player to deal with." He looked at her. "Not to mention 5ft 7 of karate black belt. We'd make a formidable team."

"Mmm," she said and returned her gaze to the coffee.

"Well, I guess we'd better head for the hospital. Unless you're going to drink that?"

"No, I'm fine."

They stood up and walked back to his Beemer in Filchers' car park.

"That's definitely the end," Sam said as they were putting their seat belts on. "No more Ollie. I think I made my position clear."

It was Luke's turn to laugh. "I don't think you could have made it clearer," he said. "You're free and single again."

She glanced at him, a slightly sad look in her eyes as if she was regretting something.

"I assume you're happy it's over?" he said.

She nodded but her eyes looked glassy as if she was about to cry again.

What was that about?

He could never understand women.

Luke started the engine and they headed towards Weston.

It was a short drive and fifteen minutes later they walked into A&E where a nurse took them to Helen's cubicle.

"And where are my grapes?" was Helen's first comment, as Sam and Luke kissed her on the cheek.

They pulled up a chair on either side of the bed. Helen was sitting up and looked a touch pale but then she didn't exactly have a rose-tinted complexion.

"You seem to be on form," Luke said. "How are you feeling?"

"Like a wee fraud…" She touched the top of her head. "…and as if I'm halfway to being a Mohican."

Her hair was notable for a shaved strip about four inches by two inches on the left, in the middle of which was a line of red.

"How many stitches?" Sam asked.

"Twelve."

"Can you remember what happened?" Luke asked.

Helen shook her head. "Not much. Bob told the paramedics we had a few drinks on his narrowboat, went for a walk and that was when I missed my footing and fell into the canal. What a numpty!"

"Who's Bob?" Sam asked.

Helen's smiled turned sheepish and he was sure her cheeks would have flushed if they'd had the ability.

"A friend. We met on Tuesday at the film studio and he invited me back for drinks."

After his conversation with Cora an hour earlier, Luke knew 'friend' could have more than one meaning, but it was Sam who asked the question.

"Is Bob more than a friend?"

"Ach, not really."

Sam laughed. "As would any friend."

Helen snorted. "Get away with you. Anyway, nothing

can come of it. He thinks I'm Helen Livingstone and that my dress sense is closer to Marilyn Manson than Marilyn Monroe. The fact that Bob hasn't been to see me since he called the ambulance tells you everything." She hesitated. "Did they catch whoever it was who killed that poor wee girl?"

"Not yet," Luke said, "but the Dumpy Dumper body turned out to be an anti-environmentalist by the name of Scott Finlay so that links the two murders."

"Do you think it could be Andrea Mason?"

"She's got to be a suspect. Did you see anyone else at the filming that you recognised?"

Helen was about to answer when the nurse who had shown them in reappeared.

"You're free to go, Helen."

"Grand. Thanks, Jenny." She turned to Luke. "Luke, you couldn't drop me off at home could you?"

"Of course. Then you need to spend a few days at home resting up."

"Not on your Nellie. I'll be in bright and early tomorrow. We've got some whiteboarding to do."

Chapter 50

Josh was loading four sausages onto the grill pan when Leanne called over from the lounge area.

"Not too many beans for me please, Joshy, and only one egg."

"You're sure one sausage is enough?"

"Okay, you've convinced me. I'll have three."

"What?"

"Don't worry," she said with a chuckle. "One will be fine."

Josh was relieved. He needed three sausages to prepare for his day at Filchers.

Not that he found working in the Ethics Team a chore. No. His days were brillianto. Never would he have dreamed when he started work as Edward Filcher's assistant that he would end up where he had.

"You need the energy," Leanne said, apparently reading his mind. "Given that you're now a high-powered underwear operative."

"I do indeedo." He realised what she'd said. "Eh! It's undercover not underwear."

"You're concealing things from others. It's more or less the same thing."

"Stop it, Leanne." He turned the sausages over and cracked three eggs into the frying pan. "How's the studying going?'

"Okay. Russian's a challenge at the best of times but I'm getting there. Anyway, I've had enough for now. I'll get back on it this evening."

She put away her books and walked to the kitchen table where Josh had already laid out knives, forks and ketchup.

"You're on form today," she said.

"Big day. We're updating the crazy wall after what happened this week. Two murders and they're linked."

"Not to Earth Conflict though?"

"No, but it spices the day up knowing we're on the edge of something big."

He turned the sausages again and flipped Leanne's egg.

Today was definitely a crucial day. What had been a relatively low-key investigation into two environmental groups had become a case involving double murder. Not that Sow the Wind or Earth Conflict were implicated, but given the interests of the two dead people it was certainly possible.

If so, he wondered who he would have down as the murderer.

The person he disliked the most was definitely Shannon. She had it in for him for no apparent reason. However, if he'd learned one thing from Luke it was not to jump to conclusions.

If it wasn't Shannon, could it be one of the other members of Earth Conflict that he'd met? Nick had been the most pro-violence when they'd spoken at the Community Centre, with Finn and Shannon close behind, while Brett had appeared to be pleading for peaceful protests.

Then there had been that man who had stood up and asked a provocative question. Bob something. Matthews, that was it. Bob Matthews. He'd been the one to instigate the argument and it was him who asked Brett to step outside.

On balance, Josh decided he'd plump for Brett. He was all too pleasant and his argument for peaceful action had to be a ploy to draw attention away from himself.

The microwave beeped and he plated up their sausages, eggs and beans.

"Thanks," Leanne said as they took their seats. "Looks scrummy."

"It is," he replied through a mouthful of sausage.

Leanne's phone rang and she looked up at the wall clock. "It's only eight. I hope nothing's happened to Mum or Dad."

She put down her cutlery, returned to the lounge and answered her phone.

"Hello. Leanne."

Josh watched as she listened to the response from the caller. She seemed confused and after a few seconds turned to him and shrugged her shoulders as if to say that the caller was mad.

"Is it a nuisance call?' he asked.

She waved her hand to shush him.

"No. I'm Leanne," she said emphatically to the person on the other end. The caller said something and although Josh couldn't make out the words he could tell it was a woman.

"Yes, of course, I'm sure," Leanne said. The caller said something else. "You are as well. Right. I understand" She listened again. "No, I'm not George's mother. I think you've got the wrong number."

It began to dawn on Josh what was happening. 'You are as well' was the big clue. He swallowed his mouthful of sausage and watched as it played out.

Shittedy-shit-shit.

"Did you say George Bailey?" Leanne asked. "What did he look like?"

"I think you should hang up," Josh said, a note of desperation in his voice. "She's clearly got the wrong person."

"Wild hair but attractive," Leanne went on. "Mmm. I might know who you mean. Did you say that the two of you agreed you ought to meet up? That's nice." She paused, covered the mouthpiece with her hand, glared at Josh and hissed, "You've got some explaining to do."

She returned her attention to the caller. "I'm sorry,

Leanne, but George has moved on permanently." She emphasised 'permanently' in a way that worried Josh more than a little. "If I get a new number for him I'll be in touch, but I don't think that's going to happen." She glared at Josh again. "He's got several personal problems to deal with."

She hung up, put the phone back on the table and put both hands on her hips.

"Well?"

Josh swallowed. He wasn't fond of Leanne's teapot pose. It never boded well.

"She asked for my number and I didn't want to give it to her," he said, his voice an octave higher than normal.

"So you gave her mine?"

"It was the first number that came into my head."

"Do you want to see her again?"

"Of course I don't."

"Isn't she attractive?"

No, no, no.

He wasn't falling for that question again. The other Leanne was pretty but if he admitted it then the hole he was digging would grow even bigger. There was a better answer, surely there was.

"Well, Josh. Did you find her attractive?"

"That's not the point, Leanne. You've got to remember that I was in my underwear…"

"What!"

"Not underwear." He gulped. "Undercover. I was in my undercover role. I had to be George and she, well, she seemed to like me and because George is single I had to…"

He stopped as he realised Leanne was grinning. She shook her head and returned to the table.

"Am I forgiven?" he asked.

"I understand what happened now and, yes, you're forgiven." She shook her head, still smiling. "If you had a brain, Josh Ogden," she added as she picked up her knife and fork, "you'd be dangerous."

Chapter 51

There was a round of applause when Helen walked into the Ethics Room.

She smiled and gave a mock bow.

"Wowza!" Josh said as he spotted her shaved patch. "Great haircut."

Luke walked to the centre of the room. "Right, guys," he said. "A lot has happened since we last got together. Our investigation into two environmental groups is now linked to a person who is possibly a serial killer."

Josh put his hand up.

"No need for the hand, Josh."

"Sorry." He blushed slightly and pulled his arm down. "Isn't a serial killer when there are three or more murders, guv?"

"That's right, son. A third body was found in a shallow grave in woods near Shepton Mallet yesterday afternoon. It was a man and the post mortem is scheduled for later today. And before you ask, he hasn't been identified yet."

"How do you know it's the same killer?" Maj asked.

"We don't, not for certain. However, my working hypothesis is that it is." He paused. "As you all know, I was already helping the police on the Dumpy Dumper case, which was then combined with the investigation into Erin Douglas's killing. Avon and Somerset are taking the lead but if there's anything, anything at all, that leads us to believe someone we've encountered in Sow the Wind or Earth Conflict should be suspect we need to let them know."

"Is DI Gilmore the SIO?" Helen asked.

"Unfortunately not. It's DCI Bramley."

"That girt great lump!" Maj exclaimed.

"I know you've encountered his bad side before, Maj,

and believe me, Applejack doesn't have a good side. However, we're stuck with him. All we can do is ensure we do our very best to help him and his team find the person responsible." He gestured to the whiteboard. "Helen, do you want to take the reins back?"

"Ach, no," she said. "Maj is doing a grand job."

Maj wheeled the board to the centre of the room.

"We should start by restructuring it," Luke said. "At the moment it centres on the two environmental groups. We need to be focused first and foremost on the murders."

"I see what you mean," Maj said. He removed the post-its and photos and erased the various lines connecting them. The only words left were 'Project Greta' at the top in the middle.

Immediately beneath these he wrote 'Scott Finlay', 'Erin Douglas' and 'John Doe' next to each other.

"That's a good start," Luke said. "Please can you add Sow the Wind, Earth Conflict and Globo Energy as headings about halfway down. Clearly, the killer may not come from one of those three organisations but at the moment that's all we, the Ethics Team, have to go on. The police team will doubtless be looking at other environmental groups, the victims' families, and so on."

"It's unlikely to be someone from Globo Energy though, guv," Josh said, "given that Finlay and Douglas were anti-environmentalists."

"You're right, Josh. However, although it's unlikely it's not impossible. Someone at Globo could have a grudge against them for some reason. I'd prefer not to rule anyone out until we're absolutely certain they're innocent."

Once Maj had added the three new headings he stuck back the photos and post-its they had up before. Andrea Mason and the MP Curtis Pinnington went under Sow the Wind while four names went under Earth Conflict: Finn O'Sullivan, Shannon, Nick and Brett. Globo Energy had three names: Liz Rathbone, Daniel Craven and Henry

Lavers.

"Josh," Maj said, "can you draw Earth Conflict's logo again?"

"Sure."

Josh took the pens from Maj and drew a blue circle and added a red 'X' over it.

Luke nodded his approval. "Now we need to mark the connections. Finn O'Sullivan was in a relationship with Andrea Mason and he was in Sow the Wind before starting Earth Conflict."

Maj drew a line from Finn to Andrea forking off to Sow the Wind itself.

"We also know that Andrea was at the studio when Erin Douglas was killed, and that she had an affair with Henry Lavers."

Maj drew two more lines linking Andrea to Erin and to Henry.

"That certainly puts her at the centre of things," Sam observed.

"It seems to," Luke acknowledged. "Helen, Josh can you update us on your encounters with Sow the Wind and Earth Conflict, please? Helen, you go first."

"Aye, I'll do that. I'll start with the Sow the Wind meeting last Monday. There were a dozen or so there and I met Andrea Mason, although to be honest the woman I talked to first seemed to be the organiser. Her name's Jackie and if I were to guess I'd say she's nudging fifty."

Maj added her name beneath Andrea Mason's.

"Anyone else of note?" Luke asked.

Helen cast her mind back. "Two people asked provocative questions. One was called Paul. He's thirty or thereabouts and looks a lot like Finn O'Sullivan only a wee bit cleaner. The other man didn't give his name. He was older and well-built with thick stubble and a mass of brown hair to his shoulders. Both seemed to be advocating violence and not that subtly either."

Maj added 'Paul' and 'Stubble-man' beneath Jackie's name.

"Did you see either of those two men at the studio?" Luke asked.

"I think I saw the guy with stubble, but I can't be certain. I must admit I was busy talking while we were waiting."

"You didn't see Paul though."

Helen shook her head. "No, but there were close to two hundred people there. I didn't see Jackie either which surprised me. Andrea walked past a couple of times but I would have expected Jackie to be with her since she came across as the power behind the throne."

"Did you see anyone leave their seats prior to the murder?"

"Not that I noticed. Aside from Bob, that is."

"Bob being the man who called the ambulance for you."

"Aye."

"Bob Matthews?" Josh asked. "Tall, sixty or so?"

"That's him. How did you know?"

"He was at the Earth Conflict meeting. It was him that caused it to be abandoned. He stood up and asked a question they took proper offence to."

"Maj," Luke said, "Can you add Bob Matthews to the board, please? He's connected to both Sow the Wind and Earth Conflict. Put him under Earth Conflict for now but draw a line between him and Andrea Mason." He looked over at Helen who was looking distinctly unhappy. "Best draw a line connecting him to Erin Douglas too."

"It cannae be Bob," Helen pleaded. "He's lovely. He called the ambulance for me and…" She stuttered to a halt. "Excuse me." She stood up and rushed out of the room.

"Do you mind if I…" Sam said, gesturing to the door.

"Of course not," Luke said.

Sam stood up and hurried after Helen.

Josh looked at the door, then at Luke and then back at the door.

"What was all that about, guv?"

Luke smiled. "Why don't you get the coffees in, Josh? We'll resume when Helen's feeling better."

Fifteen minutes later Josh returned with a tray of drinks.

He passed Luke his double espresso. "Any sign of them yet, guv?"

"Sam messaged me to say they'll be up soon."

"Do you know why Helen ran out like that?"

"I have a suspicion, son. I can't say more than that."

It was only a couple of minutes later that Sam and Helen returned.

"I'm sorry about that, guys," Helen said. "I lost my composure." She smiled tentatively. "Sam and I have had a good chat though and I accept Bob has to be a suspect, especially since he was near the Ladies when Erin Douglas was killed. I'm hoping my faith in him is justified but..." She shrugged her shoulders.

"Josh," Luke said. "Please can you tell us what happened at the Earth Conflict open meeting you went to? I gather it was explosive."

"You betcha. Finn, Shannon, Nick and Brett were all there and when, ah...' He looked over at Helen before continuing. "...Bob Matthews asked his question all hell broke loose."

"Can you remember what he asked?"

"He asked Finn O'Sullivan if he'd left Sow the Wind because they wouldn't use violence. Before Finn could answer Shannon said, and I quote, "You're fucking stirring it", then Nick came in on her side. This prompted Brett to leap to Bob's defence and next thing I knew all five of them had stormed outside."

"Did you follow them?" Sam asked.

"No. I was stuck with Leanne."

"Leanne was there?"

Josh nodded. "And her son Hunter."

"What?"

Luke decided to intervene at this point. "I'll explain later, Sam, but it's not what you think. Thanks for that, Josh."

Josh put his hand up again.

"What now?"

Josh turned to Helen. "The other man who spoke at the Sow the Wind meeting." He pointed to the whiteboard. "The one we've called 'Stubble-man'. Can you describe him in more detail?"

"Aye. Late thirties, maybe forty. Long unkempt brown hair."

"Did he have an accent?"

"Not really."

"What was he wearing?"

Helen smiled at the memory. "A jumper that puts your wee George Bailey outfits in the shade."

"Was it green, blue and red checks?"

"Aye. How did you know?"

Josh beamed from ear to ear. "It's Nick. It has to be."

Maj drew another dotted line connecting Nick to Sow the Wind.

"Well done, Josh," Luke said. He sat back and looked at the whiteboard. "We've got a fair bit to go on there, but there are also a few gaps. Maj, could you look into Curtis Pinnington please?"

Maj nodded his agreement.

"We also know next to nothing about Jackie, Paul, Shannon, Nick or Brett. We don't even know their surnames. Helen, please see if you can find out more about Jackie and Paul."

"Aye. I'll do that."

"Josh, you see what you can find out about the other three."

"Gotcha, guv."

"Sam, please can you find out as much as you can about Bob Matthews?"

Sam looked across at Helen before answering. "I'll get right on it."

"As for me, and much as I don't want to, I'll catch up with DCI Bramley and see if what we've found helps their enquiries."

Chapter 52

Helen had told Sam all she knew about Bob Matthews when they'd left the others in the Ethics Room. He'd told her he was divorced, had been living on a narrowboat for eight years and was an occasional actor but made most of his money from working on other people's boats.

Sam began by searching for 'Bob Matthews Actor' and was rewarded with a photo of a man who looked to be in his early fifties. She could immediately see why Helen had been attracted to him. He had neat, salt-and-pepper hair but his standout feature was his smile. It was broad and made all the more endearing by a dimple in the centre of his chin.

She smiled.

'Silver fox' were the words that came to mind. No wonder Helen was smitten.

Clicking on the photo took her to a theatrical agency. There were two more studio shots and a brief résumé, with 'The Bill' given prominence and no acting roles since 2008.

She tried searching on Facebook and Instagram but although there were plenty of 'Bob Matthews', there were none that sounded like her man.

Sam sat back in her seat. She seemed to be at a dead end as far as online information was concerned. What other avenues were there?

She walked over to Helen who looked up as she approached.

"Problem?"

Sam shook her head. "No, but I wondered if you knew the name of Bob Matthews' narrowboat?"

"Ach, I'm sorry. I was a wee bit pickled by the time we got back there. It was long and narrow, I remember that much, but then they all are, aren't they? It was moored two or three hundred yards from the pub if that helps."

"Which pub?"

"The Old Lock and Weir near Keynsham."

"Thanks."

Sam decided to drive out to the pub over the weekend. If he'd moved she'd speak to other boat owners and see if they knew him.

She was about to ring Liz Rathbone when her desk phone rang.

"Hi, Sam," Leanne said. "There's a man in reception asking to speak to you."

For a second Sam feared it was Ollie then realised Leanne had met him so it couldn't be.

"What's his name, Leanne?"

"He won't give his name. To be honest I think he's more than a little tipsy. I told him to sit on the sofa and he did, then he lay down and I think he may be asleep."

"But it's not even eleven!"

"I know."

"Did he say anything?"

"He mumbled something about a gazelle. Does that mean anything to you?"

"Can you describe him?"

"He's well-built, about Josh's height but more muscular and probably ten years older. Still handsome though."

"Even though he's old?"

"Yes. I mean no, I mean…" Leanne laughed. "I made a Josh of that, didn't I?"

Sam returned her laugh. "I'd never thought of using Josh's name like that but it might enter my repertoire now." She paused. "Are you sure that man said 'gazelle'? Could it have been 'Jazelle'?

"Could have been. He's slurring his words."

Sam sighed. "I thought as much. It's Tony, my ex from a while back. I'll come down and have a word with him."

"I'd be quick if I were you. Edward Filcher's just walked into the building and he's spotted him."

"I'll be right there."

Sam rushed downstairs to find Filcher standing over Tony and poking him in the ribs with the index finger of his right hand.

"Up," he said. "Up, up, up." Each 'up' was accompanied by another poke, but Tony wasn't stirring.

Filcher called over to Leanne.

"Who is this man, Lena?"

"It's Leanne, Mr Filcher."

"Eh?" He looked down at Tony as if expecting him to have sprouted breasts.

"I know him, Mr Filcher," Sam said, now out of breath from having raced downstairs.

Filcher looked up at her. "I see, ah…"

"Sam."

"Yes. Sam. I know." He waved his hand over Tony who was now snoring. "Friend of yours?"

"No."

"Thought you said…"

"He and I used to be an item."

He harrumphed and raised an eyebrow. "Item, eh?"

"A long time ago."

"Indeed. Mmm." He gave Tony another poke. "He can't sleep here." Filcher bent down so that his hooked nose almost touched Tony's forehead. He sniffed loudly then shot back upright. "Damned blighter's drunk." He glared at Sam as if this was her fault.

"It appears so, Mr Filcher. If you leave it to me, I'll get rid of him."

"Yes, do. Drunk! Pah!" He turned, said, "Make sure Samantha deals with him, Lena" to Leanne as he passed her then marched to the lift to take him to the Executive Floor.

Sam called over to Leanne. "Is the Olive Grove Room free?"

"Yes, it is. Do you want a hand to carry him in?"

"No need. I know how to wake him."

She bent down, grabbed Tony's crotch and squeezed hard.

He shot up into a sitting position, screamed "Whazza fuck!" and cupped both hands around his testicles.

"Come with me, Tony," Sam said.

"There was no need…"

"Now!" She grabbed his arm, pulled him upright and half-led and half-dragged him to the meeting room.

Once there he flopped into a chair.

"She th-thumped me," he said.

"Thumped you?"

"Jazzy. She's thum…" He burped and the room was filled with the smell of vodka and stale lager. "Thumped me."

"She dumped you?"

"Iss what I said." He looked across at Sam who was wondering, not for the first time and almost certainly not for the last, what she had ever seen in him.

"Loves you anyway, Sammy," he went on. "Always 'n' forever. You're my girl."

"I am most definitely not your girl, Tony."

"Yeh." He waved his hand in her general direction. "You're my girl."

"I don't know why I'm asking this, Tony, because it seems blindingly obvious, but why has Jazelle finished with you?"

He burped again and covered his mouth with his hand. For an awful moment, Sam thought he was going to vomit but he managed to hold it in.

After a few seconds, he swallowed and took his hand away.

"She said…"

A phone started to ring and Tony reached down to his jeans but lacked the dexterity to retrieve it.

Sam bent over, pulled his phone out, ignoring his squeals of delight, and clicked to accept the call.

"Tony, I love you," came the voice at the other end and she instantly recognised the smoke-filled estuary accent. "Sorry I said that. I love your wedding tackle and the way you…'

"Jazelle," Sam said quickly before she continued in this vein. "It's Sam here."

"Oh. Sammy. Are you and Tone back together?"

"We most certainly are not. Where are you?"

"At work."

"Can you come and get him, please? He's turned up at my office and he's very intoxicated. It's Filchers off the Lower Bristol Road."

"Aw. Bless him. Tell him I wasn't serious. Tell him…"

"Jazelle, stop! How quickly can you get here?"

"I'll have to ask Mr Jefferson."

"Book a taxi and be here in ten minutes or I'll call the police."

She hung up, looked over at Tony, who was now snoring again, and returned to Leanne.

"His girlfriend's on her way," she said. "Please call me if he's not gone in fifteen minutes."

Leanne smiled. "I will, Sam."

Chapter 53

Sam rang Liz as soon as she got back upstairs.

"Hi, Liz. It's Sam Chambers."

"Oh, hi. That's good timing. I've just come out of a meeting with Henry."

"All okay?"

"Kind of." She lowered her voice to a whisper. "It's difficult to talk because I'm in an open office and Daniel's only a couple of cubicles away."

"Why don't we meet for lunch?"

"That would be great."

Sam's instinct was to suggest the Salamander but she was worried she might see Ollie.

"What about The Architect?"

"Beneath the old Empire Hotel? Suits me. 12:30?"

"See you there."

Sam hung up and went over to Luke who was growling under his breath and hitting the keys of his computer harder than was strictly necessary.

"Having fun?"

He looked up and grimaced. "I hate spreadsheets."

She smiled. "And I love them. Do you need a hand?"

"Would you mind? These inbuilt formulae are driving me up the wall."

"No problem."

She wheeled her chair over next to his and as she did so their thighs touched. She immediately felt her cheeks turning pink.

Stop it, Sam, she thought. *You're being stupid. He's your boss. Get over yourself.*

"What's the issue?" she asked, trying to keep her voice level but conscious of how close they were to each other.

How could she be enjoying their physical proximity while simultaneously feeling so uncomfortable?

Because she was stupid, that was why.

Be professional, woman, for goodness sake. Act your age.

"It's that tab," he said, pointing up at the screen. "I click on it, enter the number, and then the totals in that one…" He pointed again. "…seem to change as if they've got a mind of their own."

She spent a couple of minutes working her way through the forms to understand how they worked, aware all the time that Luke was watching her intently, and fighting to keep herself from blushing again, and then the next ten minutes explaining what was happening.

"Thanks for that," he said when she'd finished.

She pulled her hand away from the keyboard, inadvertently touched his and pulled it away in shock.

"Are you okay?" he asked.

"I'm fine," she said, swallowing and wheeling her chair back a couple of feet. "I've arranged to see Liz Rathbone at lunchtime. She wants to update me after a meeting she had with Henry Lavers this morning."

"Good. Let me know how you get on."

Ten minutes later Sam set off for the city centre. She decided to walk rather than get the bus.

She needed to clear her head.

Liz was in the entrance hallway when she reached The Architect. It was a very grand building and they shook hands before walking through to the main room, a large, high-ceilinged space.

"I don't suppose you have a booth available?' Sam asked the nearest waitress.

"You're in luck," she said. "We had a cancellation."

She showed them into a cordoned-off corner where a table was laid for two.

She gave them each a menu. "Can I get you two ladies a

drink?"

"Prosecco, please," they said in unison, prompting both of them to laugh.

"Make that a bottle," Sam said.

"It is Friday," Liz replied.

"So, how's everything going?" Sam asked once the waitress had left.

"Much better, thanks. Henry seems to have softened his view of me."

"In what way?"

"We met this morning. It was ostensibly to discuss your project, but as soon as we sat down he apologised for being so brusque and for what he'd said to HR."

"That's good."

Liz nodded. "He told me he'd been out of order but blamed it on our not seeing each other any more. He said he'd loved every moment we'd been together."

"Was he trying to rekindle the relationship?"

"Get me back in the sack you mean?'

There was a cough and they both looked up to see a waiter who was no more than eighteen or nineteen standing at the side of the table. He had a bottle in his hand and was trying to pretend he hadn't heard anything.

"May I?" he asked, gesturing to Sam's glass but avoiding eye contact.

"Please," Sam said.

He filled their glasses, put the bottle into an ice bucket and left.

Both women laughed.

"You were saying," Sam prompted.

"No, I don't think he was trying to rekindle anything. Henry told me, as he has before, how he broke up with me because he felt so guilty betraying his wife. He begged me yet again not to tell her."

"Is yours the only extra-marital affair he's had?"

"Oh yes. Definitely."

How little you know, Sam thought. *Henry has had a fling with Andrea Mason and is probably a serial adulterer.*

"Were you pleased when he finished it?"

Liz thought about this for a moment. "I was upset and disappointed at first, but it didn't last long. The truth is I never had any real feelings for him. I let him seduce me when we were away together at a conference and it was all about the sex."

She hesitated before continuing.

"It's not as if I even like Henry. Why I did it is beyond me." Sam could see that tears were starting to form and passed her a tissue. "I've been a complete bitch, Sam. Poor Ellen. I find it hard to look her in the eyes now after what I did."

"Screw him," Sam said.

A smile returned to Liz's face. "I did."

"Ahem."

They both looked up to see the young waiter had returned, his cheeks now red and his eyes focused firmly on the centre of the table. "Can I get you any food?" he said in a monotone.

They ordered a salad each and he topped up their glasses and left.

"I don't know what that poor waiter thinks of us," Liz said as she sipped her bubbly.

"Did you get around to talking to Henry about our project?"

"Yes. I must admit I laid it on a bit thick about how good your team are. Especially you. I told him you were very smart and if there was anything to uncover you'd find it."

"That's very good of you."

"Sam, do you mind if I ask a personal question?"

"Not at all."

"Your boss, Luke. He's very attractive. In looks and personality."

Sam smiled, not wanting to say that she agreed.

"You're very lucky." Liz went on.

Sam raised an eyebrow. "Lucky?" She raised her glass to her lips.

Liz nodded. "How long have you two been going out?"

Sam spluttered, spraying Prosecco everywhere.

"Sorry. Have I touched a nerve?"

"No." She wiped her mouth with a tissue. "Not at all." She swallowed. "I was surprised, that's all. Luke and I aren't in a relationship."

"You're not?"

"No."

"Really? The way you look at each other and the chemistry between you... I was sure you were an item."

"No. Never have been and never likely to be. Ah, here's our food."

Chapter 54

"Have you got a mo', Luke?" Maj asked.

Luke grinned. "Anything to save me from this bloody spreadsheet." He closed his laptop. "Sam showed me how the blessed thing worked before lunch and I'm all at sea again now. I think I'll leave it until after the weekend."

Maj wheeled his chair over.

"I've been looking into those three MPs."

"And?"

"As you know, they're all linked to Sow the Wind. Curtis Pinnington is named on their website as a supporter, John Gilbey was at the studio for the filming of 'Answer Time' with Andrea Mason, and Teddy Overton was badly injured by one of the group's activists a few months back." He paused. "I've discovered that there's more to the relationship between these three than meets the eye."

"Go on. I'm intrigued."

"All three were elected to Parliament in 2015. They're not in the same political party as each other, so you'd expect disagreements, but their encounters have been a lot worse than that. I had a look through the transcripts of their parliamentary debates on Hansard." He opened his notebook on Luke's desk. "See these dates?"

"There are certainly a lot of them."

"Thirty-four. Regular spats in the Commons between Pinnington and Gilbey and, until he resigned as an MP, between both of them and Teddy Overton. The Speaker of the House had to tell them to tone their language down on several occasions."

"Always about environmental issues?"

"On every single occasion. And the most interesting of the three is the one whose photo we've put on the whiteboard."

"Curtis Pinnington?"

Maj nodded. "John Gilbey has consistently favoured a greater commitment to environmental action while Teddy Overton has always taken the opposite stance. Pinnington, on the other hand, has flipped completely. When he first entered parliament he spoke passionately about how ridiculous the claims about greenhouse gas emissions were. He denied there was any such thing as climate change and argued regularly with Gilbey. Then he switched sides three years ago, affiliated himself to Sow the Wind and his arguments in the Commons were with Overton from then on."

"Did you find anything else out about Pinnington?"

"He was divorced from his first wife five years ago and almost immediately married a much younger woman, Louise Hansen. I found her on Facebook. At twenty-eight she's four years younger than his son by his first marriage. She posted that she was a dancer before she met him." Maj laughed. "Looking at the profiles of some of her friends I'm pretty sure she missed the word 'exotic' from that description."

"Mmm. That's all very interesting. What's your next step?"

"Pinnington is the Member of Parliament for South Mendip and he's holding a constituency surgery in Glastonbury today. It closes at five." Maj looked at his watch. "It's one-thirty now so I was thinking I might drive down, think up a good question and take it from there."

"Excellent plan. Give me a ring when you're done and let me know how you got on."

"Will do, Luke."

Maj grabbed his coat and headed downstairs, pleased that he had brought the Octavia into work rather than cycle in as he normally did.

He entered the address of the constituency office into

the SatNav. It estimated that he'd be there by 2:45 pm.

Once he'd left the car park, Maj turned his thoughts to how to extract useful information from Curtis Pinnington.

His reason for attending the surgery had to be because he wanted the MP to take action on his behalf. It also needed to be about the environment. If he did that he could spin the conversation to touch on Pinnington's links with Sow the Wind.

An idea occurred to him. He knew the address of Luke's farmhouse and he also knew that it was within the constituency boundary and in a conservation area.

He smiled to himself.

Yes, that would work.

The SatNav's estimate was accurate and it was not yet 3 pm when he parked in the car park near the ruins of Glastonbury Abbey. He'd been to the music festival twice in his twenties but never to the town itself so he was interested to see what it had to offer.

As he turned from Magdalene Street onto the High Street he realised that the shops were quirky to say the least. With names like 'Fairyland Aromatics', 'The Wonky Broomstick' and 'Buddha Maitreya Soul Therapy Centre', they sold an esoteric selection of crystals, witchcraft supplies and fairy accessories.

It was a hippy's dream!

He found the surgery just off the main road opposite 'Facets of Avalon'. It was an unprepossessing 1960s terraced house with a sign above the entrance saying 'Curtis Pinnington - Member of Parliament for South Mendip' in large black letters on a yellow background.

The door was open and a young woman looked up at him from her desk as he walked in. She was thirty or so and he immediately wondered if they shared their country of birth.

"Good morning," she said, her accent confirming that he'd been right. "I'm Sagal. Are you here to see Curtis?'

"I am, yes."

"He's with someone at the moment but only one person is waiting so with any luck you won't have to wait more than half an hour. What's your name?"

"Maj Osman."

She wrote it down on her pad. "And why do you want to see your MP today, Mr Osman?"

"I want solar panels and I'm having a problem getting planning permission."

She made another note.

"You can wait in there." She gestured to the open door to her left. "Feel free to make yourself a hot drink."

"Thanks. Ah, do you mind if I ask you a question?"

"Not at all."

"You're Somalian, aren't you?"

Sagal smiled. "That's right."

"Me too. I'm a British citizen now but I came over with my father when I was nine. The thing is, I'm wondering if the hold-up in getting planning permission might be because of my colour. Do you have many people coming in to see Mr Pinnington because they've encountered racial prejudice?"

"A few," she said.

"And is he understanding if that's the case?"

"I'm sure he is." She tapped her pad. "The fact you want to see him about solar panels will pique his interest though. I'm sure of that."

"Why?"

"He's very vocal on the need to counter climate change. He's even linked to two or three environmental action groups."

"Two or three?"

She nodded. "One of them's called Sow the Wind. They were in earlier today to see him before the surgery started."

"I've heard of them. Isn't Andrea Mason their main

spokesperson?"

She shrugged. "I wouldn't know, but the woman who came in was a Jackie Walker." She lowered her voice. "I probably shouldn't be telling you this, but they had a major fallout. I could hear them shouting at each other through the wall."

"Blimey. What was it about?"

"Something to do with money. I heard her refer to 'regular payments'."

"Perhaps she was asking him to increase his contributions to the group and he didn't want to?"

"Could be."

There was the noise of a door closing and a middle-aged woman appeared at the end of the hall.

"I'll go in and wait," Maj said.

He walked into the small waiting room where an elderly man was the solitary occupant. He was perched on one of half a dozen wooden chairs around a coffee table which was heaped with nature magazines.

"Typical politician," he grumbled as Maj sat down. "Always keep you waiting."

Sagal walked in. "You can go in now, Mr Anchovy," she said.

He stood up and growled. "It's Anthony, not Anchovy."

"Sorry. Of course. Please go through the door at the end of the hall."

He harrumphed and disappeared from view.

"Whoops!" Sagal said to Maj.

"Easy mistake to make," he said.

Chapter 55

After a few minutes, Maj began to understand how Sagal had heard so much of the disagreement between Curtis Pinnington and Jackie Walker.

Mr Anthony-not-Anchovy was not a happy bunny. Some words were lost in the thin stud wall that separated the waiting room from the MP's office, but the gist was easy to follow.

"Ruddy council…" Anthony said, followed by a series of words Maj couldn't make out, then "…bins full of rubbish…." More mumbles. "…just not good enough!"

He couldn't make out Pinnington's replies and assumed he was maintaining his cool.

Anthony's tirade went on for a few minutes longer then it went quiet and a moment later he heard Sagal's voice from the entrance hall.

"Goodbye, Mr Anthony. Thank you for coming in."

"Mmm," Anthony grumbled. "Not good enough. Told him. Told that MP." He gestured back to the door at the end of the corridor. "I told him, I did. Not good enough, I said. It'll smell like high heaven, I said. There'll be rats, you mark my words. Not good enough, I said."

He gave one more harrumph then Maj heard the front door close and walked back to Sagal's desk.

"Another satisfied customer," he said with a smile.

"We get all sorts. He's not the worst, believe me." She gestured to the end of the corridor. "You can go in now."

Maj walked to the end of the hall and knocked on the door.

"Come in."

He entered to find Curtis Pinnington seated behind a dark rosewood desk and looking much as he did in the photo on the whiteboard. He was the epitome of an English upper-class gentleman, albeit with a complexion that was ever so slightly orange. His bright red waistcoat was worn over a white shirt and Old Boys' tie, and the edges of his mouth were turned up in a smile that was as false as the matt black hair on his head.

At close quarters, it was blindingly obvious to Maj that the MP was wearing a wig, and it was with some difficulty that he managed to keep a straight face.

"Thank you for seeing me, Mr Pinnington."

Pinnington's smile remained and it had all the sincerity of his fake tan.

"Nonsense, Mr…" He referred to his pad. "Osman. I am here to serve. Please take a seat." He gestured to the chair on the other side of his desk. "I gather you have a problem with solar panels."

Maj sat down. "Yes. I live in Norton St Philip, and put in a dozen solar panels two years ago. Now I want to add six more and because it's a conservation area I need planning permission. I applied nine months ago but haven't heard anything. It's very frustrating and if I ring or email the best I get is that they're working on it."

"I see. I appreciate it may seem a long time to you, but I'm not sure that I can get much publicity on the back of a nine-month delay."

"Publicity?"

Pinnington nodded but the smile remained fixed as if it had been attached with the same glue as his hairpiece. It showed off his super-whitened teeth but didn't stretch as far as his eyes. They were deep blue and cold.

"I find that publicity is the best way to make progress, Mr Osman."

"Oh. I thought you'd ring or email them."

Pinnington laughed, but it lacked warmth. "Oh no. If I am to get anywhere with a cause I need to be visible. Visibility is everything. I have many years of experience and

I know how to make things happen."

Maj was being patronised in a way that hadn't happened to him since he had worked for Glen Baxter.

"I wouldn't call this a cause, Mr Pinnington. This is just about my new solar panels."

Pinnington shook his head. "Mr Osman, I got where I am today by backing the right horse. If we can persuade the newspapers that yours is a worthwhile cause then I'll happily go on air and make my feelings clear." He paused for a second as an idea occurred to him. "Actually, both of us together might work well. Perhaps 'Good Morning', but we'll have to make it hard-hitting and more emotive. A nine-month delay won't get me the attention I'm seeking. Where are you from, Mr Osman?"

"Bristol."

He smiled condescendingly. "Originally?"

"Somalia."

"Excellent. I can work with that. We'll tell them that the council have failed to process your application because of your ethnicity."

"I don't think that's the reason, Mr Pinnington."

"Whether it is or it isn't is by the by. What matters is that I appear on television and tell your story with you alongside me. You won't need to say anything but I suggest you wear something different."

"A suit you mean?"

"Oh no. Better if you wear the kind of clothes you might wear in Mogadishu. A white shawl over a white skirt perhaps?"

"I see. So that you and I look very different."

"Exactly. To show that I am standing up for a poor downtrodden immigrant. The fact that you're black will emphasise the point."

"I'm pleased that the colour of my skin helps."

Pinnington was oblivious to Maj's sarcasm as he imagined himself under the media spotlight. His smile was almost genuine now. "So am I," he said. "So am I."

"Actually, talking about causes, I remember now that I saw you on the TV a while back."

Even more of Pinnington's over-brillianced teeth came on show. "I am frequently on television," he said smugly.

"You were defending the Sturridge Group after one of their subsidiaries disposed of chemical waste in the River Avon."

"Ah, yes." Pinnington coughed. "That must have been a few years ago."

"I guess so, because you've moved to the opposite side now, haven't you?"

"We have to learn and adapt, Mr Osman."

"I suppose it's good that you've learned from your mistakes."

"I wouldn't call them mistakes."

"Because didn't I hear that you're now funding Sow the Wind."

"I support their worthy endeavours but I don't give them any money."

Sagal had said the MP had aligned himself with two or three groups and Maj decided to go out on a limb.

"Which do you favour more, Mr Pinnington? Sow the Wind or Earth Conflict?"

Pinnington sucked his jaw in. "How do you know about my association with Earth Conflict?"

Maj chose to ignore the question. "Or is it a case of you backing whichever of the two gets you more attention?"

"I assure you, this is not about me. I am trying to help you, Mr Osman, and insinuations that I am trying to promote myself are neither helpful nor appropriate."

Maj smiled. "I'm sorry. I'm a little confused, that's all. I'm increasing my use of solar energy because I'm a keen environmentalist, but it's not clear to me where you stand."

"That should be abundantly self-evident. As you said a moment ago, I work with two leading campaign groups for environmental action."

"And for the Sturridge Group, whose Chairman has gone on record as denying there is any such thing as climate change."

"I severed my links with the Sturridge Group several years ago."

"Was that because a pro-environmental stance gives you a better chance of furthering your political ambitions?"

"Mr Osman, do you want my help or not?"

"No, I don't think so." Maj stood up and walked towards the door, opened it and then turned back as he decided there was nothing to lose by testing one more theory.

"One more thing."

Pinnington sighed. "Yes."

"Was Oscar Briggs' attack on Teddy Overton a surprise, or were you involved in planning it?"

Pinningtons' eyes widened and Maj saw that he had hit a chord.

"I had nothing to do with that, nothing whatsoever."

One more testing question, Maj thought, and he might go over the edge.

"So Jackie Walker acted without your approval?"

Pinnington stood and advanced around the desk towards Maj. He was a cornered beast now, and his lips turned down at the edges as he prepared himself for a fight.

"You're a journalist, aren't you?" he snarled and jabbed his index finger into Maj's chest. "Which rag do you work for?" He didn't wait for an answer before continuing. "You don't know the danger you're putting yourself in, Mr Osman. Even if that's not your real name, I will find you and put a stop to what you're doing."

There was genuine menace in his voice.

"Is everything alright, Mr Pinningon?" Sagal called from her desk.

Pinnington stepped forward so that his face was inches from Maj's. "Get out!" he hissed, then laughed and there was genuine evil in it. He lowered his voice. "I advise you to watch your back."

Maj turned and walked down the corridor as the door slammed behind him.

"Was everything okay in there?" Sagal asked.

"Fine," he said. "Mr Pinnington was very helpful. Nice to meet you, Sagal."

"You too, Mr Osman."

Chapter 56

Luke was finding it hard to focus on his journey home as every profanity he had ever heard, and a large number that were completely new to him, issued from the BMW's speaker system. JD Kirk's character Bob Hoon was trying to outwit an army of fake Santas and Luke was struggling to stop himself from laughing out loud at his antics.

He was almost relieved when Maj rang and interrupted Angus King's narration.

"Hi, Maj," he said, still smiling. "How did it go?"

"I met Curtis Pinnington."

"Find anything out?"

"Yes, quite a bit. He's got his fingers into both Sow the Wind and Earth Conflict."

"That's interesting. Both of them, did you say?"

"He confirmed it. I'm also pretty confident that he's providing back-handers to Jackie Walker, though what she's doing for him I can't be certain. He went on the defensive when I suggested he might have had something to do with the attack on Teddy Overton." Maj paused. "He became quite aggressive. I thought he was going to punch me for a minute. He threatened me too."

"What did he say?"

"That I didn't know the danger I was putting myself in by speaking to him like that, and that I should watch my back. It was bluster though, I'm sure of it. He's a bully but he's a coward too."

"Okay, thanks for the update. I'll ring Helen and tell her. She's going to the Sow the Wind meeting on Sunday evening so it'll be good for her to have a heads-up. Have a good weekend, Maj."

"You too, Luke."

Luke rang Helen and told her what Maj had said.

"I'll try to spend some time with Jackie before or after the meeting," she said when he'd finished. "It would be good to find out what makes her tick."

"Good idea."

"I'm also going to see if I can sneakily take photos of her and other attendees. With Nick popping up in both groups it would be good to have images of them."

"I agree. Be careful though. You're Helen Livingstone remember, and you need to stay in character. I don't want you to take any risks."

"Ach, dinnae worry, Luke. I'll be fine."

He hung up and the phone rang before Hoon had time for more than three ridiculously-constructed expletives.

"Hi, guv."

"Hi, Josh."

"I've tried doing some desk research on Shannon, Nick and Brett but I'm not getting very far. I thought I'd go back to Southgate tomorrow to see if Finn and Shannon are there again. Is that okay?"

"Of course it is."

"Shannon's a touch intimidating…" Josh paused. "Scrub that. She scares the willies out of me. I think she's my best bet though. She's got quite a gob on her. I'll see if I can get a few minutes alone with her."

Luke laughed. "Good luck."

"Thanks, guv."

Luke ended the call and it occurred to him that he'd now spoken on the phone to all of his team bar one, and Sam was the one he'd most like to speak to.

For an update on her meeting with Liz, that was all.

Plus it would be good to talk to her, wish her well for the weekend, perhaps ask her out…

Ask her out!

Where did that come from?

He paused the audiobook and reminded himself that

she was way out of his league, had just come out of a painful relationship with a godawful twat of a boyfriend, and…

And what?

His phone rang and he looked down to see her name on the screen.

Fuck!

He answered, suddenly tongue-tied and feeling like a teenager.

He was forty-three for goodness sake.

"Hi, Sam."

"Hi. Are you on your way home?"

"Yes."

"Anything planned for the weekend?"

He thought briefly of saying, *I'm not doing anything tomorrow night if you're free*, but nerves got the better of him.

"Ben and Chloe are home until Sunday evening."

"That's great. Give them my love."

"I will. What about you?"

"Nothing much." She laughed. "I'll be on my own with a film and a bucket of popcorn tomorrow evening I expect."

"Will you? I was wondering…"

"What?"

He hesitated.

"Are you still there, Luke?

"Sorry. I was miles away. How did it go with Liz?"

And that was that. He was back talking about work, the moment gone.

Idiot!

"It went well. Henry Lavers apologised to her so she's feeling a lot more relaxed. We got on well and I suggested she join Hannah, her boyfriend and me on Monday evening. We're going to see Ghost at the Theatre Royal and I've got a spare ticket."

"Was Ollie supposed to be going?"

She laughed again.

He loved that laugh.

"You got it. Is that alright, Luke?"

"Is what alright?"

"Me mixing personally with someone I'm working with." She paused. "Is that kind of thing okay?"

"Of course it is, Sam. It's fine."

"Good. I…" She hesitated again.

"What is it, Sam?'

"Nothing. Have a good weekend, Luke, and take care."

Chapter 57

Josh was standing in front of the mirror in their apartment staring in horror at his reflection.

"Will the other Leanne be there?" Leanne asked.

"I don't think so. I certainly hope not."

Leanne grinned. "You're scared she might be, aren't you?"

He turned around to face her. "A little. She kind of tried to chat me up." He turned back to the mirror.

"Was she attractive?"

"Don't start, Leanne. I know better than to answer that one."

"Who are you expecting to see?"

"I'm hoping it'll be Finn and Shannon again."

"Finn's the founder of Earth Conflict?"

"That's right."

"And did you say Shannon's about our age?"

He tipped his head to the left and then to the right, but whatever he did his hair looked a mess. Without mousse or gel, all it did was flop. There was no sturdiness to it, no strength, no rigour…

"I said, is she our age?"

"What. Oh, yes." He tried standing on tiptoe but that made no difference either.

"And is she pretty?"

"Difficult to tell with all the piercings." He peered at his hair with his eyes slightly closed but it still looked awful. "Probably."

"Probably?"

"Yes. She's got big eyes and a small button nose. Perky cheeks too."

"Perky cheeks?"

"That's right."

There were alarm bells ringing, silently at first but they were growing louder by the second.

Pissedy-piss-piss.

Josh turned back so that he was facing his girlfriend again.

"No," he said, suddenly panicked. "No, she hasn't got perky cheeks. She's got, ah…"

"Perky tits?'

"Yes. I mean, no." He gulped. "I haven't seen them. Obviously, I haven't seen them. I mean I've seen the shape of them, through her jumper. Well, not through. It's not as if I've been staring at them."

He realised that Leanne was smiling.

"Eh!"

"You're so much fun to tease, Joshy," she said and leaned forward to kiss him on the lips. "I do love you."

"I love you too."

She smiled. "Come on. You'd better finish getting dressed. It's magic mushroom time."

*

Forty-five minutes later Josh wandered into Southgate and was pleased on two counts. First, Finn and Shannon were there, and second, there was no sign of Leanne-number-two or her son Hunter.

Finn and Shannon were standing next to the hand-decorated phone box again, but this time they were deep in discussion rather than lecturing passing shoppers.

"Ah, George," Finn said when he saw him. He was wearing the same creased and dirty clothes as previously, and Josh wondered if he slept in them. "You can help settle an argument."

"Hi, Finn."

Josh turned to Shannon who was wearing a black trench coat belted at the waist. As ever, she had rings through her upper lip, but he was sure there was something different about her.

"Hi, Shannon," he said. She nodded back and after a few seconds, he realised that she'd had her hair cut. "That's a nice style," he added. "A bob suits you."

She sneered at him. "I'm not going to shag you, *George,*" she said, accentuating his name as if to suggest it was an invention.

Josh laughed nervously. "No. Of course not. Who would, with hair like this." He gestured to the top of his head and as he did so it dawned on him that his hair was sophisticated and neat when set against Finn's matted braids.

"So what was the argument?" he asked quickly.

"Shannon said Brett deserved what he got and I disagreed," Finn said.

"What did he get?"

"A black eye," Shannon said, clearly taking pleasure from the fact. "He deserved it too. He's a loser."

"Who hit him?"

"It was that guy who stood up and asked those fucking stupid questions. Bob something."

"Bob Matthews."

She furrowed her brow, surprised he remembered. "Yeah, him. When we went outside all hell broke loose."

"Why?"

It was Finn who answered. "We're all on the same side," he said, "but some people take more extreme views than others."

"Yeah." Shannon shook her head. "But Brett talks complete shit. I swear he was trying to wind the rest of us up."

"What happened after he was hit?"

"He fell to his knees," Finn said, "and that guy Bob

immediately said sorry and helped him up. It calmed down then, although Nick was still angry with him."

"He was fucking furious," Shannon threw in. "I thought he was going to give Brett a second shiner."

"What exactly was it that Brett said to wind them up so much?" Josh asked.

"Something about knowing they were ready for violence. That he had proof of it."

The light rain had turned to sleet and now snow and it was beginning to settle.

"No one's going to listen to us in this weather," Finn said, looking up at the falling flakes. "I think we should call it a day."

"I'm meeting a friend in M&S for lunch," Shannon said, "so I'm going to grab a coffee in there to kill time until she arrives."

Josh saw his opportunity. "I'll join you," he said quickly.

Shannon glared at him. "I told you, *George*. You're not getting into my pants."

"I don't want to, Shannon."

She sighed and seemed to accept his word. "Okay, but you can pay."

They said their goodbyes to Finn and walked to M&S where, true to his word, Josh bought the drinks, a double espresso for Shannon and a luxury hot chocolate with extra marshmallows for himself.

He brought them back to the table and passed hers over.

"That's what the guv drinks," he said, gesturing to her mug."

"I thought you were unemployed."

Whoops.

"Ah… 'The Guv' is a character in a TV show."

"Which one?"

"Happy Valley."

Shannon shook her head. "I don't think so. I've seen

263

both series."

"Might have been Line of Duty then. Or something else. Yes. Probably something else." He smiled, but it wasn't returned. "Sounds like that guy Bob was bang out of order, hitting Brett like that."

"He had it coming."

"Still. I mean, we're all on the same side, aren't we?" She nodded absent-mindedly and looked at her watch "Where's Brett from, anyway?" he went on. "Is it a Gloucester accent?"

"Taunton."

He nodded. "Makes sense. What about you?"

"What about me?"

"Are you from Somerset?"

"Does it sound like it?"

She took a sip of her coffee and looked pointedly out of the window.

This was useless. He was getting nowhere and getting there fast.

He decided to take a different tack.

"You know my name's George Bailey?"

"Yes, *George*, I know your name's George Bailey."

"I was thinking how odd it would be if Brett's surname was Butler, then he'd be a famous character from a film too."

"You mean Clark Gable's character in Gone with the Wind?"

He pointed a finger gun at her. "Exactimo."

"That was Rhett Butler, not Brett Butler."

"Oh. Right."

"Nick's surname is Cage though. The same as the actor."

"Wowza! Is it?"

"No." She wasn't smiling but she looked distinctly pleased with herself. "It's Atkinson."

"I see. You were joking or something."

"It was 'or something'." She turned her attention back to the window.

"Is Nick ex-army? I saw a tattoo on his arm and it looked like a winged dagger."

Shannon shrugged. "I don't know."

"What about you, Shannon? Have you got a famous surname?"

"What do you care?"

"I'm trying to make conversation, that's all."

She sighed. "No. I haven't got a famous surname. My name's Shannon Wilson. And Brett's surname is Napier. Now will you shut up?"

"Happy to, Miss Wilson." He grinned. "More than happy to."

Chapter 58

Luke pushed open the back door and led Wilkins into the boot room.

"Sit," he said, and the soaked-through cocker spaniel dropped obediently back onto his haunches. Luke called through to the kitchen. "Chloe, would you mind bringing me a bowl of soapy water, please?"

His daughter appeared a minute or so later, looked down at the cocker, who was showing every sign that he was pleased with himself, and smiled.

"I could smell him from the kitchen. Is it fox poo?"

"You guessed it. If he'd spotted it on our way out we'd be alright because he's been in the lake, but oh no, he had to start rolling in it on the way back."

He took the bowl from her, got onto his hands and knees and started scrubbing Wilkins' back.

"He's loving the attention," Chloe said.

After a minute or so Luke studied his workmanship. "I think I've got the worst of it out," he said. "Would you mind changing this for clean water?"

She took the bowl and returned to the kitchen.

"I spoke to Granddad while you were out," she said once she'd filled it and brought it back.

"Thanks." He took the bowl, rinsed the cloth in the clean water and started washing the suds off. "How does he seem?"

"Not too bad, all things considered." She paused. "Dad, are we spending Christmas at Borrowham Hall?"

"I hadn't thought about it, to be honest. Why do you ask?"

"I spoke to Marion. She's very keen that we come."

"I'd like to, but it'll depend on Erica as much as

anything. You know what she can be like." He reached for a clean towel and used it to dry the excess water from Wilkins' back. "Given Pippa's going to be with us that's an extra four to cater for."

He stood up and shepherded the spaniel into his crate.

"You can dry off for a few minutes before I let you out, boy," he said as he passed a bone-shaped biscuit through one of the gaps in the metal frame.

"It's not even as if she prepares the food, Dad. Amy will be doing all the cooking."

He stood up, turned back to his daughter and shrugged. "What can I say?" He paused. "I'll ring Mark to see if it's okay. I'll suggest that we drive down on Christmas Day in the morning and leave Borrowham the day after Boxing Day."

"Sounds good."

They went into the kitchen and Chloe put the kettle on. As Luke spooned coffee into two mugs he heard the front door and a few seconds later Ben and Pippa walked into the kitchen.

As always, his son and his girlfriend were holding hands. They'd only been going out a few months but were now inseparable. It was obvious they were smitten with each other.

"Did you get what you wanted?" he asked

"Definitely," Ben said. He was beaming from ear to ear while Pippa looked slightly embarrassed.

Luke and Chloe exchanged glances.

"What have you bought?" she asked.

"Show them, Pips," Ben said. He let go of her hand and she held it up so that they could see the diamond engagement ring on her finger.

Chloe took hold of Pippa's hand and lifted it so that she could see the ring more closely.

"It's beautiful," she said. "Congratulations, both of you." She turned to her brother. "Well done, bro'."

Luke stared at the ring.

He wanted to say something, needed to say something, but felt incapable, his words stuck in his throat. He glanced across at his son who was gazingly lovingly down at his fiancée.

Fiancée!

That meant marriage.

Which almost certainly meant children.

No way was Ben old enough for that sort of commitment. He was a teenager, barely out of school.

"It's not as grand a ring as I'd have liked," Ben said.

"It's perfect," Pippa said.

He looked across at Luke. "Aren't you going to congratulate us, Dad?"

"Of course. Sorry." He bent down to kiss Pippa on the cheek then hugged his son and stood back again. "I'm delighted."

"You seem reticent."

"No, it's just…"

Chloe laughed as she realised why he was holding back. "Dad," she said, "has it dawned on you that Ben's a few months older than you were when you and Mum got together?"

"What? But Pippa…"

"Is older than Mum was."

"Really?"

"Really."

"Christ. I feel so bloody old." He laughed. "Next thing I'll be a grandfather."

"Not for a while, Luke," Pippa said. "Not for a while."

*

It was coming up to seven when the five of them set off to walk to the Tucker's Grave Inn.

Luke had suggested they go into Bath for a meal to celebrate, but Ben and Pippa had insisted that a cider and a takeaway was their preference.

He let his son and future daughter-in-law go on ahead, while he and Chloe walked a few paces behind. Wilkins was on his lead alongside his master and shaking with excitement as he sensed the fields ahead and the freedom that went with them.

Luke's thoughts turned to Jess. If only she could have been here for this moment.

He kept his voice low. "Mum would have loved Pippa," he said wistfully.

"I think you're right, Dad." She put his arm through her father's once they'd climbed the first stile and released the cocker. "She and Ben make a great couple."

"Do you know if they've talked about having children?"

"Ben told me that they want at least two."

By the time they reached the cider house, Luke and Chloe had dissected most aspects of Ben and Pippa's relationship and analysed their prospects for decades ahead.

Luke and Ben ducked as they entered the pub which appeared not to have changed in at least two hundred years. There was no bar, just a line of barrels on the left, a snug through the archway ahead, and an alcove on the right containing an ancient, rectangular pine table.

Luke was pleased to see that Stan was one of the three men around the table.

"Hi, Stan, Ozzie, Reg," he said, nodding to each of them in turn. "Mind if we squeeze in?"

"Course not, Luke," Reg said. He was the largest of the three by a long way, both horizontally and vertically, and had a strong Somerset accent. He nodded hello to the twins. "Ben and Chloe, isn't it?"

"That's right," Ben said. He smiled down at his girlfriend. "And this is Pippa."

"They got engaged tonight," Chloe said.

"Well done, you two," Stan said. He was in his late sixties, a thin man with a completely white comb-over and an even stronger accent than Reg.

"The drinks are on me," Luke said. "I insist."

"Mary!" Stan shouted. He had a very deep voice for a man so slight of build.

A few seconds later a middle-aged woman wearing a Mother Tuckers apron appeared.

"Right, my luvvers," she said. "What'll ye all be 'avin'?"

Luke looked over at Stan. "Black Rat for you, Stan?"

Stan nodded. "Lush. Same fer Ozzie and Reg."

Luke turned back to Mary. "Black Rats all round please."

She turned to the barrels and started filling seven dimpled glasses.

Stan and his two friends resumed their discussion, which seemed to centre on the merits of the latest John Deere tractor, while Luke, Chloe, Ben and Pippa covered a variety of subjects including wedding plans.

After an hour or so, both Chloe and Pippa disappeared to the Ladies and Luke saw his opportunity.

"Stan," he said. "Pardon my interrupting, but you know a lot about books, don't you?"

Stan nodded. "A fair bit, aye."

"Have you heard of a book called 'Armageddon Never'? A friend of mine was reading it but I couldn't find it online."

Stan snorted. "I reckons you got the name wrong, Luke. You sure it weren't 'Apocalypse Never'? Did it have polar bears on the cover?"

"That's the one."

Stan tapped the side of his nose. "Thought as much. It's by Scott Finlay. Load of old pig's wax if you ask me, but it sold well."

"Thanks, Stan. That's very helpful."

"No problem, me kidder." He held his empty glass out.

"It'll cost you another Black Rat mind."

Chapter 59

The tailor's son was worried.

Annoyed too.

He'd messaged Robin over an hour earlier and there was still no reply. It just wasn't good enough. He was the one who was paying.

This was happening everywhere in his experience. No one cared about service any more.

It had started with banks, then airlines.

Now it seemed that even hitmen had little regard for their customers.

He sent the message again.

Why have you not yet dealt with number 3?

He immediately saw the message '*Robin is typing…*' and a few seconds later the response appeared.

I will deal with her in the next forty-eight hours.

Why has it taken so long?

As I said, I had to deal with a problem.

That was several days ago.

I was interrupted.

What do you mean 'interrupted'?

I have dealt with it now, but it was more complicated than expected.

The tailor's son thought of pushing for an answer, but decided it wasn't essential he know what 'I was interrupted' meant.

He had a much more pressing matter to deal with.

Is anyone onto you?

> *Of course not. I am a professional.*

Are you sure? Have you encountered any of the following…
Majid Osman?
Sam Chambers?
Helen Hogg?
Luke Sackville?
Josh Ogden?

> *No. Who are they?*

I have had contact with one of them and I believe they are a team.

> *Are they police?*

No.

> *Do you want me to deal with them?*

The tailor's son gave this some thought.

The money wasn't an issue but they couldn't leave bodies scattered here, there and everywhere. He and Robin were already responsible for three deaths, with a fourth to follow shortly. Another five would be much too risky.

He smiled.

It was also exciting.

This was an adventure and he was gaining great satisfaction from controlling, and in some instances ending, people's lives. He had employed Robin for a just cause, but was now enjoying the whole experience.

He didn't want to be caught though, and another five deaths was too risky.

His phone pinged.

Do you have an answer?

Keep your eyes open. If you come across any of those five eliminate them.

Normal terms?

Yes. Normal terms.

Very well. I'll be in touch soon.

Goodbye, Robin.

Goodbye, Taylor.

Chapter 60

Sam was restless, bored and, if she was honest, lonely.

It was Saturday evening and she was stuck at home. Okay, she was out the next day with Hannah and Liz, but that was twenty-four hours away. Right now, she was twiddling her thumbs wishing for what might have been.

She'd dropped a big enough hint when she'd told Luke she'd be at home on her own with a film and a bucket of popcorn, but all he'd done was change the subject and ask a question about Globo Energy.

He'd finished with Cora but was evidently enjoying being single again. Either that or he had his eyes on someone else. Another senior manager no doubt. Glamorous too in all likelihood.

She sighed. There had been a time when she thought Luke had a genuine interest in her beyond their working relationship. On one occasion he had even seemed close to asking her out on a date.

That had to have been her imagination working overtime.

He just wasn't into her.

After channel-hopping for a few minutes, and rolling her eyes when a series with the title 'Naked Dating' flashed onto the TV, she decided she ought to make herself useful. Moping around in the flat was not her style and, after a few moments thought, it dawned on her that she could do her friend and colleague a favour.

It was obvious that Helen had fallen for Bob Matthews, and that in her eyes there was no way he was involved in anything untoward, let alone murder. Helen was smart and Sam had immense faith in her judgement.

She decided to find Bob and tell him how Helen felt.

He had probably been trying to locate her since the accident, but with only the name Livingstone to go by he wouldn't have been able to track her down.

She flicked off the television, stood up and walked to the side table to fetch her notebook so that she could look up what Helen had said about him. As she did so she realised that the curtains were still open. It had been dark for several hours, but she had been so self-absorbed she hadn't even noticed.

As Sam started to draw the left curtain closed she sensed a rapid movement in the road outside. It was midway between two street lamps, an area that was partly in shadow. Something had darted into the gap between the hedges beyond the pavement and it was too big to have been a cat or dog. She stared down for a second or two trying to see what it was but couldn't see anything. Whatever it was, it had vanished now.

Thinking no more of it, she changed into warmer clothes, put on a scarf and coat and went down to her car.

For a moment she thought she ought to tell someone where she was going, just in case.

In case of what?

She smiled and shook her head, annoyed with herself. Helen had to be right about Bob. And besides, if she was going to ring anyone it would be Luke and she knew he'd tell her not to go.

Her notes said that Helen and Bob had gone for a drink at the Old Lock and Weir near Keynsham, and that his narrowboat was moored close by. She looked the pub up on her phone and saw that it was less than a thirty-minute drive away. That was good. It was only just gone ten so she could be there well before closing time. She was confident the staff would know Bob Matthews, given the location next to the river and the fact that Helen had said he gained most of his income from working on other people's boats.

As she was approaching Kelston, Sam had the weirdest

sense that someone was following her. She looked in the rearview mirror and saw there were two cars behind her, but with their headlights on it was impossible to tell the make.

It was the vehicle immediately behind that was spooking her. He was much too close for comfort.

She was approaching a bend but to her surprise the car suddenly revved up and surged past, only just making it in time as a van appeared on the other side of the road and slammed on his horn.

What a nutter!

The second car was a respectable distance behind and as she watched it drew back still further.

She shook her head, pleased that the boy racer had passed her without causing an accident. No wonder she'd been spooked.

Ten minutes later she pulled up in the pub car park, climbed out and wrapped the scarf tightly around her neck. There was no rain or snow but it was well below freezing.

She hurried to the entrance, standing to one side as a young couple left and headed towards their car. They were arm-in-arm and giggling and looked very much in love.

The pub itself was busy and had a pleasant and bustling atmosphere with most people clustered as near as they could get to one of two open fires.

Sam approached the bar.

"Good evening," the man behind the bar said. He was young, mid-twenties probably, with an Australian accent. "What can I get you?"

"I was looking for a friend. Bob Matthews. Do you know him?"

"Sorry. I've only been here a week. Vera might know though."

He turned to a woman of about Helen's age who was pulling a pint further along the bar.

"Vera, this lady's asking about a Bob… Sorry, what was

his surname?"

"Matthews," Sam said. "He owns a narrowboat and I know he was moored near here a week or two ago."

Vera smiled. "I know Bob. Be with you in a sec.'

She finished serving, took payment then walked over as the young Aussie moved aside to serve another customer.

"Bob was moored outside," she said, "but he's moved on now."

"Do you know him well?"

She shook her head. "Not as much as I'd like." She smiled and winked. "Handsome fella, but keeps himself to himself. He don't talk much. Good listener though."

"I believe he works on other people's boats."

"Really. I didn't know that. I thought he said he was an engineer. Mind you, he might be telling porkies given the name of his boat." She laughed.

"What's his boat called?"

"Smoke and Mirrors." She laughed. "Perhaps he's a magician and everything he says is an illusion."

"Perhaps." Sam paused. "I don't suppose you know where he went after he left here, do you?"

"I do, as it happens. Cleeve Wood."

"Is that a long way from here?"

Vera laughed again. "You don't know the area, do you? It's about half a mile along the Avon going towards Bath."

"Can I drive there?"

"No, but you can walk. Go to the end of our car park and you'll see a footpath. Follow that and it'll lead you there."

"Thanks."

Chapter 61

The path was easy to find.

After Sam had taken four or five steps it bent to the left and was no longer illuminated by the lights in the pub grounds. She retrieved her phone from her pocket and turned the torch on.

She'd walked a few hundred yards when she heard a rustling from her left. She stopped dead in her tracks and pointed her phone into the trees, but all she saw were fleeting shadows as the light flickered from branch to branch.

She jumped in shock when there was a sudden loud screech, followed by a series of cracks and crackles. A second or two later she saw a bird, possibly an owl, fly up towards the night sky.

Tutting to herself at her stupidity, she wound her scarf more tightly around her neck to fend off the cold and turned the light off, peering forward into the blackness to where she thought the boat might be. There was no indication of any illumination, but after a few seconds her eyes adjusted and she was able to see the moonlight reflecting off the water to the right.

She turned back to the path but it was too dark to see her way forward and she was about to turn the light back on when there was another noise. It was behind her this time.

She spun around and heard a crack. It sounded like a twig snapping.

"Hello," she called. "Is someone there?"

There was no response.

It could have been another bird, but the noise had sounded like it came from ground level.

Could it be a wild animal?

Perhaps it was a badger.

She turned her light on again and shone it back down the path in the direction she had come.

Nothing.

Then she heard another noise, from the wood this time.

She twisted and the beam caught movement as something disappeared behind a tree. It was above the ground, well above the ground.

Too high to be a badger.

"Hello," she called again, a touch of panic in her voice.

Again there was no response.

"Come out. I know you're there."

She hesitated.

Should she plough on or turn back? It was only a few hundred yards to the safety of the car park. If she ran, she could outpace him.

Or was she being stupid?

Could it be a deer? It would have to be a big one.

There was another noise. She shone the light back into the trees and caught an outline.

The outline of a man half-hidden by a tree trunk.

He was big, at least six feet tall. Broad too. She lifted the phone with the thought of shining it directly into his eyes when he left the shelter of the tree.

With any luck, he'd be blinded and she could make her escape.

His head started to appear and she held her phone forwards but as she did so it slipped through her fingers and fell to the ground.

It went instantly dark.

She could still hear him. He had emerged and was moving closer.

Any second now he'd be on her.

"What do you want?" she screamed.

There was an almost silent click and she staggered,

stumbled for a foothold and fell backwards onto the ground.

The next thing she knew she was temporarily blinded as he shone his phone into her face.

"Are you okay?" he asked.

"Get that light out of my eyes!"

He moved his phone to one side and held his hand out to help her up.

She pushed it away. "What the fuck do you think you're doing, Ollie?"

"Sorry. I didn't mean to frighten you."

"You didn't mean to frighten me!" She clambered to her feet and brushed herself down. "What did you think was going to happen? It's late at night, in the middle of nowhere, and you sneak up on me."

"Sorry."

"Stop saying sorry."

"I wanted to find out who you were meeting, that's all. You weren't supposed to see me following you."

"And stalking's okay if you're not spotted, is it?"

"Sorry."

Sam gave a deep sigh. "This has got to stop, Ollie."

"What's got to stop?"

"Well, hunting me down in the middle of the night for starters." She hesitated. "Were you outside my apartment earlier?"

"Yes. I thought you were with someone."

"And what business is that of yours?"

"We're together, Sam. You can't see other people when we're boyfriend and girlfriend."

"What do you mean we're together? We're over, Ollie. Or hasn't that registered?"

"We argued at the restaurant, but couples are always arguing. It doesn't mean we're finished."

"Okay, let me make this abundantly clear. You and I are not a couple. Our relationship has ended and there is zero chance of us ever getting together again. Do you understand?"

"But we're good together."

She gave a dry laugh. "Now you're sounding like Tony."

"Is it Tony you're with now?"

She shook her head in exasperation. "Who I am going out with is nothing to do with you."

"Luke, then?"

She ignored him. "Point your light at the ground. I dropped my phone."

He shone his light down and she spotted her phone, picked it up, switched the light on then turned and headed back towards the pub.

"I'll give you a call," he shouted after her.

She turned back and marched up to him.

"If you come near me again you'll be in deep trouble. Don't forget I'm a black belt."

"Are you threatening me?"

"Yes. Well spotted."

He was pathetic.

She returned to her car and headed back to her apartment.

Chapter 62

Helen was in two minds about Bob.

On the one hand, she knew it was right to have him marked down as a suspect. He'd been at the filming when Erin Douglas had been murdered, and he'd also provoked a fight at Earth Conflict's meeting.

The thing was that he'd been such great company when they were in the pub and then back at his boat. It wasn't just that he was good-looking, though he was definitely that. He was witty and he'd seemed genuinely interested in her.

Could it have been an act? Was he using her as some kind of alibi in the belief that the police would be looking for an individual rather than one-half of a couple?

She laughed. They'd spent one evening together and she was thinking of them as a couple. How ridiculous was that?

She returned her attention to her laptop. She wanted to see if she could dig anything up on Jackie Walker before the evening's Sow the Wind meeting. Given what Maj had discovered about her back-handers from the right honourable Curtis Pinnington MP - not that it seemed that there was much that was honourable about him - there was a chance she'd done something similar in the past.

After an hour or so she gave up. Jackie shared the odd post on Facebook, and occasionally tweeted and retweeted on X, but the subject matter did nothing other than confirm her to be a keen advocate of environmental action.

She changed into her 'Helen-Livingstone-is-an-environmentalist' outfit, put on her heaviest winter coat and headed out to her car.

Ten minutes later Helen parked the Fiat in Kingsmead Square car park and walked the short distance to the Bath

Brew House where Sow the Wind had reserved the Tank Room. It was still twenty minutes ahead of the scheduled start time which would hopefully give her the chance to talk to Jackie.

She was in luck. As on the previous occasion, it was Jackie who greeted her when she arrived.

"Hi, Helen. I'm pleased to see you again."

The room was already buzzing with conversation and Helen could see at least twenty people seated at tables or standing in small groups.

"Hi, Jackie. It looks like a better turnout than last time."

Jackie nodded, clearly pleased. "The message must be getting out that we mean business."

"What you do is very important. My particular bugbear is wind farms."

Jackie frowned. "You don't approve of them?"

"Ach, no. The opposite. It's disgraceful how long it takes to grant planning consent for even a single wind turbine. And don't get me started on the height limits. Other countries in Europe are way ahead of us."

"Now you're talking my language."

"The real question is how we make them sit up and take notice. I've tried writing to my MP but he's useless."

"What constituency are you in?"

"West Wiltshire."

"No wonder, then. You'd have a better chance if you were in South Mendip. Curtis Pinnington's the MP and he's a fervent supporter of ours."

"Will he be here tonight?"

Jackie shook her head. "He's not quite that fervent. He gets us to do the donkey work." She spotted someone over Helen's shoulder. "Will you excuse me, Helen? I've just seen Paul and I want to catch him before the meeting. Let's try and talk afterwards."

"Aye, that would be grand."

She watched as Jackie walked past her and over to the

man who had been so vocal at the first meeting. So, the name of the man who looked like a cleaned-up version of Finn O'Sullivan was Paul, was it? She'd have liked a surname, but it was a start.

Helen moved to the side of the room, stood with her back to the wall and removed her phone from her handbag. She did her best impression of scrolling through messages while zooming the camera in on Jackie and Paul and taking several photos.

More people were coming into the room and she realised she needed to grab a seat before they all filled up. She eyed up a single seat at the end of the second row.

"Is this free?" she said to the woman perched next to the vacant seat. She was in her thirties, Helen thought, though it was difficult to be sure because she was very overweight.

"Yes, no problem." Helen sat down and the woman nudged her and smiled. "Exciting isn't it?" She had a strong Bath accent.

"What do you mean?"

"Being 'ere." The woman lowered her voice. "After what happened in Bristol." She slowed down her speech and widened her eyes. "The murrr-derrr."

Helen took an immediate decision not to let on that she'd been there.

"That's why we're here," the woman went on. She jabbed her elbow into the ribs of the woman next to her. "Isn't it, Trace?"

Trace leaned forward so that Helen could see her face. She was even larger than the first woman but much the same age. "Couldn't miss it, could we," she said. "I said to Millie, I said, we can't miss it. Bound to be questions, aren't there? I mean she was there, wasn't she? That Andrea Manson. She was there and she's on one side and the dead one, she was on the other. They were in opposition and then she's stabbed. I mean, it's very Agatha Christie, isn't it?"

"Mason," Helen said. "Her name's Andrea Mason."

"Or Cluedo," Millie said, ignoring what Helen had said. "In the bathroom with the dagger. Only it wasn't Professor Plum." She laughed at her non-joke. "I wonder whodunnit."

Not as much as I do, Helen thought.

A couple in the row behind were also discussing events at the studio and it dawned on Helen that this explained why numbers were up. They were like people slowing to view the aftermath of an accident on the other carriageway of a motorway. Morbid curiosity had brought them there.

All the seats were taken by the time Andrea Mason emerged from a side door and moved to stand beside Jackie.

"That's her," Trace hissed to Millie. "That's Manson."

Helen wouldn't have been surprised if the women had pulled popcorn out of their handbags.

As at the first meeting, it was Jackie who kicked the meeting off.

"Thanks for coming, everyone. I'm delighted to see so many of you are interested in Sow the Wind?"

Millie put her hand up.

"We'll have plenty of time for questions at the end, if you wouldn't mind waiting," Jackie said pleasantly.

Millie put her hand down and put her mouth to Helen's ear. "Do you know what Sow the Wind is?" she whispered.

Helen kept her voice equally quiet. "An environmental group."

"A what?"

"I'll explain afterwards."

"Ta."

"Please welcome Andrea Mason," Jackie said.

There was a smattering of applause and Andrea started speaking. As on the previous occasion, she talked in a monotone but knew how to grab an audience's attention.

Even Millie and Trace seemed interested in what she was saying, though Helen suspected they were secretly hoping for the topic to move onto the events of the previous week.

Their wishes were met when Andrea finished and Jackie invited questions.

A man at the back immediately stood up. "Andrea," he began, "you're very knowledgeable."

"Thank you," she said.

"So, who do you think did it?"

"If you're talking about the chemicals discharged into the Thames, I believe…"

"The murr-derr," Millie called out.

"Yeah," Trace added. "Whodunnit?"

The meeting descended rapidly from there. Jackie made a valiant attempt to drag the topic back to climate change and greenhouse gas emissions, but 90% of the audience weren't interested. After the fifth question along the same lines, she thanked everyone and said they'd run out of time.

Helen expected the two women next to her to be disappointed but as they stood up Trace said, "Thanks for suggesting this, Millie. I'm looking forward to telling Jan and Katie that we saw her. She's famous and we were here, with her, very close."

"Shall we ask for an autograph?" Millie said.

"Nah, wouldn't be appropriate. She'll have been traumatised, won't she?"

"Yeah, that's true. We don't want to come across as unfeeling. Not after she's been through all that. Fancy a drink?"

"Yeah. Good idea. Let's go to Wetherspoons." She looked at Helen. "Nice to meet you."

Helen smiled. "Have a good rest of the evening."

"Ta," they said in unison and she watched as they waddled to the exit.

Chapter 63

Helen waited in her seat as people streamed out of the room, leaving a few who had been too embarrassed to ask their questions in front of a large number of people.

Two men and two women stood obediently in a queue waiting for their turn with Andrea.

It was clear that Jackie was relieved when the first, an earnest-looking middle-aged man in horn-rimmed glasses, asked for Andrea's views on turning all of the UK's golf courses into forests to reoxygenise the planet. While Andrea answered, Jackie asked the three standing behind him what their questions were.

A few seconds later she sent two of them out with a flea in their ear having discovered their questions related to the death of Erin Douglas.

She walked up to Helen and shook her head. "I can't believe what people are like. The Earth is falling apart and all they care about is that woman's death." She seemed to realise her insensitivity and added hastily, "Not that it wasn't awful, of course." She hesitated. "Look, Helen. I know we said we'd talk after the meeting but would you mind waiting a few minutes? I need to have another word with Paul first."

"Not at all."

"Great. It shouldn't take long."

She went over to Paul, whispered in his ear and then led him to a partitioned-off corner of the room.

Helen waited for a few seconds and then walked casually to the partition and sat down beside it. From that position, she was able to hear every word.

She looked across at Andrea who was still talking intently to the pro-forestation man.

This was a risk, she knew it was, but she was sure Jackie and Paul were planning something and this was an opportunity she couldn't afford to throw up.

"He and I have…" Paul said then paused.

"Have what?" Jackie prompted.

"Let's call it history."

"What does it matter? He's an MP so having him as a supporter helps us."

"You don't know what he's like. He can't be trusted."

"He wants Sow the Wind to have more visibility. Surely that's a good thing."

"He wants to raise his own profile, that's what he wants. He doesn't care about anyone except himself."

"Can't we forget about his involvement and get back to discussing Gilbey?"

Paul didn't raise his voice when he responded but Helen sensed real menace in his words. "You don't fucking understand, Jackie," he said. "I'm not helping Sow the Wind if that man's anywhere near it."

"You have to, Paul. I need your help. He's…"

"He's what?"

"He's paying me to, ah, to ensure we take positive action."

"I don't believe it. That's settled. I'm going to go to his house and stop his involvement once and for all."

"You don't know where he lives."

Paul laughed. "I certainly do."

Helen could sense their discussion was on the verge of ending. She stood up quickly and walked towards Andrea. A few seconds later Paul rushed past her and out of the room.

She watched him go. Jackie hadn't appeared from behind the partition and Helen took an instant decision.

She headed for the exit.

Once outside she saw Paul turn the corner onto Norfolk Buildings. He was walking determinedly, but not so quickly that she couldn't keep up.

He'd said he knew where Curtis Pinnington lived, and she was concerned that he intended to hurt him or worse.

She rang Luke.

"Hi, Helen. How did it go?"

She explained what she'd overheard and her worries about what Paul might do if he got to the MP.

"You're to stop following him," Luke said when she'd finished. "It's too dangerous, Helen. I'll ring DI Gilmore now and tell him to find out where Pinnington lives and get a car there straight away."

"But what if it's only a few hundred yards from here? That poor wee man."

"Helen!"

"Oh dear, I think my battery's dying."

She ended the call and turned her phone off.

Paul was striding down Great Stanhope Street now. He turned right into Nile Street and Helen stopped walking.

Luke was right.

It was too dangerous, and what could she do anyway? Paul might be armed for all she knew.

She stopped walking and turned her phone back on.

Luke rang a minute or so later.

"Where are you?" he asked and she could tell he was worried.

"I've stopped following him. I'm going to walk back to my car."

"Thank goodness. I've spoken to Pete, and Pinnington lives at the top of Marlborough Buildings which is about a mile away. Where did you last see Paul?"

"On Nile Street."

"I'll pass that on. With any luck they can intercept him before he gets there."

"Let me know when you hear, won't you?"

"I will, Helen. Well done."

Helen walked back to her Fiat, unlocked it and climbed

into the driver's seat. It was only then that she realised she was shaking, and not because of the cold.

She couldn't face spending the rest of the evening on her own and pulled her phone out again.

"Hi, Mum," Ronnie said when he answered.

"Hi, Darling. I…" She realised she was crying.

"What's wrong, Mum?"

She wiped her eyes with the base of her palm. "Is it all right if I come to yours? Something's happened and I could do with some company."

"Of course. Are you okay to drive?"

"Aye. I'm not hurt, just shaken up. I'll explain when I get there."

Ten minutes later she parked outside Ronnie and Becky's apartment to find her son standing by the front door. He rushed down, opened the car door and she climbed out and into his arms, relishing the comfort that embracing him gave her.

"Come inside," he said. "It's freezing out here."

"Aye," she said. "I'll explain…"

Her phone started to ring. It was Luke.

"Well?" she said.

"They caught Paul less than a hundred yards from Curtis Pinnington's house. He put up a fight but he's now handcuffed and in the back of a van heading to the Custody Centre."

"That's grand news."

Luke gave a dry laugh. "DCI Bramley has already phoned me to say I can stand our team down now he's caught the murderer."

"Ach, if you ask me I don't think Paul's our man."

"Why's that?"

"I dinnae quite know. He's an angry young man but I don't see him as a serial killer somehow."

"Interesting. I'll let you know if there are any developments."

Ronnie led his mum into the apartment where Becky had already put the kettle on.

"Come on, Mum. Becky's making you a hot chocolate."

She looked up and smiled. "Thanks, Becky."

"No problem." She finished making it and brought it over to Helen, who had dropped into the armchair, then sat next to Ronnie on the sofa.

"What happened?" Ronnie asked.

Helen cradled the mug in her hands as she told them that someone she was investigating had set off to confront an MP. She described how she'd followed Paul for a few hundred yards before calling the police.

"What does this man Paul look like?" Becky asked when she'd finished.

"He's…" She stopped. "Actually, I can show you. I took photos when he was talking to someone earlier."

She clicked on her phone a few times and passed it over. "He does have wild eyes," Becky said as she zoomed in on one of the images. "But he could be quite handsome if it weren't for the ridiculous forked beard."

"Let's have a look," Ronnie said.

She passed the phone over and he almost dropped it in shock. His mouth opened and he looked across at his mother and then back down at the man in the photo.

"What is it?" Helen asked.

"I recognise him. It's Pinky."

"The Pinky you shared a squat with?"

"Definitely. He didn't have a beard when I last saw him but that's him." He paused for a second. "Mum, you didn't tell us the name of the MP."

"It's Curtis Pinnington. He's the Member of Parliament for South Mendip."

Ronnie smiled. "You never knew Pinky's surname, did you?"

She looked at him wide-eyed as she realised what he was implying. "You don't mean…"

Ronnie nodded. "Pinky's surname is Pinnington. Curtis Pinnington is his father."

Chapter 64

Luke dropped Chloe, Ben and Pippa off at Bath Spa railway station and then headed towards the office.

He was almost there when Pete rang.

"Luke, could you come to Portishead this morning?"

"I've got a meeting with Edward Filcher at 9:30. Can I come after that?"

"I'd prefer it if you came earlier. Applejack's going to be running around like a headless chicken when he gets in."

"Because of Paul Pinnington?"

"You guessed it. I could do with your help."

"I'll head there now." He looked at the dashboard. "I should be there by nine."

"Great. You should beat him in. Thanks, Luke."

"One other thing, Pete. Could you bring Gemma Turnbull in for a second interview?"

"Sure. Why?"

"Something she said has had me thinking. I want her to clarify something for me."

Luke hung up and called Sam.

"Morning, Sam," he said when she answered. "Good weekend?"

"Interesting."

"In what way?"

She laughed. "I'll tell you when I see you. Did you have a good time with Ben and Chloe?"

"Yes, thanks. Ben and Pippa are engaged."

"That's fantastic news." She paused. "It won't be long before you're a granddad."

It was his turn to laugh. "Nice try, but I'm not rising to the bait. Have you spoken to Helen this morning?"

"No. I'm not in the office yet. Why?"

He explained what had happened with Paul Pinnington.

"Fancy that," she said when he'd finished. "Is he still a suspect?"

"At the moment, yes. I'm on my way to Avon and Somerset HQ now. That's the reason I'm ringing."

Her reply was instant. "Yes, I'll deputise for you."

He smiled. She knew it was Filcher's 9:30 team meeting every Monday and was one step ahead of him.

Perhaps I could ask her out to dinner as a thank you, was the first thought that came into his mind, but what he said was, "Thanks, Sam. I owe you."

"I'll hold you to that."

"I'm hoping to be in the office later. Good luck with Filcher."

"Thanks. Take care, Luke."

He hung up and realised he was still smiling, though he wasn't sure why.

Forty minutes later he walked into the incident room and Pete immediately led him off to a table at the side of the room.

"I was called in yesterday evening when Paul Pinnington was brought in," he said, keeping his voice low.

"Did you get much out of him?"

Pete shook his head. "Not a lot, but I kept it brief. He'll need to be interviewed properly this morning."

"Was Applejack with you?"

"No. I rang him at home and he said he was under the weather and he'd deal with him this morning."

"Lazy sod."

"Who is?"

Luke turned to see DCI Bramley standing behind them. "Good morning, Jack," he said pleasantly. "Are you feeling better?"

"What do you mean?"

"Pete said you were poorly yesterday."

"Mmm. Yes, I'm fine." The corners of his lips turned

down. "What are you doing here?"

"I thought you might need my help."

"Thank you, but this is a police matter."

"And I'm a police consultant."

"You're a civilian, and you're treading on my patch."

"Don't worry. You're the SIO and I wouldn't dream of interfering."

"Good." He turned to Pete. "DI Gilmore, I'd like to interview Paul Pinnington now. Please can you arrange it?"

"Of course," Pete said. "Do you and Luke want to grab a coffee before you go in?"

"It will be you and me conducting the interview." He gestured to Luke. "I don't want him anywhere near it."

"I'm sitting right here, Jack," Luke said.

"The Chief insisted he be in on it," Pete said.

"She what!" Applejack twisted around as if she was concealed somewhere in the room. "When? How?"

"She came down about fifteen minutes ago, sir. I told her Luke was on the way in and she said she'd like him to lead the interview because of his skills and experience."

Applejack's lips trembled. "Lead the interview!"

"With you there as well since you're the SIO."

"I... But..." He looked at Luke, harrumphed loudly and then added "Bah!" to emphasise his annoyance before turning and leaving the room.

"I'm surprised but pleased that the Chief said that," Luke said once he'd gone.

"I'm sure she would have done," Pete said with a smile, "but I haven't seen her today."

*

Twenty minutes later Luke and Applejack were sitting opposite a sullen-looking Paul Pinnington.

He was exactly as Helen had described him, a man who

would have been handsome were it not for his ridiculous forked beard and long brown braided hair.

"I don't know why I'm here," he said. "What have I done?"

"You killed three people," Applejack said. He sneered. "That's what you've done."

Pinnington sat back and folded his arms. "You're talking shit."

"Don't talk to me like that, young man. I'm a Detective Chief Inspector."

"I don't care if you're the Queen of Sheba."

Luke decided to step in before it descended still further.

"Mr Pinnington," he said, "may I call you Paul."

"Yes, that's okay."

"Good. I'm Luke." He smiled. "DCI Bramley and I are investigating a series of murders and your name came up. We need to ask you some questions before we can eliminate you from our enquiries. I'll need to record our interview. Is that okay?"

"I suppose so."

"And you're sure you don't want a solicitor?"

"Positive. I haven't got anything to hide."

"I'm not so sure," Applejack said.

Pinnington looked at Luke and indicated Applejack with his thumb. "You need to keep him under control. Are you his boss?"

Applejack puffed his chest out. "I am the SIO," he asserted. "He is not my boss."

"I thought you were the DCI?"

"I'm both."

Luke held his hand up to stop them, then pressed the button on the recording device.

"Interview with Paul Pinnington in Interview Room 4 at Avon and Somerset Police Head Office." He checked his watch. "The time is 09:48. Interview conducted by DCI Jack Bramley and Luke Sackville."

"Are you a civilian, Luke?" Pinnington asked.

"Yes, he is," Applejack said. "I'm the only police officer here."

Luke held his hand up again before Pinnington could respond.

"Paul," he began, "are you a member of Sow the Wind, an environmental group?"

"Yes. I joined recently."

"And is it true that you advocated a more violent form of action at one of the group's meetings?"

"No."

Luke raised an eyebrow. "Are you sure? We have a witness who told us that you said it was needed to improve visibility."

"Your witness is lying."

"Okay. Moving on, how would you describe your relationship with your father?"

Pinnington shrugged. "We don't get on."

"When did you last see him?"

"A few years ago."

"And yet you stormed out of a Sow the Wind meeting with the intention of going to his house?"

"I didn't storm out."

"Why did you decide to see him last night?"

"Because he's a hypocritical bastard, that's why."

"What do you mean?"

"His claims to be green and in favour of action against climate change are garbage. He used to be paid by the Sturridge Group. Did you know that?"

"Go on."

"All he's interested in is himself. And I found out last night that he's paying Jackie Walker to do his dirty work for him. I wanted to confront him with it, that was why I was going to his house."

"Jackie Walker?"

"Yes. She's in Sow the Wind and she's the one who's

promoting violence. Jackie's the person you ought to be interviewing, not me."

Chapter 65

Paul Pinnington was allowed to go home without being charged, and Luke and Applejack returned to the incident room.

"How did it go?" Pete asked when they walked in.

Applejack smiled. "We've got our killer."

"Did he confess then?"

"Oh no. It's not Pinnington. I knew that straight away." He tapped the side of his nose. "It's my copper's nose."

"Is it?" Luke said. "I thought it was acne."

Applejack ignored him. "Have Jackie Walker brought in, DI Gilmore. She's our murderer."

"How do you know?" Pete asked

"It's obvious." He tapped his nose again. "Bring in Curtis Pinnington as well. He's been paying her to kill people."

"Bring the MP in?"

"Didn't you hear me the first time?"

"Ah, given he's a Member of Parliament, would it be wise to make the Chief Constable aware that you're pulling him in for questioning?"

Applejack hesitated as he thought this through. "As I said, I'll let you know when to bring Curtis Pinnington in. I need to run it by the Chief first. In the meantime, get that woman Walker in."

"Yes, sir."

Applejack nodded, looked briefly at Luke and then turned and left the room.

"While you were interviewing Paul Pinnington," Pete said, "an ID came through for the body found in the shallow grave. His name's Brett Napier."

"Did you say Brett?"

"Yes. Why?"

"Just a second."

Luke called Josh's mobile.

"Morning, guv."

"Josh, did you manage to locate Finn O'Sullivan at the weekend?"

"Yes. He and Shannon were in Southgate again."

"Did you find out anything useful?"

"Shannon told me that a punch was thrown when they stormed out of the Earth Conflict meeting. It was Nick and he gave Brett a black eye."

"I don't suppose you found out their surnames did you?"

"I did actually. Shannon's surname is Wilson, Nick's is Atkinson and Brett's is Napier."

"I thought that might be the case."

"Why, guv?"

"Brett Napier's dead. It was his body found in Ham Woods."

"Wowza!" Josh paused. "That doesn't fit though, does it, guv?"

"How do you mean?"

"Well, the first two killed, Scott Finlay and Erin Douglas, they're anti-environmentalists, whereas Brett was in Earth Conflict."

"Good point, Josh."

"I'll update the whiteboard."

"Thanks. I'll see you later."

Luke hung up and explained to Pete who Brett Napier was. "Josh is right," he mused.

"What about?"

"It doesn't fit. Why would someone murder two people on one side of the environmental argument and then a third on the other?"

"Unless he or she is just plain nuts."

"Mmm. I wonder if Brett found out what the murderer

was up to and was killed because of that."

"If that's the case it means our main suspects have to be the members of Earth Conflict. How many are there, Luke?"

"Only three now that Brett Napier's dead. Finn O'Sullivan, the founder, plus Shannon Wilson and Nick Atkinson. There's someone else who was at their last meeting that we need to look into as well. His name's Bob Matthews."

Pete's phone rang. He listened for a few seconds, then said, "Please take her to Interview Room 4." He looked across at Luke. "They've brought Gemma Turnbull in."

"Did you check the CCTV for Antonio Scarapucci's nighttime visits to Sainsbury's and the housing estate?"

Pete nodded. "He was caught in Sainsbury's car park at twenty past midnight and driving around the estate at just after 12:45."

"Thanks."

A few minutes later Luke and Pete walked into the interview room to find Gemma Turnbull sitting back on a chair with her feet on the table. She had again overdone the makeup, but this time her lips were a deep purple with matching mascara. The black leather tunic was gone and in its place was a black jumper over navy blue slacks.

She was chewing gum and looked first at Pete before settling on Luke. "I ought to fucking sue you for this."

"Why's that?" Luke asked.

"Dragging me out here. Lost income, innit?"

Luke pushed her legs off the table as he and Pete sat down.

"Eh! Whatcha doin' knobhead?. It's fucking ten quid for foreplay, big boy."

"Price gone up has it, Gemma?"

She ignored him.

Pete started the recording device. "Interview with Gemma Turnbull in Interview Room 4 at Avon and

Somerset Police HQ. It is 10:33. Conducting the interview are DI Pete Gilmore and Luke Sackville."

"Gemma," Luke began, "why did you lie to us about the events at the Park and Ride?"

He noticed her eyes widen slightly before she answered. "I didn't."

"You told us you saw someone putting a body into a Dumpy Bag at one in the morning."

"Yeah. That's right."

"And you're sure about the time?"

"Yeah. Fucking said I was sure last time."

"Because we have another witness who said he spotted the body between 12:20 and 12:45."

"He's lying."

"We know he's not. We've got him on CCTV."

"Maybe it was earlier. Yeah, now I think back it was more like midnight."

"How much were you paid, Gemma?"

"Whatcha mean?"

Luke turned to Pete. "DI Gilmore, am I right when I say that Gemma could be found guilty through common purpose?"

Pete nodded. "You are indeed."

"Which means she could be liable for life imprisonment?"

"That's correct."

Gemma looked from one man to the other during this exchange then leaned forward over the table and glared at Luke. "Hang on a minute," she said. "What the fuck is 'common purpose'?"

Luke smiled. "It's a concept in UK law that says if you engage in criminal activity as part of a group, you become criminally liable for anything done by any member of the group in the course of the crime. In this case, murder."

She shook her head. "I wasn't involved in no murder."

"Of course, it could be that you face a lesser charge of

aiding and abetting an offender, or possibly conspiracy to pervert the course of justice."

"Is that better?"

Luke turned to Pete. "What's the maximum charge for aiding an offender, DI Gilmore?"

"Ten years."

Gemma gulped. "Fuck's sake."

"Of course, if you help us with our enquiries, and we catch our killer, we might decide to drop all charges."

She hesitated, but only for a second.

"He didn't give me no money."

"What do you mean?"

She laughed but there was no humour in it. "The only fucking thing he gave me was that black eye."

"What happened, Gemma?"

"He booked me, like, you know, as a client. But when we met, instead of wanting Humpty Dumpty he started threatening me."

"Humpty Dumpty?"

"Yeah. It's this special thing I do. I get most of my clients that way. Kinky fuckers they are. I get an egg…"

Luke held his hand up. "It's all right, Gemma, you don't need to explain. You said he threatened you?"

"Yeah. He said if I didn't do what he asked he'd hunt me. Made it clear what that meant. Fuck, he's scary."

"And he told you to tell the police you'd seen someone putting the body in the Dumpy Bag?"

"Yeah, and to say I found that picture thing. Only he told me to say it was a woman I'd seen. A woman with, like, what's it called, raster-fer-arian hair."

"Dreadlocks?"

"Yeah, them. Only I thought I'd say it might be a man so you stood a chance of catching him."

"What name did he use to book you?"

"Robin."

"And can you describe him?"

"He had his head and face covered so all I saw were his eyes. He was a big bastard though. Broad shoulders and tall. Not as tall as you, but then you're a fucking giant."

"Anything else you can tell us about him?"

She thought about this for a second. "Yeah. He had a deep voice and sounded posh, which was weird given what he said he might do to me."

Chapter 66

Sam wondered if she should tell Luke what Ollie had done.

It had been upsetting and, until she discovered it was her ex-boyfriend, scary. She needed to talk it through with someone and she knew Luke was a great listener and would say all the right things. He was always a comfort if anything was wrong.

However, there were two very good reasons not to confide in him.

First, he would very much disapprove of her setting out on her own to locate Bob Matthews. Not because she was a woman and he thought her in any way weak. No, he wasn't like that. He'd disapprove because he'd think that doing something like that on your own was downright stupid.

He'd be right too.

Second, she hated to think what Luke would do to Ollie if he knew he'd stalked her and frightened her half to death. Mind you, the stupid sod deserved anything coming his way.

Her phone rang and she saw it was him.

"Hi, Luke. Have you left yet?"

"I'm afraid I'm not going to make it today. A lot's happened in the case and we're pursuing several leads."

She felt an immediate pang of disappointment. "What are the developments?"

"Well, for a start… Just a second." He came back on the line a few seconds later. "Sorry, Sam. I'll have to go. DCI Bramley and I are set to interview Jackie Walker and she's just arrived."

"Jackie Walker? The woman from Sow the Wind."

"Yes. I'll explain everything in the morning."

"Okay. Take care."

"You too, Sam."

She hung up and stared at the phone for a second.

'You too' he'd said.

Did that mean anything?

She shook her head.

Of course, it didn't.

*

It was coming up to six o'clock when Sam decided she'd done enough work for the day. In any case, she needed to ensure she had enough time to get ready for her evening out.

Josh and Maj had already gone home, but Helen was still working away on her laptop.

"I'm off, Helen," she said as she stood up to grab her coat.

"I'll be leaving soon too, but I want to finish this wee report first. Have a nice time tonight. I hope the show's good."

"Thanks. See you in the morning."

Once she was in the car, her thoughts turned to the evening ahead.

She was pleased Liz was coming. It meant she wasn't playing gooseberry to Hannah and Bertie but also, and more importantly, they'd got on well when they'd had lunch together and she felt like they could become close friends.

What was odd was the fact that Liz had sensed chemistry between her and Luke and assumed they were in a relationship.

She wondered if it might be worth opening up to her. If Liz knew her true feelings for Luke she might be able to offer some advice.

However, it was a big call given she hardly knew the woman. She decided it would be best to see how the evening went and play it by ear.

Liz was standing on her own outside the Theatre Royal when she got there, while Hannah and Bertie were only a couple of yards away.

"Hi, Sam," Hannah and Liz said at the same time.

Sam laughed and made introductions.

"And there I was thinking what a happy couple you were," Liz said when she'd finished, "little knowing who you were."

"And now you think we're an unhappy couple?" Hannah said.

Liz smiled and Sam could tell that she knew Hannah was joking. "Absolutely. The two of you look as if you hate each other's guts."

"That look's reserved for Ollie," Sam said. "You wouldn't believe what he did on Saturday night."

She told them what had happened and then they took the conversation into the theatre bar.

Sam was pleased with the way Hannah and Liz seemed to immediately hit it off and by the time the buzzer went, indicating it was time to go to their seats, they were teasing each other mercilessly.

The performance itself was enjoyable, and as they walked out of the theatre they discussed its relative merits set against the film. They all agreed the cast had done a great job, but that without Patrick Swayze it didn't have quite the same impact.

"We're going to have to go," Hannah said when they emerged onto Saw Close.

"Sorry," Bertie said. "It's my fault. I've got an early start tomorrow."

They said their goodbyes and the couple headed off towards Kingsmead.

"Fancy a drink?" Liz asked.

"I'd love one," Sam said. "Shall we go to The Salamander?"

"Can do, although I've never even heard of it."

"It's where Ollie and I had our first date, but I'm not going to hold that against it." She laughed. "Come on, it's just around the corner."

Once in the pub they took a table opposite the bar and Sam bought a bottle of Prosecco to share.

As at their lunch, and earlier in the evening, conversation flowed freely. There were some dark moments as Sam related a couple of the more 'exciting' investigations that the Ethics Team had undertaken, but in the main they kept things light.

They'd been there about an hour when the barman called last orders and Sam had to look at her watch to take in the fact that it was already 11 pm.

"We must do this again," she said.

"Definitely."

"Do you want to share a taxi?"

"It's okay. I live just off The Circus so it's an easy walk from here."

They finished their drinks and went outside.

"Thanks for a great evening," Liz said. "It's great to wind down, especially given the complete arse Henry's been."

"At least he seems to have got over himself," Sam said. "Let's hope he continues like that."

Liz held up both hands with her fingers crossed. "Let's hope."

She turned and headed up John Street. It was completely quiet at that time of the night and she kept to the middle of the road.

Sam was smiling as she watched her walk away, pleased that she and Liz had formed a bond. She hadn't had the courage to ask her advice about Luke, but there was always next time.

She started to turn to head towards Milsom Street, where she knew she'd easily be able to get a taxi, when she noticed Liz had stopped walking. She was some forty yards up the street and had moved onto the pavement. She appeared to be talking to someone who was hidden from view in an alley or doorway on the right-hand side.

A second later Sam watched as a gloved hand stretched out and grabbed Liz's arm. She tried to resist but whoever it was was too strong, and she was pulled off the pavement and disappeared from view.

Chapter 67

Sam didn't hesitate.

She dropped her bag and ran at full pelt up the road. Within five seconds she reached the point where Liz had disappeared from view, looked to her right and saw her friend immediately.

Liz was no more than five paces away. The alley was narrow and dark, but there was enough light trickling through from John Street for Sam to see that she was on her back.

Her attacker, and Sam was sure it had to be a man because of his bulk, was kneeling on her chest. He had his left hand over her mouth and was reaching into his back pocket with his right.

He heard Sam and looked up. A balaclava covered most of his face, but she saw his eyes widen. Meanwhile, Liz continued squirming beneath him, her muffled screams barely audible.

"Fuck off!" he shouted at the top of his voice, while at the same time bringing his right hand around and into the air. She saw light reflecting off the blade of his knife as he waved it in her direction.

She didn't move.

"You're next, bitch!" he screamed.

He turned his attention back to Liz and brought his hand down towards her throat.

Sam's karate instructor had taught her that there were only two ways to deal with an attacker armed with a knife. Give him what he's asking for, or get the hell out of there.

Neither was possible in this situation.

Liz's life depended on her actions in the next split-second, and running away wasn't an option.

Her only chance was to exert what was known in karate as 'two on one control'. He was strong, she was sure of that, but his weapon arm was his weakness.

She leapt forward, grasped his knife arm with both hands and twisted while pulling it away from Liz's throat. By leveraging the rotation in this way she was able to generate more power and force.

He tried to resist, but she had surprise on her side. He gasped as the knife clattered to the ground, then pulled his left hand away from Liz's mouth and stretched out for the handle.

Liz took the opportunity to scream for help at the top of her voice.

Sam kicked the knife out of the attacker's reach and then released his arm. He stood upright, growled, formed his right hand into a fist and drew his arm back to strike.

She almost smiled at his naivety as she pivoted on her left foot and lifted, then extended, her right leg, striking him on the side of his head with her instep.

He fell to the ground, glared across at her and then lifted himself to all fours, ready to get to his feet.

He wouldn't be as naive a second time, she knew that, and she fired another kick at him, this one not so much out of the karate manual as out of pure instinct. She caught him on the chin and his head jerked backwards as he toppled backwards into the alley wall and then slid to the ground.

He was out for the count.

Sam put her hands on her thighs, gasping for breath, and heard footsteps behind her. She turned her head to see the Salamander's barman staring in horror at the montage in front of him.

"Call the police," Sam managed to say as she inhaled lungfuls of air.

She glanced at the man now unconscious against the wall, his head flopped down over his chest.

"Ask them to send an ambulance as well."

Chapter 68

Sam had the knife in her hands and was keeping a close eye on Liz's assailant. She intended to use it if necessary should he regain consciousness.

She gave a sigh of relief when she heard the sound of a siren after no more than three or four minutes. A few seconds later, a police Volvo screeched around the corner and pulled up in front of Liz who was standing in the middle of John Street waving her arms above her head.

Two constables, one male and one female, climbed out of the car and strode over. The male officer produced an evidence bag and held it open for Sam to drop the knife in.

"I'm PC Stratton," the female officer said. She was the older of the two by a decade or more. "This is PC Davies." She looked at the knife in the bag and then at the man lying unconscious against the wall. "What happened? Did he try to mug you?"

"He tried to kill my friend," Sam said, gesturing towards Liz. "I managed to disarm him."

"Tried to kill her?" PC Davies asked in tones of amazement.

Sam nodded. "I think he's the man responsible for the murders of Scott Finlay, Erin Douglas and Brett Napier."

"Fucking hell!" The young officer put his hand to his mouth.

"Darren!" PC Stratton said.

"Sorry, but, well…" He stared at the man accused of being a triple murderer.

"You need to ring Detective Inspector Gilmore," Sam said, and decided a touch of exaggeration might be useful. "He's leading the investigation."

"I'll do that in a minute," PC Stratton said. "Darren,

let's handcuff him. We don't want to risk him coming to."

PC Davies pulled the man forward while she secured his hands. As they were doing this an ambulance pulled up and two paramedics climbed out and walked towards them.

The older of the two, a man in his early fifties, looked first at Liz and then at Sam.

"Is it one of you two who's been hurt?" he asked.

"We're fine," Sam said, then gestured towards the unconscious man, "but I can't say the same for him."

The paramedic knelt down and gently lifted the balaclava off the man's head. "Looks like he's broken his jaw." He looked back at Sam and rubbed his chin. "I don't see how he's done that when it's clear he fell backwards against the wall."

"I kicked him," Sam said. "Twice. Once on the side of his head and then his face."

The paramedic's eyes widened and he looked at her for a second or two before calling to his colleague. "We'll need a stretcher, Ron."

"Be right there."

He turned back to Sam and Liz. "Are you sure you're both okay?"

Sam looked at Liz. "Are you hurt at all, Liz?"

"Bruised where he pushed me over, but aside from that I'm fine." She swallowed. "A bit shaky but I guess that's understandable."

"I'd like you both to come to the station and give statements if that's all right?" the female officer asked.

They both confirmed it was fine.

The paramedics laid the stretcher on the ground and were about to lift their patient onto it when his head jerked up and his eyes shot open. A fraction of a second later he screamed in pain as he registered the pain from his broken jaw.

He tried to pull his arms from his back before realising his hands were cuffed together, then it dawned on him that he'd been captured and there was no escape. He scowled at Sam before blinking his eyes closed as the pain hit him again.

PC Stratton rang DI Gilmore, spoke to him for a moment or two then looked over at Sam. "What are your names?"

Sam told her and she relayed the information down the line. She and the DI exchanged a few more words and then she hung up and turned back to the two women.

"Another car's on its way so that there's someone to keep an eye on…" She paused. "Do you know his name?"

Sam shook her head. "I've never seen him before."

Chapter 69

Luke was standing at the back door waiting for Wilkins to come in after his regular last thing at night anointing of a plant pot when his phone rang. It was Pete.

"We've got him, Luke. We've captured our triple murderer."

"What? That's great news. How?"

"He had a…"

The line started breaking up and he couldn't catch the next few words.

"Sorry, I lost that, Pete. What did you say?"

"…knife …attacked a woman…"

Wilkins chose that moment to reappear. He was holding in his mouth, as he often did, a present for his master. On this occasion it was a rotten apple. Luke absent-mindedly retrieved a dog biscuit from a drawer and held it out. The cocker immediately dropped the apple and took the goodie from his hand. A split-second later it had been munched and swallowed and Wilkins sat back on his haunches patiently awaiting another treat.

"Did you say he had a knife and attacked a woman?"

"Yes… Sam…"

Luke's heart fell.

Surely not!

"Did you say Sam? Sam Chambers?"

"… Royal United Hospital… don't know his name…"

Luke ended the call and rang Pete's number, praying he was able to get an improved connection.

Pete answered immediately.

"Hi, Luke."

"That's better. I can hear you properly now. What's happened to Sam?"

"She caught our man." He laughed. "She broke his jaw in the process though and he's currently on the way to the RUH."

"Is she okay?"

"Yes. She wasn't hurt at all."

"Thank goodness. Where is she?"

"They've taken her into Redbridge House to take a statement."

"And she's definitely unhurt?"

Pete laughed again. "I assure you she's fine. The way you talk anyone would think you were a couple."

"So what's the name of our man?"

"He won't say."

"And Sam didn't recognise him?"

"No."

"Mmm. I might know someone who will."

He hung up and rang Josh.

"Hi, guv. It's Luke."

"I know who I am, son"

"No. I was telling Leanne who it is. It's you."

"I know it's me. Listen, forget all that. Can you come to the RUH with me?"

"Sure. Have you hurt yourself?"

"No."

"Ah. Right. He hasn't hurt himself." Josh paused. "Why then?"

"I'll explain on the way."

"You mean you want to go now? He wants to go now."

"Yes."

"But it's nearly midnight."

"I'll pick you up in twenty and explain on the way."

"He'll pick me up in twenty…"

Luke hung up, shut Wilkins in his dog crate, locked the front door and climbed into the Beemer.

As soon as he'd set off he rang Sam.

"I heard what happened. Are you okay?"

"I'm fine. Liz is a bit bruised though."

"Liz?"

"Liz Rathbone. He was going to cut her throat, Luke. She was lucky I was there. Five seconds later and she'd have been a goner."

"Pete told me that you didn't recognise him?"

"No. It's not Bob Matthews though."

"How do you know?"

"Too young. It's not Finn O'Sullivan either. No dreadlocks."

"In that case, I think I know who it is but I'm taking Josh to the RUH to confirm it."

He paused. Should he suggest seeing her after he'd been to the hospital? She might feel okay now, but when realisation of what might have happened hit her she'd need someone to support her.

But no, that was silly. By the time she'd been interviewed it would be the early hours of the morning. The last thing she'd want was her boss wading in. Besides, she had her mum and Hannah and she was close to both of them.

"I'll see you in the office in the morning," she said.

"Ah, yes."

"Take care."

"You too, Sam."

Fifteen minutes later he pulled up outside Josh's apartment to find him waiting on the pavement. He climbed in and they set off.

"So what's all this about, guv?"

Luke told him about the evening's events and who he thought the killer was.

"Wowza! You really think it's him?"

"I do indeed. The police will find out in the end but it'll buy valuable time if I'm right and you can confirm it."

Josh grinned.

The prisoner was in a private room in A&E. A police

officer was stationed outside and talking to a young female doctor in scrubs.

"I'm sorry, sir," the officer said as they approached. "No one's allowed in."

"He won't be able to talk anyway," the doctor said. "He's broken his jaw in two places and it's likely that he'll need MMF."

"MMF?" Luke asked.

She nodded. "Maxillomandibular fixation. The upper and lower jaw will need to be wired together for six weeks to stabilise the fracture while it heals. It's going to be extremely uncomfortable and he'll be in a lot of pain."

"That's good news," Luke said.

The doctor raised an eyebrow at this but he ignored her and turned to the police officer.

"It's PC Abney, isn't it?"

"That's right." He looked at Luke again. "Sorry, sir. I didn't recognise you."

Luke smiled. "That's okay. Listen, I only need a minute. My colleague," he indicated Josh, who was beaming from ear to ear at the thought that he was playing such a critical role, "might know who this man is. All I need is for him to go in for a few seconds to have a look."

PC Abney turned to the doctor. "Is that okay with you, Dr Lambert?"

"If they're not going to ask him to speak then yes, it's fine with me."

He turned back to Luke. "Very well then, sir."

Luke pushed the door open and Josh stepped in, then almost immediately back out again, the beaming grin even wider.

"It's him," he said. "It's Nick Atkinson."

Chapter 70

Luke was surprised to see Josh when he got into the office. He was sitting at his desk while Maj and Helen stood over him, listening intently.

He walked over. "Morning, everyone. I didn't expect you in so early Josh, given it was gone one when I dropped you home."

Josh looked up at him, his grin now appearing to be cemented into place.

"I couldn't sleep, guv. I've been telling Maj and Helen all about last night," he said. "Good result, eh?"

"Definitely."

"I was wondering if Nick Atkinson's ex-military."

"Why's that?"

"When he threatened Brett, before they all stormed out of the Earth Conflict meeting, he pulled his sleeves up." He pointed to the inside of his left arm between the elbow and the wrist. "He had a tattoo about here and it looked like a dagger with wings. I'm sure that's an army symbol of some kind."

"Hang on a minute," Maj said. "Can you draw it?"

"Sure."

Josh walked to the whiteboard and drew a downwards-pointing dagger. On either side, he drew wings that appeared to spout from the handle before bending upwards.

"That's not a dagger, and those aren't wings either."

"I take it you know what it represents," Luke said.

Maj nodded. "A friend of mine's got the same tattoo. He's sworn to secrecy about his missions but he told me which unit it represents. It's the sword of Excalibur and those," he pointed to the wings Josh had drawn, "are flames. It signifies that the unit will come back to life whenever England needs it."

"Go on," Josh said. "Don't keep us in suspense."

Maj smiled. "Our triple murderer Nick Atkinson was in the SAS."

"Wowza!"

Luke rubbed his chin as he looked at Josh's drawing. "I wonder…"

"What are you thinking?" Helen asked.

He turned to Josh. "Did he come across as someone with psychopathic tendencies, Josh?"

"Not at all. He advocated violence but he always seemed very much in control of himself."

"Mmm. I'm starting to think he was being paid by someone else, someone who wanted these people dead but didn't want to do the dirty work themselves."

"You mean a paid assassin?"

"Exactly."

"Wowza duo!"

Luke's phone rang and he saw it was Pete. He accepted the call and stepped away from the others.

"Hi, Pete. How's it going?"

"What the hell do you think you're doing?" Applejack shouted down the phone.

Luke pulled the phone away from his ear for a second, then put it back but kept it a few inches away to ensure his eardrums weren't blown off.

"Well?" Applejack went on. "What in blazes were you thinking? Tell me that, eh! Tell me that."

Luke kept his tone pleasant. "What's the matter, Jack? Are you upset that one of my team caught the murderer?"

"I… You…" He was spluttering, so incandescent with rage that he was unable to articulate his words. "I was in charge, fully in control, of the investigation. What do you mean by barging into the hospital last night demanding to see my prisoner?"

"We identified him for you, Jack."

"It's not bloody good enough. First, you send your woman after him, putting her in danger, instead of letting the police deal with it…"

"Sam is not 'my woman', Jack."

Applejack ignored him. "Then, and this is what really gets my goat, then you try to garner praise for yourself by beating us to ID'ing him."

Jack waited.

"Well? Well?"

"Have you finished, Jack?"

"No, I haven't bloody finished."

Luke waited.

Nothing.

He waited some more, but all he could hear was the sound of the other man breathing heavily and grunting.

"I've had it up to here with you, *Mister* Luke Sackville." Applejack said eventually, putting as much emphasis on the word 'Mister' as he could muster. "Hah. At least you'll be out of my hair now we've got our man. Good riddance too."

"What about his paymaster?"

"What are you talking about, paymaster?"

"I believe that Nick Atkinson is a mercenary, a hitman who was paid to do what he did."

"Don't talk balderdash."

"The investigation needs to continue. If you don't catch the man behind these murders he'll find another paid assassin to do his dirty work."

"You're talking out of your hat. I am the SIO, thank goodness, and I don't need to listen to your ridiculous theories. This is police work. Stay out of it. We've caught our murderer and that's the end of it."

"I'm sure when we interview him…"

"There's no 'we' about it. You're out of this case, Sackville. I'm putting a report into the Chief and recommending that your consultancy work is terminated immediately. I can't believe you stormed in on a prisoner like that. It shows a complete lack of respect."

"Have you finished now, Jack?"

The line went dead.

"Problems?" Helen called over.

Luke shook his head. "Nothing I can't handle."

He rang Pete's number back.

"Sorry about that, Luke. He grabbed the phone off me and I couldn't stop him."

"Where is he now?"

"God knows."

"Listen, Pete. I don't believe Nick Atkinson was working alone. I think he's a paid hitman and I suspect he'll 'no comment' his way through interviews. Are you able to get the team looking into his background?"

"Already on it."

"Good. Get them to look into his military record. He's got an SAS tattoo on his arm."

"I'll do that."

"And see if they can track down his whereabouts before these killings started. If I'm right, and he's a professional assassin, he'll be responsible for other hits. If we can find out where he's lived over the past few years we might be able to link him to unsolved murder cases."

"Good thinking. I'll get the guys onto it."

"Great. I've got another theory I want to follow up on. It's a long shot but I'll let you know if I get anywhere."

He hung up.

"Good morning, Luke," Sam said. She took her coat off and walked over to him. "Sorry I'm late in."

"Don't be ridiculous. I'm surprised you're in at all after last night. You did fantastically and you saved Liz Rathbone's life."

He saw a trace of pink appear on her cheeks.

"We've got him and she's safe now," she said after a few

seconds. "That's what's important."

He frowned. "Not necessarily." He explained his theory that Nick Atkinson was being paid.

"Can I help?" she asked when he'd finished.

"There is one thing. Could you try to track down a Jason Mullins for me? I don't know much about him I'm afraid."

She smiled. "I'll do what I can."

He returned her smile and was struck in that instant by how beautiful she looked. He'd always thought her attractive, but she was truly...

"Well," she said, tapping her notebook with her pen.

"Sorry, I was miles away. Ah, Jason is about my age and he went to Harrow."

"The public school?"

"Yes. Last I knew his parents lived near Inverness. I don't know any more than that I'm afraid."

"I'll get onto it straight away."

He watched her as she turned and walked to her desk, then shook his head and picked up his phone.

He had a crucial call to make.

Chapter 71

Luke looked down at the phone number on his pad.

Had he got it all wrong? Sure, the man had told a few falsehoods, but did it follow that he was Nick Atkinson's paymaster? What possible motive did he have?

But then again, there was the incident with the book. What he'd said could have been a slip of the tongue, but if it wasn't…

He needed a couple more pieces to complete the jigsaw. If Sam was able to track Jason Mullins down he might provide one of them, but he needed to tread carefully for the other if he was going to solicit an honest answer.

He rang the number.

"Hello," Jackie Walker said. She sounded tentative, but that didn't surprise him given the grilling he and Applejack had given her the day before.

"Hi, Jackie. It's Luke Sackville."

"Oh, hello." She lowered her voice. "I told you and DCI Bramley everything yesterday."

"Don't worry. All I'm ringing for is to see if you've got a number for Andrea Mason."

"Why? You're not going to tell her what I did, are you?"

"No. It's about something completely different."

"You're sure?"

"I'm sure. Have you got her number?"

"She's here now. We've been planning our next meeting but she's popped to the loo. Oh, hang on."

There was a short pause and then Andrea came on the phone.

"Hello?" she said and there was an implicit question in the word.

"Hi, Andrea. My name's Luke Sackville. I've been

working with the police looking into Erin Douglas's murder."

"I've already told the police everything I know. DCI Bramley interviewed me at the studio."

"I appreciate that. Do you mind if I ask you a personal question?"

She hesitated. "Why would you want to do that?"

"Believe me, I wouldn't ask if it wasn't important." He paused. "How well do you know Henry Lavers?"

"Henry who?"

"Henry Lavers."

"I've never heard of him. So, what's this personal question you need to ask me?"

"It's okay, Andrea. You've told me enough."

He was about to call over to Sam to tell her she didn't need to trace Jason Mullins when his phone rang.

"Luke Sackville."

"Hi, Luke. It's Leanne. A Mr Taylor is here to see you. He said it's urgent and that he has some valuable information he needs to share with you. Something about Liz Rathbone."

"I'll be right down."

He headed out of the office, took the stairs two at a time, almost ran to the reception desk and looked around for his visitor.

"Where is he, Leanne?"

"He said he wanted fresh air." She lowered her voice and smiled. "People often say that. It means they need a cigarette."

"What did he look like?"

"He's… Oh, there he is." She pointed through the window next to the entrance door. A man was standing on the other side with his back to them.

"Thanks. I'll be back in a minute."

Luke walked outside and recognised his visitor immediately.

"Hello, Henry," he said. "Have you come to give yourself up?"

Henry laughed. "You're very smart, Luke, but then you always were at school. You're wrong on that count though. I have no intention whatsoever of giving myself in. I've got something to deal with and then I'm booked on a flight to South America." He grinned. "I've stashed money away in a Swiss bank account and I'm looking forward to a new life."

"You said you had something to deal with. What's that?"

Henry was still smiling. "You."

He turned so that Luke could see the gun in his hand while ensuring his body shielded it from onlookers.

Henry flicked the gun to one side to indicate the car park.

"Walk ahead of me and don't try anything. Another death is neither here nor there. Head for the silver Transit."

"I wouldn't have thought a van was your style, Henry."

"There's something inside that I want to show you."

Luke started walking and Henry waited until he was five or six yards ahead before following.

"Don't dream of making a move," he hissed. "Shooting you now would give me nothing but pleasure."

Luke kept walking but slowed his pace. There was too much distance between them for him to stand a chance of disarming him, but there had to be something he could do. Perhaps if he got him talking he could distract him.

"What are you going to show me?" he asked.

Henry laughed again, and there was something maniacal about it. "You thought your glamorous assistant had been Liz's saviour, but I was waiting when she got home from the police station. She and I used to be an item. Did you know that?"

"What have you done to her?"

"What do you think? She put up a struggle but I was too strong. Poor Liz."

Luke had reached the back of the van and turned to face Henry who remained a few yards away.

"She's in there," Henry went on. "Not a pretty sight I'm afraid, but then a dead body's never pretty, is it Luke?"

"You've never been in a relationship with Andrea Mason, have you?"

Henry laughed again. "No. I told you that to help build the case against her and her type. They're low-life bastards, all of them. Trying to destroy our business. They need to be behind bars, and that's where they would have gone if it weren't for you."

"So the idea behind killing anti-environmentalists was to put the blame on the likes of Andrea Mason and Finn O'Sullivan?"

"Got it in one, Luke. Now stop blabbering and open the door."

Luke dreaded to think what he might find in the back of the van.

He opened the door…

… to find a pristine and empty space.

"What the…"

Something solid struck the back of his head. He staggered and started to turn around but as he did so a second blow hit him, on the left temple this time.

Luke's eyes closed and he fell back into the van.

Chapter 72

Sam decided that her best bet was to ring Harrow School.

It was a woman who answered.

"Good morning, Harrow School. How may I help you?"

Her words were delivered in a snooty tone and Sam knew immediately that extracting information from her was going to be a challenge.

"Hello, my name's Sam Chambers," she said in her most pleasant voice. "I'm in a bind and need to track someone down. My mother's died and I need to inform him."

"You're related to this person, are you?"

"I'm his step-sister. I haven't seen him since he was sixteen. His name's Jason Mullins."

"Is he a student here or a teacher?"

"He was a student but he'd be about forty-three now."

"In that case, I can't help."

"Don't you have records of past students?"

"Of course we have records."

"Then…"

The woman interrupted before she could say more.

"I am not at liberty to reveal personal information to just anyone who calls in."

"I told you. I'm his sister."

The woman sighed. "You could try the Harrow Association."

"The Harrow Association?"

This was met with an even deeper sigh. "Yes." A pause. "It's for old boys."

"I see. Thanks. Have you got their number?"

"You'll find it online."

The woman hung up.

She had, however, been right and it only took Sam a moment to find a number. Her call was answered immediately.

"Hello. Old Harrovians. Jeffrey speaking."

He was the complete opposite of the woman at the school itself, his voice plummy but cheerful and full of bonhomie.

"Hi, my name's Sam Chambers. I wonder if you could help me track someone down."

"I'll do my very best, my dear. I assume he's an old boy?"

"Yes." The man was so pleasant she decided there was no need to tell any white lies. "My boss, Luke Sackville, needs to speak to him."

"Does he indeed. I know Luke. Splendid fellow. Are you a fellow officer then?"

"No. He's left the police and works in the private sector now."

"I see." He paused. "Luke was in the same class as my son, you know. Please remember me to him. My name's Jeffrey Arthurcock-Brown and my son is Gerald."

For a moment Sam thought he said Half-a-cock-Brown and had to fight back the urge to giggle.

"What did you say your surname is?"

"Arthurcock-Brown. Who is it Luke's looking for?"

"Jason Mullins."

"Jason Mullins, eh? There's a name I haven't heard in a quarter of a century."

"Have you any idea where he is now? Do you have phone numbers for old boys on your database?"

"I'm afraid we don't hold details for boys who were expelled."

"Jason Mullins was expelled?"

"Oh yes, my dear. After that business with Mr Kirby, the Head of Geography, the Principal had no option.

Mullins tried to blame it on another pupil but the idea that Lavers did it was a non-starter."

"Did you say Lavers? Was that Henry Lavers?"

"Yes, that was the lad. Trying to accuse an innocent boy compounded Mullins' offence in the Principal's eyes. As if what he did wasn't disgraceful enough."

"What exactly was it that he did?"

"I was in the Parents Association so I was told, but we were all sworn to secrecy. It wouldn't have been good for the school's reputation if it had got out."

"Surely you can tell me now that twenty-five years have passed."

Jeffrey hesitated. "I suppose so, though even after all this time it saddens me to think of it. Old Mr Kirby was so upset he left the school that term and never returned. Rip had strong views on the environment but to kill his dog because of them is unbelievable."

"Jason Mullins killed his dog?"

"Yes. He was found strung up on the washing line in Rip's back garden with a message round his neck saying 'No More Motorways'. The big environmental topic at the time was road-building and Mullins was a very vocal activist and totally against it. Rip, on the other hand, believed motorways were essential for the economy."

"What about Henry Lavers?"

Jeffrey gave a dry laugh. "That's what made accusing Henry so ridiculous. Henry was very much on the same side as Mr Kirby. He had no reason to treat him so appallingly."

Chapter 73

Sam hung up and turned around to tell Luke what she'd found out, but to her surprise his chair was empty.

"Does anyone know where Luke went?"

It was Helen who answered. "He dashed out about ten minutes ago. I heard him say he'd be right down so I presume he was speaking to reception and he's got a visitor."

Sam rang his mobile but it went straight to voicemail, presumably because he was in a meeting with his guest.

What the Harrow old boy had told her was intriguing. As she thought it through, it dawned on her that there was a direct parallel between the events of a quarter of a century ago and the recent murders.

Jason Mullins, an environmentalist, had been expelled from Harrow School after it was believed he killed the pet of an anti-environmentalist.

Nick Atkinson had killed two anti-environmentalists and attempted to kill a third. As with the incident at Harrow, this put environmental activists firmly in the frame for the murders.

This couldn't be a coincidence.

The common denominator was Henry Lavers.

He had to be Nick Atkinson's paymaster.

She gulped.

This information couldn't wait. She needed to drag Luke out of his meeting and tell him what she'd learned.

She rang reception.

"Leanne, do you know which meeting room Luke has taken his visitor to?"

"He hasn't." Leanne seemed confused. "Actually, I wonder where he's got to. He said he'd only be a minute."

"What do you mean?"

"His visitor was outside, having a cigarette I think, and Luke went outside to talk to him."

Sam's heart sank. "What was the name of his visitor?"

"A Mr Taylor. He didn't give his first name."

Sam was about to ask what he looked like when she realised it wouldn't help because she'd never met Henry Lavers.

"Promise me you won't go anywhere, Leanne. I'm coming down."

She called Liz's number as she raced downstairs and was relieved when she answered after only a few rings.

"Liz, it's Sam. I need your help."

"What's wrong? You sound panicked."

"I think…" She paused. Best to be sure first. "Just a second. I'm going to put you on speaker." She clicked the speaker button as she reached the reception desk. "Leanne, this is Liz Rathbone."

"The woman from Globo Energy?"

Sam nodded. "Can you describe Mr Taylor for Liz please, Leanne?"

"Sure." She leaned closer to Sam's phone. "He's about five foot ten or eleven. Smart suit. Full beard and handsome I'd say, although I'm not one for earrings on men. He had brown hair with…"

"Hang on," Liz said. "Did you say he has an earring?"

"Yes. In his left earlobe. Actually, it wasn't a ring, it was…"

"…a silver cross."

"That's right. Do you know Mr Taylor, Liz?"

"It's Henry. It has to be."

"Just a second, Liz," Sam said and turned to Leanne, her panic increasing now. "Did you see where they went?"

Leanne shrugged her shoulders. "Sorry. I wasn't looking."

Sam ran to the door and looked outside. There was no

sign of either man.

She dashed back in and heard Liz's voice over the phone's speaker as she reached the reception desk.

"What's going on, Sam? Why is Henry calling himself Mr Taylor?'

"He's the murderer."

Liz and Leanne both gasped.

"What are you talking about?" Liz asked. "We caught the murderer last night."

"Nick Atkinson is a paid assassin. Henry was paying him to eliminate people including you."

"But…"

"I haven't time to explain. I'm worried what he might do to Luke." She turned to Leanne. "Leanne, call the police. Tell them we suspect Henry Lavers hired Nick Atkinson to kill people and that he may have abducted Luke."

Leanne got straight onto her phone.

"Liz," Sam went on, "have you any idea where Henry might go?"

"Not really. He could take him to his house I suppose, but…" She paused. "When we were having our affair, Henry took me to a converted barn he owns. I don't think Ellen knows about it. He might take him there."

"Where is it?"

"Just outside Monkton Combe. Hang on, I might have the address on my phone."

Sam squeezed her eyes closed. Was she too late? If Henry had done anything to Luke she didn't know if she could…

"Got it," Liz said. "Rosebud Cottage, Church Lane, Monkton Combe. It's not really on Church Lane though. You take a grass track off to the right about half a mile after you turn off Brassknocker Hill. The house is about two hundred yards down in the middle of the woods."

"Thanks." Sam turned to Leanne. "Leanne, can I speak to the police, please? I need to give them this address."

"They're refusing to do anything," Leanne said.

"What! Pass me the phone."

Leanne passed the phone over.

"Hello," Sam said. "This is Sam Chambers. What's going on?"

It was a woman who answered and Sam was immediately reminded of the snooty woman at Harrow School.

"I understand you're reporting a missing person, Miss Chambers, but that he's been gone for less than thirty minutes."

"He's been abducted."

"Has he?" This was delivered in a tone which made it clear she thought Sam was a crank caller and wasting her valuable time.

"Yes, by the man behind the triple murders of Scott Finlay, Erin Douglas and Brett Napier."

"By a serial killer. I see."

"Please can you at least put me onto DI Pete Gilmore? He's in the investigation team."

"Wait a minute."

There was a click and classical music started playing.

"Liz wants to know what's happening," Leanne said.

Sam shrugged. "So do I." She was getting angrier and more concerned by the second.

Two or three minutes passed then there was another click on the phone and the woman came back on.

"I've spoken to the SIO," she said, before adding in a patronising voice, "which stands for senior investigating officer by the way. He's very senior."

"And?"

"Detective Chief Inspector Bramley told me that he caught the murderer yesterday."

"He caught the murderer yesterday?"

"Correct." The woman paused. "Have you had a blow to the head, Miss Chambers?"

"Have I…" Sam squeezed her eyes closed and passed the phone back to Leanne. "Leanne, please can you try to persuade them that my concern is genuine."

"I'll try. What are you going to do?"

"I'm driving to Monkton Combe."

Chapter 74

As Luke regained consciousness his first sensation was of intense pain. He had a blinding headache too.

It took him a second or two to remember what had happened. He'd followed Henry to his van and been hit, probably by the butt of his gun.

Twice.

Instinctively, he tried to raise his left hand to his temple and it was then that he realised he was tied to a chair with both arms secured behind his back. He could feel something on the left side of his face which it took a few moments to realise was blood.

He slowly opened his eyes and squinted at Henry who was seated at a table a few paces away. He had a mug in his hand and was almost smiling.

"Welcome back to the land of the living," he said. "Although I regret to say yours will only be a short return visit."

He put the mug down, picked his gun up from the table and waved it towards Luke.

"I've been wanting to use this since I acquired it. It works just as well on tall bastards, you know." He laughed. "In through here," he jabbed his index finger against the centre of his forehead, "and then out through the back. A neat hole at the front but in the rear…" He fanned his hand out behind his head. "…whoosh! There'll be skull fragments and brain matter everywhere."

Any movement was painful but Luke knew he had to keep the man talking.

"Why are you doing this, Henry?"

"You mean why did I murder Scott Finlay and the others?"

Luke thought about shaking his head but realised it would hurt too much. "No. I know why you did that. Why do you want to kill me?"

He had to buy time. How time would help him from this position Luke wasn't sure, but it had to be better than doing nothing.

"Because you're a nuisance, Luke, that's why. You're too smart for your own good. I won't feel safe in South America unless you're out of the picture once and for all." He smiled. "This is how it's going to be, and it's a simple three-stage approach." He held up his right thumb. First, I shoot you." Up went the index finger. "Then I set fire to this barn," The middle finger joined the others. "and finally I make my escape. Simples as the meerkats would say." He grinned. "Simplicity is always best, don't you agree?"

"But why not just finish me off when you got me here? Why wait until I'm awake?"

"Not because I'm cruel, Luke, if that's what you think. No, I'm a man of principles. I feel I owe you an explanation."

"You mean you want to gloat?"

"A bit of that, yes." He hesitated. "You were always number one at Harrow, weren't you? The blue-eyed boy who couldn't put a foot wrong. Always destined to do well in the world." He laughed and gestured at the chair with his gun hand. "But look at you now. Trussed up like a pig ready for slaughter... which in many ways you are."

"They'll still catch you. There are extradition treaties."

Henry tapped the side of his nose. "Not where I'm going there aren't. I'm a meticulous planner and always have been. I've thought this through in detail."

Luke thought he heard a noise. It was the gentlest of taps and Henry was too self-absorbed to notice.

He spotted movement behind Henry's shoulder at a small window. He flicked his eyes in that direction but whoever or whatever it was had disappeared from view.

He had to hope it was someone who could rescue him. It was all the more important to keep Henry talking now.

"Which country, Henry? There's no risk in telling me if you're going to shoot me."

"You're right. I'm proud of myself, actually. I'm going to Ecuador. It's a beautiful country by all accounts."

Chapter 75

Sam crouched down beneath the window, her heart thumping.

She hated seeing Luke in this state. It was clear that he'd been badly injured. Blood had flowed freely from a wound on the side of his head and was now starting to congeal on his left cheek.

At least he was conscious.

She'd seen the gun and had to assume Henry Lavers intended to use it. But what could she do?

Hopefully, Leanne would eventually persuade the police to take some action. She might have done so already, but if a police car screamed up the track to the cottage with sirens blasting what chance would that give Luke? Henry would shoot him in an instant.

She had to act and act quickly.

Her only chance was to find a way of distracting him. He needed to move away so that he was no longer pointing the gun at Luke. If she did that it would give her time, only a few seconds perhaps but it would be better than what she had now.

If Henry was startled in his current position he would be able to lift the gun and fire in less than a second.

The fact that he and Luke were talking was a good sign. She had to assume they would continue for a few minutes at least.

The cottage was single-storey and small. She guessed it probably had three rooms inside, perhaps four. The room she had peered into was doubtless the largest and looked as though it served as lounge, dining room and kitchen combined into one. Other than that there would be a bathroom and one, possibly two, bedrooms.

Sam kept on her hands and knees and crawled along the front of the building and then turned left. There were two windows on that side, one of them high up and firmly closed, which had to be for a bathroom. The other was at the same height as the single room at the front and it was open a fraction.

Perhaps this was her chance. If it was a bedroom she might be able to open the window and crawl through, then surprise Henry from the side.

She braced herself, raised herself up and immediately ducked down again. It was another window into the largest room and she was now side on to both men. Fortunately, she didn't think Henry had spotted her, but it had been a close call.

She continued down to the end and then around to the back of the house where there was another single window and a back door, both of which she'd spotted when she'd been at the front.

She daren't raise herself to look through the window. If she did she would be facing Henry and the risk of him seeing her was too great.

The door was a problem. The top three-quarters of it were panelled with glass, leaving only a solid strip eighteen inches or so high at the bottom.

She dropped flat to the ground and pulled herself along until she was certain she was clear, ensuring she kept her body as flat as possible. Once she was past the door, she heaved a quiet sigh of relief, returned to her hands and knees and crawled around the final corner.

This was her last chance. There was a single window on this side and it had to be the bedroom. She crawled underneath it, prepared herself and slowly raised her head above the sill.

Chapter 76

Luke was beginning to feel faint.

It was difficult keeping up conversation and he wondered if he had a concussion. His mouth was dry too but he knew he had to keep Henry talking.

It was his only chance, and it was a slim one at that.

Fortunately, Henry seemed only too pleased to talk. It was clear that he was for some reason envious of him, an envy that appeared to date back to their school days.

"You were a very fast runner, I remember," Henry said. "Not that it will help you in your current position when I've got this." He grinned and waved the gun towards his captive. "Always came first in races, didn't you? Always getting awards. I'm surprised you weren't a professional athlete."

"I was a professional rugby player before I joined the police."

"Were you indeed? I hope that ended badly for you."

"It did. I was injured and had to retire early."

"Excellent. Excellent." He hesitated. "What was that?"

"What was what?"

"I thought I heard a noise. Wait there." He hesitated. "Oh, I forgot. You don't have any choice, do you?"

He walked to the front, grasped the handle, jerked the door open and stepped out. He turned left, then to his right before returning and closing the door behind him.

"I must have imagined it. Unless…"

Henry turned to look at the door to his left, then crept over to it and pulled it open, his gun arm stretched out in front of him.

"Got you!" he shouted.

"No!" Luke screamed.

Chapter 77

Sam jumped when she heard a shout from inside the house.

She had returned to the front, the bedroom window having been closed too tightly for her to be able to force it open.

Back where she started.

What now?'

An idea occurred to her and she pulled her phone from her pocket. It was already on silent, she'd done that after she'd parked the car on Church Lane, and she was pleased to see there was 4G reception.

She called up Liz's number and sent her a message.

In exactly one minute phone
Henry and distract him.

The thumbs-up reply was almost instant.

Chapter 78

Luke was relieved when Henry reappeared.

"Fooled you," he said and laughed. "There was no one there, Luke. No saviour for you today. Probably a cat, or else I imagined it." He paused. "Anyway, I think we've finished our little chat. I'd like to say it's been nice talking to you, but it hasn't."

He raised the gun, pointed it at the centre of Luke's forehead and took a pace forward.

Chapter 79

Sam crept back to the front window.

The minute seemed to go on forever. She took deep breaths to fill her lungs, using the techniques she'd been taught in her martial arts classes, an approach that helped her to stay calm and centred.

Or at least as calm and centred as was possible in the circumstances.

Henry's phone rang, and Sam swallowed then lifted her head above the sill. She saw him put his phone to his ear and then move to one side, towards the right. She made eye contact with Luke who shook his head and mouthed 'No'.

As if that would make a difference.

She moved to the front door, grasped the door handle, readied herself, then thrust it down and pushed the door open as forcibly as she could.

She leapt through the door, turned towards Henry and leapt towards him, simultaneously screaming, "YOU BASTARD!" at the top of her voice to further shock and surprise him.

He dropped the phone and lifted his gun arm but she was too quick. She pivoted, turned and kicked his arm with her right foot. It was her second roundhouse kick in anger in two days and it was as effective as the first.

There was a crack and the gun flew out of his hand. He reached for his arm with his other hand. "You've broken my wrist."

"Good."

Her karate training was left behind for her final blow as she picked his mug up from the table and swung it into his jaw. His face jerked backwards and he fell to the ground.

"Sam, untie me!" Luke called.

She stepped over to Henry to ensure he was out cold and then moved to Luke.

"With pleasure," she said as she tried to steady her breathing. She gently touched the side of his head. "That looks painful."

"Please."

She half-laughed. "Sorry." She moved behind him and undid the rope that bound his wrists.

He stood up and she returned to the front, stood in front of him and looked up into his eyes.

"Thank goodness you're okay."

"I should have done this a long time ago," he said.

"Done what?"

He bent down and kissed her.

She sighed.

At last, she thought. *At last.*

Chapter 80

Two weeks later

There was a second tree in the Library, this one covered in white and silver baubles supplemented by hanging ornaments that could have only been made by one hand.

Luke smiled.

It was clear that his niece had been busy in the run-up to Christmas.

He lifted one particularly vivid object to look at it more closely. It was roughly pyramid-shaped and painted purple and green. On the three sides she had written, 'Very', 'Merry' and 'Xmas' in broad white strokes.

It was typical Marion.

He moved from the tree to the shelves and pulled out the book he had come into the Library for. It was one he had read repeatedly when he was her age. Although larger and more garish than the leather-covered tomes that filled the rest of the shelves, he loved it all the more for its bright colours.

He took the book over to the window, stared out at the lawn that fronted Borrowham Hall and found his thoughts turning to the events of the previous few weeks.

It had been eventful, to say the least, with an incredible number of ups and downs. It was hard to believe it was only a fortnight since Sam had rescued him in the cottage in Monkton Combe. A lot had happened since then, a hell of a lot.

He sighed as he thought back to how hard it had been to finish the relationship. He'd had to do it though. It wasn't the fact that they worked for the same company. That wasn't a problem in his eyes. No, it was more that she had been, well, not his style.

He was pleased he'd ended it though. If he hadn't…

His phone rang.

"Hi, Josh."

"Hi, guv. Just ringing to wish you a Merry Christmas. I rang Helen too. She's spending the festive season with Bob on his longboat."

"It's a narrowboat, son. He's not a Viking."

"Gotcha. Got to be nicer than where Batman and Robin are though."

"You mean Taylor and Robin?"

"Yes, them. They're in HMP Bristol, aren't they?"

"That's right. Henry Lavers and Nick Atkinson are on remand and we're waiting for a court date."

The line went silent.

"Come on, Josh," Luke said. "What's your real reason for ringing?"

"I, ah… It's Christmas Day, guv. I didn't ought to be bothering you."

"Out with it."

"Well, I was telling my mum all about Henry Lavers and I realised I didn't ever ask you what put you onto him in the first place."

"It was the book."

"What book?"

"When I met him in the Francis Hotel he had a book with him. It was written by Scott Finlay, the first man he hired Nick Atkinson to murder."

"I don't get it."

"When I asked him about it Henry said, and I quote, 'The author was a leading environmental journalist'. He said 'was' when at the time no one knew Finlay was dead."

"Gucci."

"Is that all?"

"That's it, guv."

Luke hung up, looked back out of the window and then

heard a noise behind him.

"Penny for them."

A broad smile stretched across his face. He turned around and looked down into Sam's eyes.

"I was thinking how lucky it was that I finished with Cora when I did. If I hadn't we wouldn't be together."

She laughed. "And if Ollie hadn't been a complete and utter bastard…"

He echoed her laugh. "Enough said."

She gestured to the book in his hand. "What's that?"

"The BFG. I loved it when I was young. I thought Marion might like to read it."

"Good idea. Shall we go back in?"

"There's something I need to do first."

He bent down and kissed her.

After a few seconds, he broke away.

They smiled at each other and he grabbed her hand and led her back to his family.

Thanks for reading 'Sow the Wind'. It would help no end if you could leave a review on Amazon.

This is book 6 in my Luke Sackville Crime Series. If you read it as a standalone, I invite you to look at the first five books: Taken to the Hills, Black Money, Fog of Silence, The Corruption Code and Lethal Odds.

Want to read more about Luke Sackville and what shaped his career choices? 'Change of Direction', the prequel to the series, can be downloaded as an ebook or audiobook free of charge by subscribing to my newsletter at:

sjrichardsauthor.com

Acknowledgements

Thanks must first go to my wife Penny for her help, support and critical feedback on my first draft. She knows her crime fiction!

My beta readers provided excellent feedback as always. Thanks to Chris Bayne, Deb Day, Denise Goodhand, Jackie Harrison, Sarah Mackenzie, Irene Paterson, Allison Valentine and Marcie Whitecotton-Carroll.

Thanks also to my advance copy readers, who put faith in the book being worth reading.

Yet again Samuel James has done a terrific job narrating the audiobook, while Olly Bennett designed a great cover.

Last but not least, thanks to you the reader. I love your feedback and reading your reviews, and I'm always delighted to hear from you so please feel free to get in touch.

BEACON OF BLIGHT

Only the truth can save them

Luke Sackville's Ethics Team is stretched thin across multiple investigations. At first, these appear to be separate and unconnected, but soon they discover links suggesting a web of organisations that make money by exploiting innocent people when they are at the lowest point in their lives.

Further work reveals that one person is behind these operations. Ruthless in the extreme, they are prepared to do anything to avoid detection. Luke has to act quickly to prevent their reign of terror from being brought to a murderous conclusion.

Beacon of Blight is the seventh book in the series of crime thrillers featuring ex-DCI Luke Sackville and his Ethics Team.

Out 4th February 2025 - Order your copy now

mybook.to/beaconofblight

ABOUT THE AUTHOR

My name's Steve. I've never been called 'SJ', but Steve Richards is a well-known political writer hence the pen name.

I was born in Bath and have lived at various times on an irregular clockwise circle around England. After university in Manchester, my wife and I settled in Macclesfield before moving to Bedfordshire then a few years ago back to Somerset. We now live in Croscombe, a lovely village just outside Wells, with our 2 sprightly cocker spaniels.

I've always loved writing but have only really had the time to indulge myself since taking early retirement. My daughter is a brilliant author (I'm not biased of course) which is both an inspiration and - because she's so good - a challenge. After a few experiments, and a couple of completed but unsatisfactory and never published novels, I decided to write a crime fiction series as it's one of the genres I most enjoy.

You can find out more about me and my books at my website:
sjrichardsauthor.com

Printed in Great Britain
by Amazon

50259583R00202